AN UNNATURAL WAY TO DIE . . .

The plain wooden coffin was laid out in the center of the barn, supported by bales of hay at the head and foot.

James was finding this more and more curious. The body had been here since dawn, almost eight hours now. Alone. That struck him forcibly. There was no tender parting and farewell here . . .

"Because of the circumstances I think that I should look at the deceased now." He didn't ask permission. Violet glared. Lily and Rose fell back as James lifted the lid of the coffin and stood it against a bale of hay.

His somber thoughts were pierced by a shriek from Rose.

"There's blood! Blood!" she cried before she collapsed . . .

BLOOD
is
THICKER

ANN C. FALLON

POCKET BOOKS

New York   London   Toronto   Sydney   Tokyo   Singapore

An *Original* Publication of POCKET BOOKS

POCKET BOOKS, a division of Simon & Schuster Inc.
1230 Avenue of the Americas, New York, NY 10020

ISBN: 0-671-70623-3

First Pocket Books printing June 1990

10 9 8 7 6 5 4 3 2 1

POCKET and colophon are registered trademarks of
Simon & Schuster Inc.

Printed in the U.S.A.

To my husband John

Chapter One

Mr. Sweeney rubbed the large red knuckles of one hand with the reddened fingers of his other and then held both hands near the steaming electric kettle. The back room of the little shop was cold and dark in the gray Irish dawn.

"Tea, Brendan?"

"Right, Da!" his son called from the front of the shop.

Mr. Sweeney opened the box of Lyons Green Label and shook a palmful of the loose tea leaves into the warmed pot. While the tea sat stewing, he took down a naggin of whiskey from the shelf with the stores of paraffin and poured a capful into his own mug. He filled both mugs and brought them out to the shop.

"Papers late today?" asked his son, who took a split second to look up from the counter where he was sorting the mass of post. Letters and packets and parcels were piled high on either side of him. He carefully held each piece up to his good eye and then placed it in the appropriate pile.

1

"Sean will be here any moment now," he said to his father as he took his mug of tea and stirred it vigorously. A splash fell on one of the parcels and the ink began to spread.

"Damn!"

Brendan dreaded Tuesdays. Tuesday was Old Age Pension Day in Kilmartin, County Wexford, and the safe was bulging with cash. Brendan, who, with his father ran the local shop, also ran the small branch post office, which was housed in the front corner. So on Tuesdays not only did he have to sort the mail before Sean arrived on his bicycle to deliver the first round, he also had to pay out the pensions and stamp the pension books and chat ceaselessly to a day-long stream of retired locals. Tuesday was always a day of irritation made more burdensome by his fears of the post office being robbed by IRA terrorists.

"Why are those bloomin' papers late today?" grumbled his father as he peered around the posters that hung faded in the small dusty window. He looked at his pocket watch and then at the clock on the wall.

"The five-thirty is twenty minutes late, and it's not even raining," mumbled Mr. Sweeney into his mug. He stamped his feet to get the circulation going. Suddenly, headlights swept through the shop, announcing the arrival at last of the bus from Dublin. It drew up at the bus stop in front of the shop, and the conductor tossed the roped bundles of papers onto the rough pavement. With a tip of his cap he withdrew and the bus rumbled off.

"Bloody bus company. Hah! Nothing changes."

Brendan smiled. He'd heard his father say the same thing every morning for virtually the last twenty-five years, since he was a small boy. It was true. Nothing changes.

The small old man looked like a sprite in the early morning light, hopping out the door to carry in the load of newspapers. For a man of seventy years, he was remarkably strong. He cut the strings with his kitchen knife and worked at top speed to sort the

2

newspapers into piles, setting the bulk aside for sale to the passing trade, but more important, marking the name of the relevant subscriber at the top of each in the remaining pile. He watched the clock, he watched the window, he watched for the brightening light. At six A.M. by his clock he unlatched the front door and the shop was officially open to the public. As he turned he heard the knob rattle. But he didn't acknowledge it. He beetled around the far side of the counter, smiling to himself as he lifted the flap of wood, lowered it, and then stood at the ready.

"Mr. Sweeney!" said a reedy voice.

"Mr. Sinclair," replied Mr. Sweeney, looking up in mock astonishment at the tall, angular figure that peered down at him like a heron.

"Papers late today, Mr. Sweeney?"

"Indeed they were, Mr. Sinclair."

"I don't suppose . . ." said Mr. Sinclair, thinking that he had caught Mr. Sweeney out at last.

"But of course, your papers are ready . . ." Mr. Sweeney handed Sinclair his four papers. Three English and one Irish, the latter a token gesture to the country his parents had adopted.

"I see . . . well, I thank you. And now if you just let me have a tin of Three Nuns. Ran out, exceedingly tiresome. Must have a morning pipe, you know. Gets the blood running . . ." He turned at the sound of a car outside. "I say, would you credit that?"

Brendan and Mr. Sweeney looked up from their tasks and followed the direction of Mr. Sinclair's beaky gaze out the window.

"A hearse, is it?" Mr. Sweeney moved quickly to the door. Brendan, with his appalling sight, saw nothing but a blur beyond the dusty windows. "What's the alarm?" he asked, surprised at the reaction of his father.

"It turned, Brendan, it turned into the lane!"

Sinclair and then Mr. Sweeney hurried outside and watched the hearse as it carefully made its way up the narrow stony lane. Sean the postman was pedaling

3

furiously up the road. Where the lane met the road, he crossed over to the shop. His pink eyes in his broad white face were popping.

"It overtook me just off the main Dublin road, but I followed it," he told them breathlessly. He was a plump man to undertake such a strenuous pursuit. ". . . I never imagined it would be turning into Moore's!" The three men stood in silence. Sean produced a questionable handkerchief and dabbed his sweating face, Sinclair filled his pipe automatically, and Sweeney once more rubbed his stiffening hands. They lost sight of the hearse where the lane curved and was shrouded by hedging, but they still stood, waiting.

The black hearse was very new. It was still colored the traditional black, with silver-trim filigree on the roof, but it had opaque windows at the sides and rear. The hearse slowed on the gravel of the circular drive in front of the large granite-fronted manor house that was known as Moore's. With a whirr the rear door opened automatically, and with a louder whirr a flat panel slid out. Two young men jumped from the front of the car and lowered the plain wooden coffin onto the gravel. Seconds later the hearse drove off, even as the panel whirred back and the door clicked shut. The car accelerated, the noise of its tires now rumbling across the quiet fields on either side of the lane. Without stopping, it swerved out of the lane and onto the road.

"Harvey's—of Dublin."

"Not a'tall! Smith's—out of Wexford."

"Neither. They were local. Fred told me only the other night at the Drooping Well that his brother-in-law had just bought in a new car for the company." The other two men looked skeptically at the third.

"Pity Brendan couldn't see it, he might have known," mumbled Mr. Sweeney as he turned into the shop.

"Da?"

4

"Most strange, Brendan. A hearse it was, seemed to go up to the farm and then came back. Probably made a mistake in the address."

"A pretty alarming mistake," said Sinclair.

"Well, glory be to God, we're standin' here," said Sean excitedly, "and someone could be dead up at Moore's."

But they continued to stand, ruminating like the cows in the fields around them.

Violet Moore strode down the center aisle of the cowshed, her boots splashing in the streaming waters. She pulled her anorak tight around her neck, sheltering against the steam rising from the backs of her beautiful beasts. Brushing aside wisps of steel-gray hair, she watched the young man bent to his work. Queen Maeve swished her tail.

"Liam," Violet said sharply.

"Miss Moore," returned a voice.

"How is Maeve milking now?"

"Much improved, Miss Moore, much improved," the voice drawled.

"Deirdre has mastitis. I want no more of it."

"It happens, it does that," the young man replied diffidently.

"It doesn't happen at Moore's, I tell you."

Liam stood. Despite the cold of the dawning day, he was stripped to the waist, sweat and condensing steam rolling off his body. He detached the milking unit from the teats and moved slowly around the cow and on to the next. His slow, rhythmic movements maddened Violet, and she fleetingly regretted hiring him. But he was good, very good, with her cattle. It was his wry smile that was not so good. She started to speak again but refrained. She recognized a free spirit and knew if she pushed too hard, Liam would drift off into the light of day, as he had drifted in from the port of Wexford one late summer afternoon.

"Today's yield will be up, by the looks of it," Liam commented matter-of-factly. He thumped the switch on the wall and Deirdre's udder wobbled from side to side as the milk was squeezed alternately from each teat.

"I'm glad to hear it," said Violet as she walked on down the shed, patting a beast here and rubbing another's underbelly there. Yes, she loved her beasts.

She crossed the cobbled yard to the dairy barn. Both pasteurizing units were in operation, and the black tubes throbbed with a life of their own. Milk flowed into the large stainless-steel tanks, where it was heated to 161 degrees, then passed through the coolers and on to the clattering, packing machine, to be fed into hundreds of cartons. Delicious, cool, pasteurized nonhomogenized milk. She smiled. Kevin, the farm manager, was tearing open a brown box packed with flattened triangular cartons. Randomly he took out a fistful, flicking through them with his thumb.

"These bloody things are still sticking together. Banjaxes the machine. I'll have to phone . . . Morning, Violet," he called over his shoulder.

"Good morning, Kevin," she replied.

Two scrawny boys, their school day still ahead of them, packed the milk crates furiously, filling them and stacking them near the door of the modern barn. Violet's pride and joy, the new barn stood in stark contrast to the surrounding house and outbuildings, which looked in the half light as though they had grown from the rock of the ground—mottled gray and brown, covered with moss, ivy, and lichen—and a fine mist now moving in from the surrounding fields.

"Kevin, tell Liam to put the cattle out to grass in the lower field, but only until noon. I don't want them to get too giddy. It's early days yet, despite the growth."

"Right you are," replied Kevin, smiling at the tenderness in her voice as she spoke of her cattle. She knew how they would lift their heads on this their first spring morning out to pasture. How they would sniff the air and move warily at first, stiff and strange after their winter of confinement in the cowsheds. For nearly three months, they had been housed.

"Moira is about to drop. I've got the calving stall ready. Shall I call you?"

"Call me." Violet looked up as she saw Paddy, her milk deliveryman, hovering inside the door of the dairy. The scrawny boys scrambled to drag the milk crates outside.

Paddy stood aside and then came toward her reluctantly. She liked his subservience. And then again, she didn't. So obsequious, she thought.

"Yes." She spoke sharply, angry even before she heard his request.

"Miss Moore, I think you'd better come 'round the front."

"The front? Is it the truck?" she asked in alarm, visions of undelivered milk flashing before her.

"It's not the truck, but there's something you should take a look at . . ."

"Where's Lily then . . . or even Rose?"

"Ah, now you won't be wanting to alarm Rose . . ." Violet glared at the man.

"Lily!" She raised her voice, trying to locate her sister amongst the numerous outbuildings.

There was no answering voice. "Probably with the hens—if she's out of bed at all!"

"I think it would be best if it was yourself, Miss Violet."

Violet Moore marched out of the barn and across the second yard, then cut around the rear of the house. She wrenched open the wooden door built in an archway in the wall that surrounded and protected the main house and farm buildings. Her three dogs came yelping at her heels, eager for their morning run. She passed down the side of the house and rounded the corner, Paddy hurrying behind.

At first she didn't see the simple pale wooden box. It seemed to blend in with the gray and tawny gravel. It was some sort of crate, but as she moved closer she slowed and then paused.

The dogs raced up behind and then went forward to sniff at it.

7

"Sit!"

Lily came up beside her, and then Rose, who gripped her arm.

"Violet . . . what does it mean?"

At first Violet didn't answer, the four of them stood, a silent group surrounding the simple coffin. Then, at last, she spoke. "Fetch Kevin," she said to Paddy, "and have him bring a claw hammer and the tire lever."

Kevin worked quickly, hands trembling, his heart thudding in his chest. He wasn't quite sure if he should even be doing this, but then, perhaps it was a bad joke. There was no need for the police to witness a joke in such bad taste. No, a joke it was, and they'd keep it quiet, just amongst themselves. He pried up the nails on one side and then, drawing breath, forced the lid back and quickly turned his head.

"Jesus, Mary, and Joseph!" gasped Paddy. Kevin crossed himself and stared hard at the clouds scudding above them. Lily turned away as Violet moved forward slowly, Rose sheltering behind her. For an instant Violet hesitated, and then bending down, she peered at the composed gray face of the man in the coffin.

"Oh, God," she whispered hoarsely. "Jack."

"No, it cannot be," cried Rose. "Not Jack. Not my Jack."

Lily came to put her long thin arms around Rose and pulled her away. The three sisters stood silently in the rain, now pouring down.

Violet stepped back from the coffin and turned to Kevin.

"Don't let the cattle into the fields today . . . And Kevin, get this box into the barn."

—— *Chapter Two* ——

As the burgundy Citroen CX sailed along at cruising speed, James Fleming leaned back and smiled. This was a promising start to the week.

Dun Laoghaire. Bray. Wicklow. Arklow. Gorey. The small towns of southeast Ireland flashed past to his right as his attention was caught on the left by breathtaking views of the coastal waters sparkling in the early morning light. Smugly, he sped for a stretch alongside the Wexford train. He recognized it easily as a GM 141 class, the older type of locomotive. Yes, thought James, it was good to get out of the city. He had been working at Fitzgerald's, the Dublin law office, for quite a while without a break, and he knew he was starting to get the wanderlust again.

James smiled to himself. He would never have credited Gerald Fitzgerald—the senior partner, and a difficult man at the best of times—as being sensitive to the needs of his staff. Perhaps Gerald, who had been the Moores' family solicitor since St. Patrick was in knee breeches, had indeed perceived his restlessness. Obliged to go to London, it was James he had chosen to travel down to Wexford to attend to the Moores.

Well, it would be routine enough, thought James. A dead brother, three spinster sisters on a country estate. An old Protestant family. It would be a simple matter to handle the funeral arrangements for them, muddled and unworldly as they probably were.

The Wexford countryside was looking its best. Fertile fields unrolled on either side of the road, shimmering a soft green gouache—early growth which in summer would feed the county's renowned dairy herds.

The Moores owned a dairy farm, James recalled from the file, but he was not familiar with their village of Kilmartin. Gerald was from the same place. James vaguely remembered him talking about Kilmartin over dinner the night he had been made a partner in Gerald's small Dublin law firm. The Fitzgeralds came from strong Protestant farmer stock. Gerald probably went to dances and church fetes with the Moore sisters, thought James. His portly build, encased in a three-piece suit and bursting his waistcoat at the seams, made picturing him as a raw, bespectacled youth a little difficult.

That dinner at the Gray Door had been splendid. The cold borscht to start, and the tender baby ribs, which melted in his mouth. He recalled asking the Russian chef for the recipe for the marinade. And the man had given it to him too. But the third bottle of Bordeaux had erased it from memory.

James sighed. His breakfast of sausages, eggs, two rashers, and a slice of black pudding at Bewleys seemed a long time ago. Black pudding—an interesting euphemism for coagulated pigs' blood, he thought. He glanced around him, trying to orient himself. A road sign indicated a small village ahead, and he accelerated. And then he slowed. The village consisted of a crossroads with two pubs and a shop.

James parked the Citroen at an angle to the curb,

got out and stretched his long, lean body. He ran his hand through his thick, light brown hair and rubbed his face and neck. He shook one leg and then the other, shaking the creases out of his expensive and well-cut chalk-stripe suit. Dismissing the two plastic-looking pubs at a glance, he entered the shop and purchased a couple of bread rolls, a quarter pound of Irish cheddar, and two slices of Limerick ham with a lovely trimming of pure white fat. The sullen girl who served him placed them in a bag without a word.

He drove on, seeking a more attractive pub, and covered the next twenty miles well over the speed limit. Yet he was still overtaken, the second time by a farmer with a bale of hay in his trunk. The one characteristic that the Irish farmer shared with his counterparts on the continent was the incredible speed at which he drove on the narrowest of roads.

James was surprised when he came quite suddenly upon the village of Kilmartin. After one long S bend in a particularly lush area, the road straightened to reveal a pretty little village clustered around a cross-roads. James quickly noted with approval the charming architecture of the little Anglican church. It stood on a small rise, with its churchyard laid in front like a somber apron. He slowed as he passed a row of houses sitting cozily shoulder to shoulder on the broad pavement. The spire of the Catholic church rose up at the far end of the village, but before he reached this landmark, he spotted the local pub with the intriguing name of the Drooping Well.

The bar was cool and dark, with red Formica tables and aluminum-legged stools that scraped and racketed on the Spanish flagging. Cheery wrought-iron lamps dotted the walls and swung over the long bar. James was amused at the pub's striking resemblance to the myriad little bars that dotted the Mediterranean island of Ibiza. Someone here has been on a few sun holidays, he thought wryly.

"When you're ready," James called. In answer he heard movement from behind a striped curtain at the

11

end of the bar. And then silence. James seated himself on a bar stool and stared at himself in the mirror. At last a big, gruff man came out to him.

"A pint of Guinness."

The man took a pint glass and pulled the spigot.

"I haven't had any lunch, but if you could let me have a knife and a plate . . ." There was no reaction from the barman, but James knew country bartenders well enough to wait. However, after five minutes he began to wonder if the man had heard him.

The pint stood on the drip tray as its head settled. James debated with himself. If he asked again, he ran the risk of offending the man. If he didn't and the man hadn't heard him, he would be left pulling the bread apart and eating out of the bag. Or worse, being glared at by the man himself. James rattled his bag gently and was just about to open it when the barman reappeared with a fresh trout, cooked to perfection and garnished with a sprig of fresh parsley.

"Caught it this mornin'," he said succinctly, and added, "you won't get the likes of that in Dublin."

James glimpsed the man's own kitchen behind the curtain and his lunch on the table. Silently, the man finished pulling the pint, laid it reverently on the bar, and returned to his meal.

James enjoyed the fish and a second pint while he casually studied the bar's patrons. The young man in the corner, with the bottle-thick glasses, amused him, speaking earnestly to his very upper crust companion. James wondered idly if Jack Moore, now deceased, had frequented this companionable little pub. Refreshed, James returned to his car and drove slowly until he spotted the lane that should lead to Moore's farm. He pulled the car onto the right shoulder and stopped.

It was a lifelong habit, one that bespoke James's orderly, observant nature. He held his map against the wheel, but really was noting the small shop cum post office, the green mailbox to its right, the bus stops on either side of the road. He watched as the bread van unloaded its delivery of sliced pans and turnovers. He saw the turf, machine cut and stacked at the door of the garage that adjoined the ancient shop. He saw movement in the window of the shop, and in his mirror observed two or three women stepping from their front doors, not acknowledging each other, intent on sweeping the steps or studying the flowers in the small front gardens that ran the length of the row of houses.

Typical, thought James. Country people were notoriously nosy. Even a strange car stopping briefly could draw their attention. But then, his burgundy Citroen CX even drew attention in Dublin. He folded his map with elaborate movements, put the car in gear, and turned up the lane to Moore's.

"Miss Violet Moore? I am James Fleming. Gerald Fitzgerald asked me to come down to help . . ."

Violet Moore opened the door wider and stepped back as James entered the flagstone entrance hall.

"Mr. Fleming." Violet extended her hand, and James was surprised at the strength of her grasp.

As they walked toward the drawing room, James offered his condolences.

"Yes, yes," answered Violet abruptly, "now if you'll please excuse me, I want to see to some things in the kitchen."

James stood with his back to the fireplace and rocked on his heels as the fierce heat toasted his legs. He took a few seconds to revise his expectations. Violet Moore was no simple country spinster, but a woman who impressed with both her physical and personal strength. The large drawing room betrayed these characteristics. Here was no shawl-covered piano with framed photographs of distant cousins and long-dead relations, no flowery curtains and chintz-covered chairs. There were, as he noted, one or two good paintings from members of the Royal Irish Academy hanging on the hessian-covered walls. There was a tasteful three-piece suite of Scandinavian design which toned beautifully with the heavy woven toast-colored fabric that dressed the windows. A nineteenth-century rolltop desk stood in the corner, covered with neat stacks of business correspondence. A bowl of hyacinths sat in early bloom on the low coffee table. No, this was not what James had expected. And now his curiosity was aroused.

He took the heavy silver tray from Violet's hands as she reentered the drawing room. The aroma of fresh coffee filled the large, bright room. Violet poured in silence, asking only if he would take a drop of whiskey in his coffee. She fetched the bottle from the well-stocked sideboard.

Everything to hand, thought James, signs of an orderly, an active life. He waited for Violet to speak. When she did not, he began to ask a few leading questions.

"I understand that Mr. Fitzgerald has been your family solicitor for many years," he said encouragingly.

"Quite."

"I know from him that he was most regretful that he could not come down himself. He had an extremely pressing situation to deal with in London, a situation which he assured me that only he could attend to . . ."

"Yes, he mentioned some such issue on the telephone."

"Well, Miss Moore, I will do my best to stand in for him . . ."

"I'm sure you'll do as well as another," Violet replied, and refilled their cups.

James paused for a moment, musing. He seemed to be pulling teeth here. He was beginning to sound to himself like a barrister grilling a witness.

For the second time he wondered at her delay in getting to the point. Thinking he might have underestimated her grief and ability to cope, he took the initiative.

He placed his coffee cup down with a gesture of finality. "Miss Moore . . . I think Gerald told me that

14

your brother died here at the house. If you'll permit me, I'll begin now to make the necessary arrangements. I took the liberty of locating a few undertakers in the telephone book. Perhaps, if you'll tell me whether you have a preference, I'll make a few calls?"

Violet seemed to hesitate.

"I take it that a doctor has been called . . . or perhaps was with him when he . . . when he passed away." James realized suddenly that he didn't even know the cause of the man's death, and he paused.

Violet Moore sighed and then abruptly stood up.

"I think that—"

She was interrupted by voices from the doorway.

"Vi? What does he say? Oh, oh dear, oh dear . . . ." Rose rushed into the room, breathless and plump, her wispy, faded hair askew, her small hands twitching the gray and pink cardigan around her little body. James smiled. She was at that moment more like the White Rabbit than any pantomime figure. He waited to see if she'd pull a watch from her gaping pockets.

"Rose!" Lily's firm but kindly voice followed Rose from the hall. Her tall, thin frame wavered in the doorway and then she came forward, bringing a sense of calm to the group. She was followed in by a young man.

"Mr. Fleming," Violet Moore said, "my sisters, Rose and Lily. Oh, and this is Kevin Manning, my farm manager."

Kevin nodded, smiling broadly, relief in his eyes. Oh, thought James, this man seems awfully glad to see me.

"Well, what does he say?" demanded Rose again, petulantly. "Is it all over with? Can it be done?"

"Rose," whispered Lily, "I really doubt it can be done that way."

"But it must, it must. And in our own plot—"

"No!" said Violet, almost shouting. "Certainly not in our own plot! I forbid it."

Rose started to cry into a crumpled tissue. Kevin

15

stood looking awkwardly out the window. He turned, caught James's eye, and raised his eyebrows significantly.

"Vi . . ." Lily spoke in her modulated voice. "Time is passing. It's been hours now . . ."

"Of course it's been hours . . . we had to wait for Mr. Fleming." She glared at James, seemingly blaming him for the long drive down from Dublin.

"Well," said James cheerfully, "I am here now. If someone would—"

"Of course. I was just about to bring you, Mr. Fleming, when my sisters interrupted. If you'll come this way."

They made an awkward parade as they fell into a loose line behind Violet. She strode ahead, leading the way through small interconnecting halls, through the vast farmhouse kitchen to the cold room, then out the back door. They quickly crossed the courtyard between the house and the barn, dodging wild, bright raindrops which were falling from a blue sky. "March weather!" grumbled James half to himself. The whole journey was accomplished in an uncomfortable silence. As they approached the barn, James's thoughts became wilder, but nothing had prepared him for what he saw as his eyes adjusted to the dim interior.

The plain wooden coffin was laid out in the open space in the center of the barn, supported by bales of hay at the head and foot.

"Lay a jug of whiskey at my head and feet . . ." The words of the old Irish waking song flung themselves into his thoughts. He shook his head.

Rose had started to cry again.

"Miss Moore?" James directed his look at Violet, but she remained silent. He wanted some answers now.

"Mr. Fleming, at dawn this morning I was summoned to the front of my house by my deliveryman, Paddy. When I came around to the front from the barn, I saw this coffin lying on the gravel near the doorstep. Kevin opened it. After my sisters and I

16

ascertained that it contained the dead body of my brother, I had the box brought in here. I rang Fitzgerald, as you know, and told him that my brother had died." She stopped, apparently having said all she had to say.

The silence was heavy, but the air was sweet with the smell of the hay, the smell of a summer long since past. "And throw the chaff into the fire . . ." James whispered. He glanced at the faces of the people standing with him, all heads bent as if in silent prayer, all but Violet's.

"Well, Miss Moore, I must admit this is not what I was expecting."

"I assure you, Mr. Fleming, neither was I."

"You must help me here," said James more firmly. "I need some more information before I act."

Silence.

"Did you phone the police?"

"I did not."

"When did you last see him? Alive."

"I couldn't say. At least twenty-five years ago."

"Twenty-five years ago?" echoed James.

"Twenty-seven," interrupted Rose. "Twenty-seven years!"

Again there was silence.

"You are certain it is your brother?" James asked.

"At first I was not." Violet glared at Rose as her sobs grew louder. "But on a closer look, I knew it was he."

"He did not live in the vicinity then, I take it?"

Violet shook her head but failed to elaborate. James wondered why the others did not speak. He looked appealingly at Lily, but she glanced quickly away. Rose, head bowed, was sobbing into a handkerchief.

"And you were certain at that time he was dead?" he asked.

"Yes, quite dead. There was no mistaking the look of death on his face."

James was finding this more and more curious, but the presence of the dead body spurred him into action. The body had been here since dawn, it had been lying in the barn for almost eight hours now. Alone. That struck him forcibly. No one with the body. The body itself banished to the barn with the feed, sweet as it was, for the cattle. Ah, there was no tender parting and farewell here.

"Because of the circumstances, I think that I should look at the deceased now." He didn't ask permission. There seemed no reverence here. But he was mistaken. Both Lily and Rose fell back, and Kevin sighed such a sigh as to be heard. But he came forward and, together with James, lifted the lid and stood it upright against a bale of hay.

"Oh, Jack, oh my darlin' Jackeen." Real sorrow filled Rose's voice as she moved forward to stroke the dead man's face and smooth the lapels of his overcoat.

James considered the corpse before him. The gray, thin face was cold and dead, composed in death, a handsome face, that of a man around fifty. The knot in his tie sat well in the white linen collar. The overcoat was of rich Donegal tweed, the hair groomed, the skin smooth.

He whispered a short prayer and then wondered at the death of this prosperous man, at the manner of his coming to this house, at the manner of his coming to his death.

His somber thoughts were pierced by a shriek from Rose as she suddenly moved back from the body.

"There's blood! Blood!" she cried before she collapsed.

When James returned to the drawing room, the three sisters and Kevin were all standing ashen-faced, tumblers of brandy in hand. They seemed to be huddling near the fire for warmth, although James found the room stuffy now.

"From what I could see, there is a wound in Mr. Moore's chest," he said. "There was a great deal of . . . blood. The overcoat was not . . . bloodied, and seemingly concealed the wound and the bloodstains on the shirt and suit from our view. If Rose . . ." He

18

hesitated, looking at her. "If Rose hadn't . . . Well, we will deal with what has to be done."

"Which is what?" snapped Violet.

"Which is, we wait for the police," answered James, looking sharply at her.

"You had no right—"

"I had the responsibility, Miss Moore. Your brother is dead. Every aspect of this situation is—to say the least—unusual, if not bizarre. Of course the police have to be informed. As an officer of the court, and," he added more kindly, "as your solicitor per diem, I have to handle this situation accordingly."

"Mr. Fleming." Rose spoke for the first time directly to him. "Do you think, do you think . . . oh, it's too terrible to contemplate . . ."

"What Rose needs to know, and so do I," said Lily softly, "is this: do you think that Jack might still have been alive this morning when Vi . . . when we found him out front? Do you think if we had helped him then, he . . . ?" Lily shuddered.

"As you helped him twenty-seven years ago," hissed Rose to Violet.

James saw Violet lift her hand to silence Rose.

"That he might still be alive?" finished James. "I don't know, Miss Moore," he said gently to Lily. "Let us hope not, for his sake."

"For all our sakes," said Kevin.

"The police no doubt will bring the examiner with them," explained James. "It is, as you can see, not merely a question of a death certificate. I admit at first I thought that once a doctor ascertained the cause of death and signed the certificate, we could have gone ahead with the funeral arrangements, but . . . well, now I'm afraid there will be questions, and you must be prepared for a delay."

"And scandal," said Violet bitterly, "the scandal." She stood apart from the others, glaring first at them and then at James. "My purpose in calling you was to avoid just such scandal. If Fitzgerald had come himself . . ." She nearly spat the words at James.

"I assure you, Miss Moore, once Gerald or any solicitor had noticed the blood, there would be no other course. If it hadn't been Rose and myself, the doctor would have called the police."

"What need did he have for a doctor? We could have buried him in the fields."

"That's enough, Violet!" said Lily.

They all fell silent again. The sound of tires on the gravel only increased the tension in the room.

As James went toward the door to admit the police, he addressed them all. "I advise you to describe simply and accurately what happened today. This situation is very serious. Your brother was murdered. For his sake and yours, this matter must be cleared up."

James stood in the driveway surveying the rolling fields and breathing in deeply the cool air of the waning day. The setting sun lent a piquancy to the scene, a melancholy. The air was still, a few birds calling sleepily to their new mates as darkness fell. After the surprising and terrible events of the day, James welcomed the hush.

He walked down the drive, aimlessly kicking stones out of his path. He had been favorably impressed by the local police. They had been efficient as they silently went about their tasks. The medical examiner had arrived in his own car and checked the body over superficially. He had said that it seemed death was caused by the wound in the chest. A grizzled, cross old man, he had not been more forthcoming. And not in the least consoling. Still, he couldn't be expected to say more until the postmortem was completed. The body was removed by Feeney's Undertakers to Wexford General Hospital. James took his small notebook from his inside jacket pocket and consulted it. He wanted to check that he had made careful note of all the details. He sighed. He was genuinely too tired to return to Dublin. He was even too tired to drive the five miles to the nearest country hotel. He had decided to take advantage of Lily Moore's suggestion that he stay the night.

James opened the gate in toward the field and then latched it behind him. It was pleasant to walk in the quiet fields. The grass was short and the heavy evening dew barely wet his shoes.

He sighed again. He would have to ring Gerald in the morning. He hadn't wanted to bother the old man at the end of what was probably a long, strenuous day in London. What did Gerald make of Violet Moore? he wondered.

Violet. Lily. Rose. James thought of those parents long dead who had named those three baby girls after flowers, no doubt wishing for them each a life of beauty, of grace, of love. No doubt wishing for them one day families of their own, little baby flowers of their own. James mused. Maybe he would have had baby girls or baby boys of his own by now, if things had worked out with Teresa. He smiled at the sentimental picture he had created of himself and Teresa with a babe in arms. A girl. It would have been a girl. He saw the evening star and made a wish on it, as he always did—when he chanced to see it.

He hopped the dry stone wall that divided the field from the road, and continued dondering along the lane, heading toward the main road. Violet. No, she was no shrinking, hidden little thing. Instead—more like the words her name resembled—violent, violate. Such strength, such anger. So very much the head of all she surveyed, her sisters included. Did that include the brother too? He had hoped for more information when the police had questioned the sisters. He recalled their answers.

When their brother Jack had left home some twenty-five odd years ago, he had gone to England. He had corresponded with the sisters from London, and when he moved on to America, they virtually lost touch with him. It was an old story. Were the parents dead then? James was more curious than the police for all the small details. Why had the young man left

Kilmartin? Safe to assume there were no prospects on the farm. Or perhaps he had aspirations? He had struck James as looking like a businessman, smooth-skinned and rich. Perhaps he had left Ireland to seek his fortune, first in London and then in Boston. Like the hundreds of thousands of Irish before him.

And then—nothing. No word, for months. Perhaps the odd card, and then silence. They didn't even know if he had married or if there were other family members somewhere, worried and frantic . . . Violet didn't seem interested, but Rose did, and Lily too. Rose had clearly missed him the most. She had spoken affectionately of Jack as she remembered him, a young boy close to her own age. She had praised his skills around the farm, his way with the animals, and would not be silenced by Violet when she talked of his love of the land.

Lily had little to add. She had, however, been able to produce a Christmas card sent nearly ten years after he'd left home. She had even saved the envelope, which was postmarked Boston. The police would start there, of course, as well as the Irish ports and airports.

Nothing had been found on the body that would identify the man. No papers of any kind, and no money. Their first thought was robbery, and the absence of the usual things a man carries in his pockets lent weight to that idea. But if robbery had been the motive for the murder, then why did the murderer choose this bizarre method of getting rid of the body? James's mind reeled with questions and he felt the need to unwind. Suddenly he found himself back at the Drooping Well, where he had eaten lunch all those long hours ago, when he had breezed in so confidently from Dublin.

He chose to sit this time in the lounge, in a corner. He knew that he would be quickly identified as the Moores' solicitor from Dublin, and he didn't want to engage in any close questioning by the locals.

James could see the bar from the lounge. It was filled to capacity with a talkative crowd, thick blue smoke encircling the heads of people as they drank their pints. He spotted his trout-cooking barman from lunchtime, ordered a whiskey and settled back, allowing the fatigue to flow out of his body. He thought again of the call he would have to make to Gerald, and could hear the old man firing questions at him. One of the major characteristics of all lawyers, that. Curiosity masked as professional concern. James smiled. He suffered the same malady.

He loved his job. And he loved the life it had brought him, full of incident, rich in detail. He thought of those early years when he was clerking in Fitzgeralds'. He had looked forward to the day when he held power in his own hands. He had moved up to title transfers and searches. In a way, he had loved that. He enjoyed the central idea of property, of ownership, of tracking title deeds and, in the course of that, unearthing so many wonderful, intricate stories. Property was a passionate concern of the people. He had quickly come to realize the enormous truth behind the old truism: Irish people loved the land, their property, in a mystical way. Through conveyancing he had moved on to wills and estates. And now he was in his element. True, much of it could be routine. Quite ordinary people sensibly making their wills and disposing the bits and pieces of their lives amongst their families. But the gems, fewer in number perhaps, made up for the routine nature of his work.

It was the large estates, the family disputes. It was the disposal of property out of the family. It was the dredging up of all the details, of finding long-lost relations who were named beneficiaries in some old bachelor's will. These were the human mysteries that intrigued James. The intricacies and entanglements and priorities of peoples' lives, which were revealed in the making of the wills and in their execution.

And then when he had had his fill, James was in a position to arrange his schedule and take off for three or four weeks at a time. If he hadn't been able to do that, he could never have indulged his passion for train travel. Yes, this was to be the year of Peru. In fact he had forgotten about the shots, and realized he had better see to that soon. And a visa. Peru had no embassy in Ireland. He would have to apply to their consulate in London for that. This was a trip that Teresa would have objected to strongly. No sense of adventure, that was her problem. Another girl would have jumped at the chance.

He ordered his final whiskey. It wouldn't do to return to the house too late. He had become cognizant of the early hours kept by the household, dictated by the needs of the cows and the milking schedule.

He walked back briskly, relaxed and ready for the day ahead. Lily had waited up for him. He was later than he realized.

"Not to worry, Mr. Fleming. I have difficulty getting to sleep, and I don't rise as early as my sisters. I do very little of the manual work on the farm." She briefly touched her chest, as if indicating a weak heart. "No, my part in this business is the paperwork, the accounts and so on." She sighed gently; a disappointed sigh, thought James. "And the hens, of course!" she added, smiling.

She led James into the big kitchen, her gentle voice pointing out the old range-style cooker, the hooks in the ceiling where fresh-killed game used to be hung, the mechanical bellows in the now defunct fireplace, and the warming oven in the wall which they still used to let their yeast bread rise. She wasn't merely polite. Her conversation flowed easily, her ideas interesting and her voice murmuring mellifluously. It was one of the most soothing, well-modulated voices James had had the fortune to hear, and he encouraged her to talk. She made coffee on milk, and the sweet taste brought back strong memories of his college days when he indulged himself similarly after an evening of study. As Lily's voice flowed on like a low sonata playing background to his thoughts, he wondered what in this whole situation had triggered off so many disparate thoughts and memories. Fatigue, he decided, unconvinced. And although Lily seemed inclined to talk, he drew himself gently away.

His room upstairs and down the end of a long, narrow corridor was quite spartan. But it was the size of the room itself that dwarfed what would have been adequate furnishings in a more modern house. There was a single bed with a cozy, old comforter in red and brown stripes, a bedside table, two fireside chairs at the small fireplace, a towel stand, and a marble-topped washstand, of the type now seen only in good antique stores and upscale country inns.

He switched off the bedside lamp and undressed by the light of the small fire that glowed in the grate. Wrapped in the duvet, he sat for a long while at the window, the heavy chintz curtains thrown back to reveal the brightness of a country sky at night. Even with the window closed he could hear the howl of a dog, the sharp yelping of what he took to be a fox, and other, to him unidentifiable, sounds of nature carrying on its life. He had traveled far. To Russia, to India, to vast countries and high plateaux. But he had yet to encounter the quality of loneliness that filled the Irish countryside, by day and by night.

—— *Chapter Three* ——

The news of the events occurring daily at Moore's Farm spread along the route of Paddy's milk truck. And although the outlying village was alive with gossip and rumor, it was the row of houses nearest the farm and Mr. Sweeney's shop that fathered the most piquant analysis.

Paddy had come to the farm only in recent years, and as a consequence, was the most disinterested disseminator of information. There are two types of Irish country people: those abundantly endowed with the gift of imagination, and those who are not. And Paddy fell into the latter category. He enjoyed his current notoriety, however, as the man who had first set eyes on the coffin that early spring morning. But he never embellished the story. Each day he would merely report to his customers the bare facts. And so with their milk and cream he also delivered the latest movements of the Moore family. There was no betrayal in this. And although the Moores mightn't like it, they would not have expected anything else. Paddy told the neighborhood about the body, and about himself and Kevin removing it to the barn. To the barn, mind you! That caused more stir amongst his listeners than the actual discovery of the coffin itself. And then he was able to tell of Mr. Fleming, from Dublin, who had come down and who had stayed the night. Now, that wasn't news. Hadn't the whole of the pub seen him on the night in question? Paddy, being as he was, was not chagrined, and merely continued to report what he saw.

Eileen O'Grady's information was infinitely more satisfactory. Eileen did out for the Moores—that is, she was their daily help who cleaned and cooked and washed. She had been working up at Moore's for donkeys years; in fact, as a young girl she had known Jack. When she first left the convent school at fourteen, she had gone to work in the dairy barn and often used to see Jack when he came in from school. A fine-looking lad he was, she always said, full of life, full of fun. He used then to speak of the farm and what he would do when he came into the property. And now he had come back to his own place, as unexpectedly as he had gone.

Eileen embellished on the current events, although for the most part they needed no embellishment. Few believed that Violet was cast down with grief and that Rose herself was at death's door, but the stories were good and Kilmartin enjoyed them for the romances they were.

"Brendan! God bless the poor souls up at the farm, but you wouldn't know Miss Violet, she's gone so thin." Eileen stood in the crowded shop, well-aware of her audience, but nonetheless addressing her remarks to Brendan alone. Brendan nodded encouragingly, for that moment resembling a friendly, curious St. Bernard dog.

"Ah, I'll need a packet of J-cloths as well, Brendan," Eileen examined her list, "and some Vim, a packet of Sunlight Soap, mmm, and some vinegar for the windows . . . God bless them up there, they're in a bad way. A good spring cleaning will bring some needed fresh air into that house, I tell you. Rose took to her bed even before your one—what's his name—Fleming, went back to Dublin."

"But Mrs. O'Grady, we all know that now . . ." Brendan let his phrase hang in the quiet air of the shop. He expected more recent information from Eileen and he hadn't got it. In his mild way, Brendan could elicit all kinds of details. And he liked to be accurate. Between taking calls on the official post-office telephone for some of the neighbors whose phones had yet to be connected, and taking telegrams for all and sundry—but mainly the guests at the local hotel—and then again, between sorting the mail and having an interest in who was receiving what, Brendan knew far more about his neighbors than they would have guessed. But to his eternal credit, the things that he knew and the things that he found out rarely went beyond Brendan himself.

As if in answer to Brendan's unspoken criticism, Eileen leaned forward and, in a conspiratorial whisper, announced to the assembled crowd that the police were expected at the farm this very afternoon. She might have told more but for the disgruntled complaining of Mr. O'Dwyer, who had come in to buy a single stamp and had now been standing in the queue of shoppers—who had not come in for stamps —for nearly half an hour. The shoppers let him jump the queue. O'Dwyer was a mystery to his neighbors, as he seemingly took no interest in the current affairs of Kilmartin. And he stood like an incubus silencing the excitement of the small crowd. But despite his lack of curiosity, O'Dwyer knew everything that John, his neighbor on the left, knew. And that was considerable. John and O'Dwyer were to be seen on any fine day confabbing over the hedge that divided their two back gardens. On a hot day they were to be seen confabbing over the low wall that divided their small front gardens. And although the only converse he held with anyone else consisted of "It's a grand day, missus," or "There's no toleratin' this weather," O'Dwyer could build a nest in your ear, if he chose.

"Of course the police are comin' up here again," snapped O'Dwyer. "Isn't it a murder they have on their plate?" He turned on his heel with his stamp in hand and left.

No one till this point had spoken the word murder, and it sent a chill through the people in the shop.

"Ah, God rest his soul," said Eileen seriously, and she took her parcels and left the shop.

"It's a bad business," said Mr. Sinclair sententiously, in the shop for the third time that day.

Brendan's trade had increased appreciably since Tuesday, with people coming in for items they could easily have done without. But it was one of the places in the village where a bit of news might be gleaned. For those of the village who did not frequent the pub, it was either that or wait until Sunday after Mass or after Morning Prayer—if you were Protestant, that is—where news could be garnered and satisfyingly analyzed. The morning rush finally ended, and Brendan and Mr. Sweeney drew a mutual sigh of relief.

"Tea, Da?"

"That would be very welcome," answered Mr. Sweeney as Brendan disappeared into the small back room to plug in the electric kettle.

"What bickies are we having today?" he called.

"Whole Wheat, I think, but with the milk chocolate," Mr. Sweeney replied as he took down the two round packets of biscuits from the shop shelf and slit the paper with his knife. It was just past one o'clock, and he took the key from the pocket of his dusty waistcoat and locked the glass cage that sat in the corner of the shop. He sighed as he did so. The cage was an awful curse. All steel and bullet-proof glass. He'd never get used to it. At seventy he was too old for new tricks. On the other hand, he had got used to the time lock on the safe. He shook his head at the memory of how he'd take the receipts for the day's work at the small post office and stash them under the counter—and it had been safe enough for all those years. But not now. Not with the IRA robbing post offices in nearly every county in the country. He glanced up as a sudden gust of rain struck the front window of the shop. Oh, he'd got used to the safe. But the cage now was hopeless. The grill in the window was too low. His customers couldn't adjust to bending down and hollering through it, and now that he was just a little hard of hearing, he couldn't get used to it either. What's more, the little tray was far too small to be practical, especially paying out the pensions and the child allowance. Did they think up at the General Post Office in O'Connell Street in Dublin that all he did was sell the odd stamp? He was humphing to himself when Brendan returned with the steaming mugs.

Trade was relatively slow at lunchtime, and Mr. Sweeney and Brendan took turns eating lunch in the small kitchen at the back of the shop, but they always began their break with a reviving cup of Lyons tea, the Green Label blend.

"I saw the unmarked police car go up the lane," offered Brendan.

"Did you indeed?" Mr. Sweeney was full of interest. "And when?"

"Oh, about an hour ago. It was when I was getting out the two bales of turf at the front, you know, for Mrs. Byrne."

"Mrs. Byrne? How could she manage . . . Mr. Byrne usually gets it for her."

"He had to go in to work early today, I saw him on the bike as I was opening this morning. Mrs. Byrne is pretty inventive. She brought up the wheelbarrow, and lifting the turf in and out is no problem for her . . . I wonder if they came bearing news or came with more questions?"

"News, I hope. They must be worn out with questions," replied Mr. Sweeney. "And what can the Miss

Moores tell the police? Jack is gone this twenty-seven years."

"Did you know him, Da?" asked Brendan.

"Oh, aye, I knew him. Of course he was younger. I knew the whole family. Your grandfather was still alive then, and he used to do a roaring trade with not only the Moores, but all the big farms around here."

Brendan sighed to himself. They could still be doing a roaring trade if his own father had been more enterprising and not merely content to let things roll along. Things would be different when he took over himself some day.

"I remember when Jack went away because it was the spring and they were very busy up at the farm. They were calving, and they still had the sheep then. It was lambing time too. Everyone was surprised he had taken it in his head to leave just then when he was most needed . . . but he was young. Youth is heedless of such responsibility." Mr. Sweeney peered at his son of twenty-seven years and then continued.

"Anyway, it was the spring that you were born, and it stayed in my mind . . . for some reason or other. Of course, old Moore was dead, long dead, and the mother, well, I think she was dead a year or two. I do know that it was Violet who was running the farm. She used to come down here to do her business. Of course, there was no manager then, just herself with Rose and Lily and Jack all making it work. It wasn't easy. But she did a splendid job. Although I never agreed she should have given up on the sheep. But then, farming is difficult enough."

"Well, perhaps she wanted to concentrate her resources on the dairy end of things," commented Brendan.

"That's true, I imagine, looking back. After that she really made the dairy a going concern. They always did wholesale, but she brought in the retail in a big way. In fact, we were her only retail outlet for her milk. Father encouraged her, I remember, to go into the delivery business. For a single woman she did well, although she sorely missed Jack at the time. He would have been a big help to her in those early days. She was bitter. She would never mention him. Of course, I would know when they'd get a letter. When he first went, there was a letter a week, postmarked from London."

He paused to peel his apple, which he accomplished in a single movement with his pocketknife, leaving a continuous curl of skin on the counter.

"There was a gap. Rose or Lily would always ask me if there were any letters. Violet never did. After a while there were letters from America. Different cities, you know. Then just the occasional letter, always from Boston. I assumed from that that Jack had settled there . . ."

"And then they stopped, did they?" Brendan prompted.

"And then they stopped. We all thought that he had no doubt married and settled down. It was common then, Brendan, even more so than now. The men would leave, and then lose touch . . ." Mr. Sweeney sighed.

"Well, according to Eileen, Violet Moore said that he never did marry," Brendan said, resuming the conversation.

"Now that's a surprise. But the police couldn't be mistaken about that, it's too easy to check. Paddy's brother-in-law, the policeman, told him yesterday that all Jack's papers and luggage and passport were found in his room at the Shelbourne. The Shelbourne, that's Jack all over. The poshest hotel in Dublin. I'd say he enjoyed coming back and staying in style . . . Who would believe it? Dead after only a few days."

"Well, if they had the passport and the return plane ticket, they must have an address," concluded Brendan.

"Aye. And it would be easy enough to check with the Boston police . . . at least to see if there was family out there."

"No, Eileen told me, no family, no wife, no one," insisted Brendan.

"Strange, that . . ."

"Strange?"

"It's strange to me anyway," said his father. "I remember Jack was a grand one for the girls. In fact he had been very involved just before he left."

"With a local girl?"

"Mmm, what?" Mr. Sweeney plucked a banana from a bunch on the counter. "Oh yes, a local girl, there was some scandal or other." He retired to the kitchen with his banana and apple and a wedge of cheddar cheese, leaving Brendan to cope for half an hour with the few soggy patrons that the March wind blew to their door.

James Fleming picked up the phone in response to his secretary's buzz. His mind was traveling on the narrow-gauge tracks that twisted between the Peruvian Andes. A thousand adventures among ancient civilizations were about to unfold.

"Your mother on the line."

He thought rapidly. He had neglected to mention the Peru trip to his mother. She considered this railway nonsense an aberration brought on by advancing bachelorhood. He would have to tell her. And she would want to see him. Surely he was booked solid night and day for the forseeable future.

"Mother!"

"James!"

No, he couldn't possibly make the church fete on Saturday. No, nor the Gaiety Theatre on Thursday. No, not even the wine and cheese party at the museum. But yes, all right, he was free on Sunday. Yes, he would ring her on Friday to confirm.

James tapped his hand on the desk diary. He had to get his shots on Saturday. He was fortunate that Dr. McCormak was willing to take him then. With any luck he'd be deathly ill with the reaction to the small pox vaccination and could legitimately miss this bloody drinks get-together at his mother's. He looked up guiltily when his secretary came in. Maggie flirted briefly with him as she went over his schedule for the day. He had a lunchtime meeting at the Berkeley Court, but grimaced when the wind flung the rain against his window. It couldn't be helped. The contact was important; he might be able to bring in the business of a large estate. Gerald would be pleased if he pulled this one off. And they did serve excellent lamb at the Berkeley Court.

"Any word from Mr. Fitzgerald?"

"Oh yes, I should have told you. He rang this morning from London just after the office opened . . ."

"Did he . . . ?"

"No, he didn't comment that you weren't here. Another one of your late nights, I suppose," Maggie flashed a knowing smile that James chose to ignore.

"Well . . . ?"

"Well? Oh, he was in a dead rush. He said to tell you that you were to hold down the fort, that the probate was more complicated than he had expected, that you were to pull in the fish at the Berkeley today . . ." James looked up quickly, impressed yet again with Gerald's control of the minutiae of the practice.

"And . . . ?"

Maggie checked her notebook. "And that was all for you . . . Of course, I have volumes for the other three partners as well."

"Nothing about the Moores?" James asked, surprised.

"Oh, wait, yes, sorry. When the body is released for burial, you are to attend the funeral in his absence and take care of flowers, etcetera."

"Nothing about the murder?" James had sent Gerald the salient details of Jack Moore's death on the fax machine.

"Nothing."

"Are you sure?"

"Nothing."

"When is he returning?"

"He says he doesn't know. Could be away the whole week, maybe longer," she answered with a grin.

When Maggie left the office, James rapidly scanned *The Irish Times* for the day. If he had missed the funeral, Gerald would be . . . but no, there it was. The Anglican Church, Kilmartin, funeral service Friday, three P.M. Burial private, Wexford Town Cemetery.

That means they released the body to the family, thought James. When he left Moore's Farm, he had given Violet the number of the undertaker he'd dealt with. They were an old Wexford firm, very respectable and very discreet. Through the undertaker he had arranged to purchase, at Violet's insistence, a plot in a new cemetery outside Wexford town. He turned again to the death notice. Yes, it was there and not in the family plot in the churchyard that Jack Moore was to be buried. Violet was to have her way after all. James thought of Rose's tragic face and Lily's sad one. He checked his desk diary and penciled in the funeral. He wouldn't mind spending some time in the village. There were still some questions of his own he'd like to find the answers to.

"Maggie, I'll be going to Wexford on Thursday afternoon, and I'll be back on Friday evening . . ." He paused as she put him on hold. "And Maggie, arrange for appropriate flowers to be sent from Mr. Fitzgerald and the partners to the Moores. You'll find the death notice in today's paper. Jack, Jack Moore of Wexford."

He put down the phone, drew out his private notebook and made a few jottings. Yes, he'd like this bizarre situation to be put to rest, for his own satisfaction, if not for Gerald's, before leaving for Peru. He had carefully gone over his schedule on his return from Wexford. Something about that trip had made him both restless and energized. He wanted to be up and doing. He thought he saw a real possibility to take four weeks off from the firm in May. His own cases would either be concluded or could be put on hold for that month. He certainly had the time coming to him. Gerald would surely be finished in London. Although there were so many probabilities in the situation, he felt he had assessed things accurately. One of the two juniors could take care of his ongoing work while he'd be ongoing from Lima to Huancayo, 120 miles of track twisting through the rarefied air of the Andes. And then on from Huancayo to Cuzco. He would invest in a new rucksack at Johnston's of Wicklow Street. He would get his shots and get deathly ill and miss his mother's cocktail party on Sunday.

A nervous sun peered from behind the bundling clouds of March as James stepped out the front door. A nice lunch at the Berkeley, and all's right with the world.

James was surprised to see the number of cars parked outside the house when he arrived at Moore's Farm to accompany the three sisters to the church. Violet Moore had given him the impression on the telephone that it would be quite a small group of mourners.

"Mr. Fleming, I'm happy to see you again!" Kevin strode toward James, slapping the Citroen on its flanks as if it were one of his cows. His look of relief was even more evident this time. "That's a grand car you have. Very swank."

James smiled. Somehow Kevin looked all wrong in his three-piece tweed suit, biceps straining the seams, his bright red face beaming over his tight collar. But by the time James had got out of his car, he realized that Kevin was visibly troubled.

"It's a bad business, this," muttered Kevin. "I don't believe they should be upsetting Miss Moore today of all days . . ."

"Who?" asked James, intrigued.

"It's not so much the local men, though God knows they have been in and out of here all week. It's this pair of special police from Dublin I object to."

"The Special Branch! When did they first show up?"

"About an hour ago . . . no warning, nothing."

"Did you catch a name?"

"It's one Detective Inspector O'Shea. Pleasant enough. I know his name since he collared me this morning in the new barn. Had a few questions. Introduced himself. Pleasant enough, as I say, but . . ."

They entered the hall and James heard the booming voice. He had met O'Shea a few times but was certain the man would not recall their fleeting encounters over the years in Dublin. But he did.

"Fleming! Glad to see you again. How's the train trekking?" O'Shea was a big, hearty man with a sonorous voice. He gave people an instant feeling of security.

"You've a great memory there," answered James affably. "Peru is next on the agenda. I hope to take the train that runs at the highest elevation in the world."

"The devil you are. Great stuff! Great stuff!" The two men strolled into the drawing room, which was empty but for O'Shea's sullen-looking assistant. "Where's Fitzgerald these days? Not retired is he?"

James explained that Gerald was on business in London.

"Pity," remarked O'Shea. "He's from these parts. Might have been able to shed some light on the situation."

"Mmm. Any news on Jack Moore's previous history?" asked James.

"Well, that depends on what you've already heard. We know that he arrived two days before the body was found here. He came through Dublin Airport on a flight from London. We're a bit puzzled that he didn't take a direct flight from Boston. On the other hand, he

37

only made a connection at Heathrow. He didn't stop over at all . . . Tell me now, do you know the family long yourself?"

"Not really." James was deliberately vague. "He didn't have family there . . . in Boston." James hazarded this comment knowing that if Jack had, the body would have no doubt been flown back to the States.

"No. Apparently he was a successful businessman but he didn't have family. We're working with the Boston police to check on his friends. It seems he liquidated all his assets in the States—the Internal Revenue Service there is going to forward the details. But we already know now that he sold his contracting firm for a good price. And the way things are out there, he might have had stocks or investments. We're waiting to get the whole picture."

James's ears pricked up. This was something that hadn't occurred to him. If Jack's estate was substantial, Violet Moore might just ask him to manage the situation for her. If indeed there was no family, then Jack's three sisters might well be the beneficiaries. He beamed to himself, already relishing the thought of one or two trips to Boston. He'd never been to Boston, but he knew of a nineteenth-century eccentric who had built fifty miles of track in eastern Massachusetts just to tour his cranberry bogs. Had an 0-4-2 steam locomotive and several open-ended Pullman cars. That was style. And this enthusiast's delight was only a few hours' drive from Boston. He started guiltily when the three sisters entered the drawing room, somber in black mourning dress.

As Violet paused to speak to O'Shea, Lily drifted over to James.

"Mr. Fleming. I'm glad to see you here, but I was wondering . . . is Gerald Fitzgerald with you?"

James thought he detected a note of longing, or was it dissatisfaction? He stiffened, slightly offended. "I'm afraid not, he's still detained in London. But I know

38

that he would have wanted to be here with your family."

Lily nodded.

The undertaker's limousine was now at the door, and James was asked to ride with the sisters. He saw other cars leaving the farm, Kevin's amongst them. Violet was bitter during the short ride to the church.

"It's outrageous, I tell you. They could have come yesterday, they could have come tomorrow. But today! O'Shea knew it was the day of the funeral." Rose wept softly, but Lily was conciliatory.

"Violet, I don't think they can pick their moment. He has to come down from Dublin when he's free to do so . . ."

"Yes . . . yes . . . I suppose it's for the best. The sooner this mystery is cleared up, the better. I cannot bear the scandal. If they solve this today, at least the gossip in the village will die down. With luck it will be a nine-days wonder."

James pondered, not for the first time, Violet's reactions. Even taking into account the Irish penchant for saving face, he did think that at least her curiosity at finding the murderer of her only brother would outweigh her sense of scandal.

They all fell silent as the car pulled in through the gateway of the picturesque church and drove slowly up the graveled path to the side door. The hearse was already at the door, and once the family was seated, the men would bring in the coffin.

James attempted to keep his mind on the service, out of respect for the deceased, and for the most part he did so. But he hadn't known the man, and found his mind wandering. Something seemed to be stuck in the back of it, some detail nagging at the edges of his memory. He tried to clarify it, to no avail.

He observed the congregation. The small stone church was full, each of its long wooden pews creaking under the burden. Without warning, the organist switched from the Bach to a hymn James didn't recognize. Everyone got up. Violet, flanked by Rose and Lily, stood erect in the front pew. James, positioned a few rows back, concentrated on Rose, but she was steady on her feet. Several well-heeled types were amongst the general village population. Then James spotted Mr. Sweeney and Brendan from the shop. And Kevin and his wife. And Paddy with his, looking distinctly under the weather.

The nagging thought returned, even as the clergyman addressed the congregation. James listened intently as he spoke of Jack Moore, a man he obviously had not known. He smiled at the irony of the situation and thought of the numerous funerals he had attended. Funerals where glowing words were spoken by one man about another, in most cases by a man who had never really known the other. Form and substance. So much of what was significant in life was governed solely by form and not by substance. Did it trivialize events, perhaps even emotions? he wondered. Violet, now . . . she was breaking with form. And in a dramatic way. True, outside the environs of a small Irish village, the question of where a man was to be buried might seem slight. But her decision was of epic proportions in its context. She wasn't keeping up form. Jack, her only brother, was to be buried in a new, and worse, a public cemetery far from his birth place. And not in the family plot barely a hundred yards from where his sisters now sat.

What, he wondered with increasing intensity, was the bad blood between Jack and Violet Moore? What had such a powerful hold that even in the face of his death, in the face of his murder, she would not bend? She would not bow to her sisters' obvious desires to have Jack buried in the family plot in their own parish church. She would not bow in the face of the speculative gossip of the surrounding countryside, even though she seemed to live in dread of that very gossip. Yes, she was an intensely private person who was now leaving herself open to unceasing speculation as to her motives.

James's attention was caught again, and he focused his wandering thoughts on the clergyman's summation. He was naming the bereaved sisters individually, offering to each in turn consoling words appropriate to their personalities. Or so he thought. Oh, yes, he'd be careful to do that, to say the right things to some of the most wealthy and substantial members of his parish, members who without doubt had contributed to every fund-raising event this man and his select vestry could devise. Substantial. Was this the only substance that countered mere form? Shakespeare was mistaken. It wasn't the deeds that lived after men, it was their money—that was the substance the world recognized. And who better than James to know the truth of that; he who spent his working life helping people distribute their wealth from beyond the grave. Writing wills and probating wills and executing wills. And did that apportionment of wealth, that allotment of what the world called substance, parallel the dying's portioning out of affection to the inevitable survivors? Love parceled out in the form of property and belongings, stocks and shares, silverware and jewelry?

The congregation was rising, and James suddenly realized the service was nearly over. The undertaker's men were standing by the coffin, ready to move the trolley, on which it rested, slowly up the aisle, on silent wheels.

That was it! The undertaker's men. Surely they would know—who had contacted them, where had they picked up the body, where indeed had they coffined the body? He stirred restlessly in his seat. He wanted to get back to the house to speak to O'Shea. He stood up as the pews began to empty in an orderly fashion, and as he followed, was surprised to see O'Shea at the back of the church. A very large man trying to look inconspicuous and failing.

When they exited, the people gathered on the steps to offer their condolences to the Moore sisters. But Violet brushed such niceties aside and headed straight for the funeral car. Rose and Lily, however, remained. James stood nearby. He noted that the assembled crowd of friends, neighbors, and business acquaintances were with one accord warm and sincere in their expressions of sympathy to the two sisters. He watched as Lily graciously accepted the handshakes and kind words and then capably invited old friends back to the house for refreshments, after the private burial in Wexford's new town cemetery. Many of the congregation asked either Rose or Lily if they could also speak with Violet; many looked around inquiringly to see if they had missed her somewhere in the crowd and confusion at the door. Some, as they passed the funeral car in which she sat, tipped their hats or waved gloved hands gently, solicitously. James found it hard to reconcile Violet's perceptions of her jackel-like neighbors with these polite and appropriate expressions of respect if not, in this case, grief.

James watched as Rose, a bit addled, a little bit muddled in her grief, was greeted warmly by a number of women; members, he discovered, of the Irish Countrywomans Association, of whose local branch Lily had been a founding member.

Nothing was said the entire journey to the cemetery. The hearse and their car slowed passing through each village, as caps were removed and people crossed themselves out of respect to the unknown dead. James observed each sister in turn, each silent and preoccupied.

The new cemetery was painfully so, with sapling cypresses, mud everywhere, and three yellow excavators parked just yards from where they stood. The graveside service was mercifully brief, with even the clergyman seeming anxious to be done and away from the terrible emptiness of the place. Lily kept her arm around Rose, supporting her as they both stood a little distance from Violet. There were no tears.

It was with a great sense of relief that James alighted from the funeral car into the brisk fresh air and armed both Lily and Rose into the house. Sandwiches and tea were served in the seldom-used dining room, and the people who had come back for the wake spoke quietly amongst themselves. Violet, after a few broken conversations, left; ten minutes later, as James was sipping a welcome cup of tea, he spied her through the window, crossing the yard, dressed in her anorak and boots. Eileen, however, continued to move among the visitors with trays of sweets, while Kevin, looking uneasy, stood at a side table pouring drinks with a heavy hand.

James was surprised yet again to see O'Shea mingling with the guests, and curious when he beckoned him with a sober look.

"Fleming," said O'Shea brusquely, "when this group disperses—which I hope will be sooner rather than later—I am going to question the Moores."

"But you've been through all that. Surely today of all—"

"Must be done. And done today," O'Shea cut in.

"But it's routine questioning, surely."

"Pardon me, Fleming. I'm telling you this since you are, I take it, their solicitor, acting in place of Gerald Fitzgerald. Personally, I would have thought a murder serious enough to merit the old man's presence."

James bridled. "O'Shea! I am here in a professional capacity. But I assure you that having got to know the Moore sisters, I am also taking a personal interest in this case. I can speak on their behalf, and I assure you that they are anticipating a speedy solution to this tragic murder of their brother."

O'Shea smiled wryly. "In that case, I'm glad I spoke. I think you should be present when I question them."

"Of course. But before we get to that, I've been wanting to ask you about this hearse business. Have you located the undertaker who delivered the body here?"

"We're working on it, we're working on it."

O'Shea's tone was dismissive, and James reluctantly let the matter drop.

O'Shea questioned Rose first, and James had the strong feeling he had done it merely to get Rose out of the way. Between her sobs and tears she had little to tell O'Shea about Jack except what a grand lad he had been and what a happy childhood they had shared. Her mind seemed locked in a time warp where the remote happy past was far more vivid to her than the unhappy present.

"If he hadn't gone away then, this wouldn't have happened," she repeated, seemingly illogically connecting the two events. "He could have stayed on here, and in the end he would have married Kathleen and we would have had little babies, fat little babies in the house. Oh, I would have loved his fat wee babes just as my own—" Rose fell into a paroxysm of weeping, and O'Shea and James stood helplessly by. She turned and ran to the door, calling to Lily, who came quickly.

"That's quite enough, Mr. O'Shea." said Lily, her mild demeanor lending even more force to her words. She looked reproachfully at James. "Young man, I think you could look after our interests as well as Gerald would."

She brought Rose to her room, and on her return she took a seat by the fire, composed once more.

"Mr. O'Shea," she said, taking the initiative, "we have all been questioned by the local police. We were all questioned at the inquest. And I, and my sisters also, have given statements to your assistant. I really don't think that we have to undergo this ordeal again!"

"Miss Moore, believe me when I tell you that I sympathize with your situation. And I imagine you are tired after the strain of the funeral. But I think you'll agree that a speedy end to this situation would be a great relief to all concerned." O'Shea glanced at James, who nodded.

"Very well, Inspector."

"I only have one or two very specific questions. Firstly, concerning the murder weapon. We believe that the murder weapon was a carving knife from your own kitchen. Can you tell me when was the last time you saw that knife?"

"No, I cannot," Lily said simply.

O'Shea leaned back in his chair.

"Now, Miss Moore, I'd like you to recall the day and the evening before you all found the body of your brother . . . Can you think of any unusual—let me say, any out of the ordinary—occurrences in or around the farm?"

Lily shifted in her seat and then withdrew an untipped cigarette from her pocket. O'Shea leaned forward to light it. She inhaled deeply, looked at James and then at O'Shea.

"There was one odd thing . . ."

"Go on," said O'Shea keenly.

"It happened the night before we found . . . Jack's coffin. I had meant to ask Violet about it, but the events of that day knocked it out of my head. Not having seen Jack for so many years, and then to see him again dead . . ." Lily's voice trembled.

"I was very restless that night, which is not unusual for me. I had been reading, and I must have dozed off, because my book had fallen off the bed. I think now that it was the noise of the book hitting the floor that woke me. Whatever it was, I couldn't go back to sleep. I got up and turned off the light and walked over to my window. I felt some fresh air might help me. I started to open the window on the right-hand side when I glanced down into the yard.

"I thought I had seen some movement. In fact, I thought I had seen Violet. I peered through the glass, and indeed it was Violet. I was so relieved. You see, I sleep so badly that I was relieved to think I had slept through the night. When I saw Violet, I assumed she was on her way to the milking and that it must be near dawn. I continued to open the window, but it was quite stiff, and as I stood there, I saw her stop. She seemed to be speaking to someone. It was a man. And again, thinking it was time for the milking, I assumed the man was Kevin." Lily paused and smoothed her skirt. She seemed preoccupied.

"And was it?" asked O'Shea.

"Well, the extraordinary thing was that just at that moment the telephone rang in the hall downstairs. I didn't want it to wake Rose, so I rushed down to answer it . . ."

"Yes?" said O'Shea impatiently. James looked at him inquiringly, but O'Shea ignored him.

"Well, you see, it was Kevin on the telephone. He was calling with a message for Violet. He might be late coming in, in the morning, because his car had broken down or something. And he wanted to warn her to expect trouble with the calving of Moira. In case she went into labor during the night."

O'Shea looked blank. "The carving of . . ."

"The calving," interjected James. "This is the calving season."

Lily continued. "Kevin was apologizing for ringing so late, and I thought that that was a bit odd, still believing that I'd just seen him with Violet in the yard . . . in fact, still believing it was dawn. But as I stood there at the phone, I looked up at the grandmother clock and it was only half-twelve. No doubt Kevin will remember his call. He doesn't keep such late hours as a rule."

"So what you're saying is—be careful now, Miss Moore, this is very important—what you're saying is that you saw your sister Violet in the barn with an unidentified man between midnight and twelve-thirty?"

"I will say it was a man I didn't know."

"Was it your brother Jack Moore?" asked O'Shea.

Lily lowered her head and sighed. Silence filled the room. Ominous. Disturbing. James jumped as the telephone, as if on cue, rang shrilly in the hall outside the door. He went to answer it. It was for O'Shea. Lily didn't look at them as she passed through the hall and into the kitchen.

O'Shea spoke for some moments and then hung up. He lit a cigarette, then called his assistant from the kitchen and asked him to come inside to take notes. And he asked Eileen to fetch Violet.

When Violet appeared, she was still wearing her boots and anorak, her face perspiring.

"This bloomin' business of the funeral has upset all our routines," she addressed them abruptly, "and I've neglected the cattle. Moira is finally about to drop her calf. Kevin's going to need me. I can only spare you a few minutes." She glared at O'Shea and then at James.

O'Shea spoke. "Miss Moore, I'm afraid this is a very serious matter. I need your full attention. I am going to caution you now. As you see, your solicitor is here and my assistant will take notes."

James was as startled as Violet. What O'Shea was suggesting was ridiculous.

"Two pieces of information have just come to hand, two pieces of information that fit quite neatly together, I'm afraid. Firstly, a witness has placed you in your dairy barn at the approximate time of Jack's death."

"Yes." Violet looked at O'Shea quizzically.

"Secondly . . ." O'Shea took a long pull on the stub of his cigarette and threw it behind him into the fire. "Secondly, the knife which my men discovered in the same barn some days ago—"

"What knife?" Violet exclaimed.

"A kitchen knife . . . a kitchen knife which your own, er, woman, Eileen O'Grady, identified as belonging to your kitchen."

"Eileen? When did you . . . I don't . . ."

James cautioned Violet with a wave of his hand not to say any more.

O'Shea waited, but Violet remained silent.

"Furthermore, I have just been informed that this knife, found in the barn, is certainly the murder weapon . . ."

Violet swayed slightly, and James moved to put a supporting hand beneath her elbow.

". . . and that your fingerprints and only yours were found on the knife. I'm afraid, Miss Moore, that I must bring you to the police station to formally charge you with the murder of your brother, Jack Moore."

———— *Chapter Four* ————

Gerald Fitzgerald looked somber as James concluded his report.

"But I thought the body was only in the barn after it was discovered at the front of the house. The murderer hardly killed Jack in the barn and then had a hearse drive it around to the front."

"Agreed. But O'Shea didn't deign to explain his thinking to us. It seemed enough that he had the murder weapon with Violet's fingerprints on it, and only hers. That the body was found at her house. That she was seen at the barn with an unidentified man by her own sister at the approximate time of Jack's death. And that the knife was found hidden in the barn."

"Did Violet offer any explanation?" asked Gerald.

"No, she said nothing. Nothing at the bail hearing and nothing since she's been released."

"You took care of the bail?"

"Yes, there were no problems there," replied James. Gerald was silent. James glanced around the comfortable sitting room. The furnishings indicated both Gerald's prosperity and his taste. Or perhaps his wife's taste. James remembered Mrs. Fitzgerald as a kindly, maternal woman who had taken a warm interest in his early career. He missed her gentle humor. Gerald had changed after her death. He had become more remote in the past year, and everyone at the law office had noticed it. Since they had had no children, James reflected, Gerald must feel loneliness even more sharply.

"Gerald, old man, let me leave you in peace. We can discuss this—"

"Nonsense, I have too many questions. Firstly, I must say this. I think you very remiss in not attending the inquest in Wexford, mmm?" Gerald glared at James and shifted in the big wing chair to a more upright position. He seemed to be coming to life again, as the color flooded his face.

"I've close-questioned myself about that, Gerald," James said seriously. "When I left Moore's Farm that morning, after having telephoned you in London, there seemed no question of the family being involved in Jack's death. The coroner had called the inquest for Wednesday. The body was still to be examined and the postmortem performed. I should add that it did stay in my mind during that week. I rang the coroner and learned from him that they were only calling on Violet, Kevin, and Sean to give testimony. In fact, that evening I rang again and was told that no other person had come forward with information that was new. The jury returned an open verdict—that Jack was murdered by person or persons unknown. Not in my wildest dreams did I think that Violet had anything to do with it. And I might add, I still don't."

"Your loyalty to our client is impressive, James, after so short an acquaintance."

"I'm not sure it's loyalty at all, Gerald. Strangely enough, it's a gut feeling—call it a fancy of my own—but I don't think Violet capable of such an act."

"I'm amazed to hear it. As I remember Violet, she is a tremendously capable woman, a very determined woman, perhaps I might even call her a ruthless woman."

"Are you telling me you believe she did it?"

"Well, actually no. One doesn't like to think of one's longstanding clients suddenly as murderers. However, we must deal with the reality of the situation. Obviously O'Shea considers her to be the murderer. He's shrewd and generally successful, good at his job. If he has charged her, then it is with good reason. She had the means—the knife, of course. And apparently, according to Lily's still dubious statement, Violet had the opportunity. But that's assuming a lot. Lily did not identify the man as Jack, now, did she?"

James's face brightened considerably. Listening to Gerald seemed to get things back into perspective.

"And then there's motive, Gerald. What possible motive could she have had? O'Shea has nothing there, or he would have hinted at it, I'm sure of it!"

"Right! Now listen to me. Firstly, I am putting you in charge of the case. I know, now that I'm back, you probably assumed it would fall in my provenance. But I am not feeling well—with this heart thing of mine. More importantly, you have been, as it happens, Johnny on the spot. Further, you have some empathy with the Moores. And finally, I think we need your active involvement in the case. There are a number of things I want you to do down in Wexford, and you are more able than I to make flying trips in your most suitable car." Gerald smiled at James.

"Now, while you're here I want to call Lincolns Inns and see if we can get hold of Madigan. So pour yourself another brandy and one for me—it has great medicinal properties." He winked at James and turned to the phone at his elbow.

As James poured out two healthy measures of Hennessey into the Waterford Crystal snifters, he considered Gerald's idea. James didn't know Madigan well, since he'd never had occasion to be involved in a criminal suit, and he wondered at the wisdom of calling in the renowned barrister. It was like a signal to the man in the street that the accused was probably guilty. James even felt that way himself. Madigan's fame was based on often successfully defending what seemed to be hopeless causes. There was a suspicion even in the Inns of Court that many of his clients had indeed been guilty and had been set free on mere technicalities and loopholes cleverly manipulated by Madigan. James sighed. He did not want to see Violet tarred with the same brush, tainted in advance by an association with Madigan.

Gerald looked somber when James handed him his brandy, and he drank it down at a gulp.

"Madigan can't do it for us. He claims he has too many briefs as it is, and a number of those are no doubt capital cases. We'll have to call Sheridan. He's sound and experienced, but . . . well, Madigan's brilliance and fire just aren't there." James nodded, relieved. Sheridan was indeed solid and middle of the road. Convinced as he was of Violet's innocence, James did not believe she needed the Machiavellian maneuvering of Madigan. Or the public interest his presence would immediately generate. But as he left Gerald's that night, he had a twinge of regret, and hoped that his new client would not suffer adversely for the lack of Madigan's ingenuity.

"But James, it's such a change for you. So exciting! Now just put the smoked salmon sandwiches at the back of the dining room table, that's it."

"A change from what?" James felt his voice rising as he helped his mother set out what she fondly called canapes.

"Oh, you know, James—from all that dull office work you do . . . I'm sure there's more to the law than clerking . . . now put the cucumber sandwiches at the front, there we are."

"You know, Mother, I've been a partner for some years now, and—"

"Oh, but darling, of course, of course. Gerald is so generous. Of course he would do his best for you. But now this. This case will be in all the papers. We'll finally see your name in print. I'm certain that Gerald will give you a lovely raise and perhaps a lovely little promotion as well. Now, your father at your age . . ."

James tried valiantly to block out his mother's voice. It was always the same. He wondered yet again how his mother sailed blithely through life, getting all the essential details wrong and yet getting the larger picture so often right.

He heard her high-pitched voice from a great distance—calling from the African Room, her name for the room in which she housed all the trinkets she had carried back from what to her was still the dark continent. The room was bright and airy, with a bay window letting in the morning sunshine. He wished that this room had been here during his residence in the house. His mother suffered from that peculiarly Irish disease of "adding on." To date she had added on three rooms to the original house, and was now considering converting the garage.

She was arranging glasses on trays and trying to find space on the sideboard amongst the twenty or so carved elephants that reposed there. A lion looked benignly down on their heads from an embroidered cloth.

"Now, James, when you're serving the drinks—"

"The what!" James's voice was definitely an octave higher whenever he visited his mother. "I thought I was a guest?"

"Don't be ridiculous, James, you're my son. Now, in Africa, of course, we'd have a native boy. And since your brother Donald can't get away from his rounds, as he says, you'll have to do."

James thought dark thoughts about his younger brother, now a junior medical resident, but certainly senior to James in sensibly wriggling out of his mother's parties.

His mother was the most popular woman James

knew, and this was borne out yet again by the crowd of corpulent, well-dressed friends who were massed on the doorstep. James greeted them as he admitted them into the reception hall.

"James!" most of them exclaimed, as though they hadn't seen him for a generation. With his arms piled high with coats, he could barely shake hands.

"Just popping in . . . service was so very long this morning. Absolutely parched. Vivienne . . . Vivienne . . ." The swarm of thirsty church-goers buzzed into the drawing room from the hall as James sighed and threw the coats on the hall stand. He had spotted a few younger types—in fact, young women. His mother was going to try again.

The babble of voices rose around his ears as he poured large drinks and made small talk. Through the mass of bodies he had spotted a young, attractive woman perched uncomfortably on the arm of one of the fireside chairs. Eventually he carried two stiff "G and T's" to her side and introduced himself.

She looked up gratefully and then shrugged. She was balancing a plate of cucumber sandwiches in one hand and a cup of tea in the other.

She smiled an engaging smile and told him she was Hilary. And then she shrugged again.

James hastily pulled over one of the many small wooden tables that represented an elongated elephant with a sort of rimmed tray stuck to its back.

"We might as well make use of one of these beasts of burden."

Hilary laughed, and suddenly James was conscious of his mother's eyes upon him. From afar he heard again her high-pitched voice.

"You've met, you've met! How perfectly extraordinary! Now, Hilary, isn't he just all I've told you? Your aunt and I think you two are just perfect together. James, don't slouch your shoulders like that." James watched as an embarrassed blush crept up Hilary's neck.

"Young people need to be taken in hand," James's

mother barreled on. "After all, James is getting a bit long in the tooth—oh, heavens, what am I saying? But of course—child bride, child bride, I always said Mr. Fleming just robbed the cradle when he married me. Now, Hilary, we can't say that about you. This business of women having careers. Much too silly. Marriage and babies, that's what I say—"

"What is it that you do, Hilary?" James's cool voice cut through his mother's matchmaking. But without taking any notice of him, she had moved on, urging cucumber sandwiches on her tipsy morning revelers.

Hilary struggled to her feet, placing her refreshments on the mantel. "Well, actually, I'm an executive secretary with the Peat Board . . ." As she said it she laughed merrily once again, and James suddenly felt very aware of her cornflower-blue eyes and the mass of auburn hair that fell to her shoulders in wonderful disarray.

"And I know what you do. Why, we all do . . ."

"Oh, yes," replied James hesitantly.

"Of course. You're senior partner in that big law firm. In fact, according to your mother, you are head of the firm in all but name. She tells me that Mr. Fitzgerald is practically in his dotage, and but for you, the firm would be dying with him."

James wasn't sure if Hilary spoke tongue-in-cheek. Had she already got the measure of his mother?

"In that event, she'll probably have told you about my black belt in karate . . . which happened to be an orange belt in judo," James added wryly, and watched her face.

"But of course." She smiled.

James decided he could do worse than while away the remainder of the party in Hilary's company—and avoid his mother. At least for now. He gestured toward the garden door of the African Room.

"Then let's step outside to the jungle, and I'll show you some of my better holds."

* * *

James regretted his decision to drive down to Wexford on St. Patrick's Day. Never before had he realized that every village and town celebrated after Mass with a parade of its own, no matter how ragtag. His jaw clenched yet again as his CX was forced to crawl behind slowly moving marchers and floats.

Eventually he reached Kilmartin and pulled in at the Drooping Well, only to discover that it was closed for the extended holy hour. Irritated and tired, he drove on to Riders Inn, a small country hotel some miles distant which he had heard good things about from Gerald and where Maggie had booked him a room.

Two hours later James sighed and stretched his feet out to rest them on the fender of the large hearth fireplace. St. Patrick's Day had improved rapidly once he had reached Riders. The remains of an enormous afternoon tea lay scattered on the table at his side. He stretched like a fat cat, full of scones and butter and jam, wafer-thin sandwiches, and fat raisin buns. More holiday makers entered the peaceful country parlor. James stirred and regretfully left his seat.

Upstairs in the cool, sparsely furnished room, he gazed out the small window over the basin as he washed. Just a hint of pale green had touched the leafless trees that bordered what would soon be a lush garden. White wrought-iron benches and tables stood lonely, waiting for the summer. Yes, he would definitely return to this place, he mused, when he needed respite from his labors.

The small oak bar he had spotted earlier drew him back downstairs. He was just diving into a large "G and T" and a 1957 issue of *Country Life* when a voice broke in on his solitary enjoyment. He looked up, slightly annoyed.

"Compliments of the house," said a stout woman with pale gray hair pulled tightly into a bun. "It's Mr. Fleming, isn't it?"

James accepted the second gin and tonic and asked

the woman, who was both owner and manager, to join him.

"Many thanks," James said genially. "I've only been here an hour, Mrs. . . . ?"

She smiled. "Rider, believe it or not."

"Mrs. Rider. And I know that I will be returning many times."

"Well, Mr. Fleming, I can tell from your car and your appearance, you're not a commercial traveler. Perhaps you are . . ."

"A solicitor—for my sins, as they say. Actually, I should be in Kilmartin, but I underestimated the holiday traffic. I think I'll have to hold off my visit until tomorrow. And no harm done, since I've been seduced by your teas and am looking forward to your dinner!"

"Kilmartin? . . . That's a mere stone's throw from here. Sure I know it well—" She broke off suddenly. "Well, Mr. Fleming, I suggest that you walk in our gardens before dinner. There's a stretch in the evenings now, each day a cock's step longer than the day before. The air will whet your appetite." She left abruptly, leaving James puzzled.

But his unspoken question was answered that evening after the splendid dinner of grilled lamb chops, new potatoes drenched in butter and parsley, and some impossibly early fresh peas. Mrs. Rider joined her guests in the sitting room for coffee as heavy and grainy as only Irish country people made it.

"It occurred to me that as you are a solicitor, you were somehow involved in the recent unpleasantness they've been having in Kilmartin," said Mrs. Rider as she handed him his coffee.

"To be honest, I am," said James, heaping brown sugar into his coffee from the silver bowl which Mrs. Rider offered him.

"I am an old friend of the Moore sisters," she said guardedly.

"Ah, I understand. Well, I am acting as their

57

solicitor and I've come down to do a bit of work on the case. I'm doing some background work, actually."

"It's a terrible scandal here in the county, Mr. Fleming, as I'm sure I don't have to tell you. But then, I detect a Dublin accent."

"True, true. I don't know this area well, although I'm getting to like it. If there's anything you feel you could tell me about the Moores . . ."

"I hardly think . . ." Mrs. Rider, as edgy as a thoroughbred horse, began to move away.

"I mean, if you think it would be of help to Violet Moore. You were saying earlier that you were friends." James smiled encouragingly as Mrs. Rider sat down.

"Well, first I can assure you that I do not for an instant think Violet committed this horrible murder. It's ridiculous to even picture her plunging a knife into a man's chest, let alone into her own brother!"

"I agree," said James, "and not just because she is my client."

"Glad to hear it. Obviously you can't know Violet as I do. You see, we were in boarding school together. It was a small Protestant residential school for girls—since closed, I'm afraid. We were there together for six years, and after that we kept in touch for, oh, I'd say ten, with perhaps a twice-yearly visit. She was very bright. I always thought she should have gone on into a profession, but nothing would shake her determination to stay on at the farm.

"I had mixed feelings when her mother died and left the farm to her, and the others, of course. I felt that she would never escape the farm. But that was the foolishness of youth. As time passed I realized she had no desire to leave, it was her one true love—her passion, you might say. We drifted apart after my marriage to Captain Rider. Violet was at my wedding, but later, when my children came along, our interests diverged. In latter years we've met only at the races or the odd auction, the occasional party. But she never changed from that determined young woman I knew."

"Can you tell me, Mrs. Rider, had there ever been anyone special in her life?" James was inwardly thrilled to come upon this chance to find out about Violet Moore's early life.

"No, not to my knowledge. At the time when all of us girls were starting to go out socially, doing a bit of traveling, going up to Dublin in some cases to take up jobs, she remained on the farm. Then there were those few years when there was a flurry of weddings. She always attended, she always seemed in great form. The rest of us girls tried to arrange dates with brothers, escorts at weddings, you know the thing. But she never . . . well, she never did click with anyone in our circle. I think she scared the boys off. On the other hand, any number of the girls in our general circle were absolutely mad about Jack. He was younger, but it didn't matter, he was a lovely looking lad, big, strong, lively. But he had no time for us!"

"Why was that?" James's ears pricked up at the mention of Jack.

"Well, I do recall that he was gone on a girl, as we used to say. She certainly wasn't in our circle. That I do remember. But she was a local girl, from one of the outlying farms around Kilmartin. I can't recall her name; I'm not sure that I ever met her. But wait . . . wait . . ."

James waited, hopeful.

"Yes . . . It was Walsh! In fact it was the same name as some of my distant cousins in the north. I remember working out at the time if they were related. I have it . . . Kathleen Walsh!"

"Do you know if she is still in the area?"

"Oh, I have no idea. It's all so long ago. The things I'm recalling now are from that period of time that seemed so full of high emotion and sudden passions, courtships and engagements and pretty country weddings. But you're closer to that time of one's life than I.

59

"We were all in the whirlwind days of meeting our partners in life. What I remember is that Kathleen had a huge family of brothers, and that Jack was—unfortunately, in some opinions—mad about Kathleen. Why he or she broke it off, I have no idea. Of course she was Catholic, so her family mightn't have been too keen. I don't suppose Violet would have been thrilled either. Anyway, one day they were madly in love, and the next day he was gone."

It was midnight when James sat at the small dressing table in his room, quickly jotting down notes of what he had learned from Mrs. Rider. Despite the long day, he felt elated. The cool of the room was stimulating after the warmth of the oak bar. He found his mind racing . . . he was enjoying his new role as sleuth.

On reviewing the information he had gleaned, he wondered again at his mental excitement. He was building up a picture of the victim. But what in the end did the doings of Jack Moore at the age of twenty have to do with his death? James sighed. Somewhere in his gut he sensed that the clue lay in the past. He only hoped that it did not lie in Violet's past as well.

Jack, it seemed, had loved Kathleen. And he had gone away. And in all those following years he had never married. Had she been his only love—in all that time? James's thoughts drifted to Hilary.

No! There was no comparison. He could never forget Teresa. He would never forget, either, how she had fallen out of love with him. But had she actually said that? He had bought her ticket. He had waited for her on the platform. And then, at last, she had arrived. Late. And only to tell him she couldn't go, wouldn't go. But he went ahead as planned, on his Siberian Express trip across Russia. Alone. It was only for six weeks, but when he returned she told him she had met another man. God, it was four years now. She was married, she had a family already. And he was here brooding alone, his life on hold. Could it be you only love like that just once? He shook the thought away. He stretched out on the bed and fell asleep dreaming of a big country breakfast.

As James approached the tenth cottage in the row of twelve houses that sat so cozily just a few yards from the lane to Moore's Farm, he smiled. The residents had certainly done a lot with a little. Eileen O'Grady's house, for example, was painted a deep cream and the stone window ledges and door were trimmed in a brick red. James had to bend down to fit his tall frame through the open door.

Eileen gave James a quick tour of her house and extensive garden to the rear. It was a traditional cottage garden, examples of which James had only ever seen at botanical shows. Although it was early spring, much of the garden was a riot of color, provided by daffodils of every shade of yellow, shy primroses, and some early and vivid tulips. The fruit trees were showing blossoms too, especially the cherries. A row of hawthorne trees in white and pink screened the garden from the wind that raced across the open fields at the back. Eileen took great delight in showing James her spuds and onions, already planted in neat rows. Her herb garden, although a bit barren this early in the season, scented the air with its rosemary, chives, and mint.

"I must say these houses are deceptive," said James when they returned to the sitting room. "From the front I thought they would be small indeed!"

Eileen laughed. "Everybody who comes the first time says that, Mr. Fleming; you're not alone. Sit yourself down. These cottages were built in 1820," she said proudly. "The fields at the back hadn't been drained then, and it was marshy, wet land—perfect, it seems, for the growing of flax. There was a mill here, built by a Dutchman, I think. The foundations are still there where it crumbled away. He was an enlightened man and built these cottages for the workers, who grew the flax and prepared it to be made into fine Irish linen."

James noted the signs of nineteenth-century architecture, including the dutch oven beside the fireplace. He noted too the enormous picture of the Sacred Heart with the small red electric light burning in front of it. It was the largest picture in a room full of pictures and photographs. After they were settled, he got to the point of his visit.

"Mr. Fleming, I'd do what I can to help Miss Moore," said Eileen in response, settling her small, chunky print-clad body into the chair. "But all I can tell you is that the knife the police showed to me was the very knife I had used in that kitchen many a day."

"Well, then," said James, "can you say for sure when was the last time you saw it?"

"Indeed and I can. I had bought the family a good-size roast for their Sunday dinner. I put it in the oven myself on Sunday morning when I came in from Mass. It would have been ready with the roast potatoes when Miss Violet and her sisters came in from Morning Prayer."

"And did you serve the dinner?"

"Oh no. On Sundays I only prepare the meal. Lily would do up the vegetables, and Miss Violet always carved the meat, whether it be flesh or fowl."

"And did you see the knife after that, after Sunday?"

"No, I didn't. I clearly remember looking for it when I came back in Sunday evening to do the washing up. I remember knowing there was an empty space in the knife rack on the kitchen counter." She shuddered.

James waited as Eileen pottered out to the kitchen to make tea. His first call in Kilmartin had not been helpful to Violet's case. Eileen, he could see, would make a useful prosecution witness.

"Eileen, I've heard a little about Jack, about Mr. Moore, actually about his early life here in Kilmartin . . ."

"Well, now, I didn't know him very well. We were in different social circles in those days—him being a Protestant. O' course I'd see him up and down the lane, maybe goin' for the bus or goin' back and forth with the hay or the silage on the big trucks. Sometimes I'd see him on the tractor crossing over the road to the bottom fields."

"In that event, I suppose you didn't know of his friendship with Kathleen Walsh?"

"Oh, now, we all knew of that around here. My eldest brother, Kieran, hung around with one of the Walsh boys. Oh, it was a big family, sir, five brothers and then a little slip of a girl comin' along at the end of the day. They doted on her, I can tell you. A sweet dark-haired thing. They was fierce jealous when she started going around with Jack. Y'see, the mother was dead. An' the boys, they had got used to her looking after them. They needed a woman on the farm, it's a big working farm, still is, and a crop farm." Eileen refilled his cup and offered him a slice of fruit cake. "And there was another thing. The Walshes, they were Catholic . . ."

"And do you think that was the reason that Jack and Kathleen didn't marry?"

"Well, I'll put it this way, neither side was willing to see that wedding take place. Violet certainly did not want the two farms coming together in any way. I do sometimes think that's why she never married herself . . ."

"I don't understand."

"Why she never married herself? It's as though she couldn't bear to share the farm, or even expand it by means of marrying into another of the landed families hereabouts."

James cordially continued to listen as Eileen began to talk about her own children, all of them in England now. He could afford to relax a bit, he felt, having found a small piece of the puzzle.

But getting information out of Mr. Sweeney at the post office was another story. James had waited patiently as the old man served his postal customers. He was impressed with the glass and steel cage that housed the branch office, and thought to himself at what cost the GPO had installed these up and down the country. Only to be undercut, he smiled wryly, by the likes of Mr. Sweeney, who conducted most of the postal business outside the booth, on the shop counter, scurrying back and forth to get the required stamps and to make change in the separate cash drawer. Sweeney had a huge range of stock, among it items James hadn't seen since he was a child. Boxes of wax firelighters and paraffin sconces. Ten glass bottles filled to the brim with the old-style penny candies and boiled sweets. He had tinned meats, side by side with writing materials, jars of cigars standing on the counter with baskets of fresh eggs from the local farms, slabs of sticky brown gurr cake and unwrapped loaves of bread. The boxes of milk cartons reposed on the neat, even stacks of turf. In a mere twenty square yards Sweeney's shop housed items to meet every possible casual or immediate need. The whole atmosphere gave James a wonderfully strange sense of security.

James couldn't resist buying a chunk of the gurr cake. The sticky taste of molasses, raisins, and currants brought back a happy memory of when he and a boyhood friend with their red lemonade and gurr cake—survival food they called it—took the train to Killiney one hot summer day and climbed the head where it jutted out into the sea. There they had lain in the grass and counted the Dublin trains as they passed under the tunnel that cut through the granite rock of the tiny finger of land.

The last customer gone, Mr. Sweeney brought James to a small, comfortably furnished back room with two overstuffed chairs and a chintz-covered table, with a set of white and blue striped Delph china standing ready for use. The kettle was coming to a boil, and Sweeney proceeded to make a mug of tea strong enough for a mouse to trot across.

James sensed that Mr. Sweeney knew a very great deal about his neighbors past and present. On the one hand, James admired his unwillingness to chat with a total stranger, but on the other, he found his reticence frustrating.

But the sum of what he learned from Mr. Sweeney was directions to the Walsh farm, something James could have discovered for himself. As he was leaving the little room at the back of the shop, Brendan approached in a conspiratorial whisper. While James ostentatiously purchased two local papers and a second slab of gurr cake, Brendan explained his father's attitude.

"Mr. Fleming, I trust that you are only doing your best for Miss Moore. My father's always been a reticent man. It's one way to survive in a country town, as I'm sure you'll appreciate."

"Brendan, anything you can tell me would be a help right now. You must see that as an outsider I am at a loss. Sometimes I might not be asking the right questions, and that's when I need people to offer me information."

Brendan hesitated. "I'm not sure I can tell you any more than my father, except . . . well, except the morning they found the body up at the farm, we saw . . . I mean . . . the hearse was seen."

"What! You actually saw the hearse?" James's enthusiasm was not exactly professional in manner.

Brendan smiled. "Yes. My father and I were here in the shop. Mr. Sinclair and my father saw the hearse turn into the lane and return. At the time, of course, we were curious. But the car was so quick, we thought it had taken a wrong turning. Later we figured that it was the very car that had delivered the coffin we heard about."

"Did you tell the police?"

"No. Unfortunately they didn't question us," Brendan added, disappointed to have been left out of the excitement. "Sean, our postman, had already spoken to them."

"And O'Shea, the detective from Dublin?"

"No, he didn't question us either. We weren't called at the inquest because Sean was, and after all, he had got the better view, I suppose, having followed them on his bike. Mr. Sinclair, now, he felt he'd got a good view, and was only dying to be called at the inquest. But he wasn't. He was quite annoyed."

As James returned to his car, he realized that the police hadn't made much of the hearse. The postman had apparently given his evidence at the inquest, and that was enough for them. James felt discouraged. Perhaps he was beating a dead horse over this issue of the hearse.

He decided then that there was nothing for it but to visit the Walsh farm. The answer was there, he now felt certain. How he would pry out that secret—of that James was less certain.

Brendan smiled as he saw Mr. Sinclair hustling into the shop.

"But why hasn't he called to interview *me?* And where has he disappeared to, that's what I want to know! You are sure, Brendan, that you mentioned I saw the hearse?"

"Well, I said it as clearly as I could," Brendan responded, a little annoyed at Sinclair's inference.

"Whom were you hoping to see?" Mr. O'Dwyer had glided in to the shop and startled both Brendan and Sinclair.

"That Fleming character. I fully expected him to come to question me about the hearse I saw . . . we saw."

"Hoping for your moment in the sun, Sinclair?" said O'Dwyer dryly as he waited for Brendan to make up forty-four pence postage out of the odds and ends in his glassine-paged stamp book. Patrons of the branch office rarely got a single stamp in the denomination they required.

"Of course not. I wish only to do my duty."

"Too bad you hadn't thought of that when the inquest was held." O'Dwyer's tone was teasing.

Sinclair's voice rose to a shriek. "I wasn't called to it! How many times do I have to tell you people that?"

"What is it this time?" Three heads swiveled to observe Kevin standing in the open door of the shop. Their curiosity on seeing him was palpable, and Kevin laughed a hearty laugh.

"Recent events have certainly livened up the gossip in this half-barony."

"I don't think that's appropriate, coming from you." Mr. Sinclair drew his thin frame together, distaste in his voice.

"Oh, drop it, Sinclair. You're as nosy as an old cat. And you've a lot of company. Everyone in the row houses is positively demented to know what's going on. Eileen can't walk three feet without being attacked. And Paddy's milk round takes two hours longer to get through, what with one customer after another demanding news."

"Well then, what is the news? You should know, if anybody."

"Ah sure . . ." Kevin looked serious for the first time. "Life goes on, as it should. Miss Violet is up to her eyes with the calving. She— We— None of us really talks about it up at the farm. And anyway, she'd hardly discuss it with me." As he talked, Kevin helped Brendan drag out two enormous bags of commercial fertilizer from the corner.

"I'll leave you with this, though it's not news. Miss Violet . . . well now, she certainly could kill a fly." Kevin smiled broadly at his own little joke. "And I've seen her put down her dogs over the years, and a horse, without it taking anything out of her. But her brother, now, there's not a snowball's chance in hell of her takin' a knife to her brother."

"You mean you know that for a fact?" Sinclair inquired in his thin voice.

"I know it like my own name. I've worked with her

many a year, since I was a lad. I know because I know what family means to her, I know what that farm up there means to her. Do you think she'd jeopardize that farm for anything?" Kevin's face grew florid.

"Then if they're so great on family, why did Lily say what she did?" O'Dwyer's serious voice broke in on Sinclair's mumblings.

"How the hell . . . ?" Kevin dropped the sack on the floor. "Oh, what's the point, everybody knows everything in this place. I suppose Eileen . . . ?"

"Not a'tall. It was Rose herself who told me, after a fashion. I met her at the coop market on Saturday morning. She was full of it, told everyone within earshot. I fear this whole business has pushed her further into that foggy, foggy dew. What does interest me is, how is Violet taking it? Her own sister doing the dirty on her."

"What 'dirty'? Lily merely told the police she thought she saw Violet with a man at the barn."

"A man she said was you!" said Sinclair.

"And which wasn't. For Jaysus sake! That should show how important her statement is. She thought she saw Violet and meself. And I'll tell you it wasn't me. So if the man wasn't me, then maybe the woman wasn't Violet!"

"Interesting, Kevin," remarked Mr. O'Dwyer caustically. "But we know it wasn't you, because there's real evidence. The vet spoke to you. Your wife presumably can vouch for you. And Lily herself said she got your call on the phone."

"Well, I see that the whole village knows all my movements anyway!" said Kevin heatedly. "But that doesn't weaken my argument. My point is, Lily thought it was me until she knew otherwise. She might have done the same over Violet. She might have thought the woman was Violet until she knew otherwise."

"In that event, who was it?"

"How the hell should I know? I'm demented thinkin' about it."

"What does Violet Moore say?"

"I heard she said she was in her room. And of course there's hardly a witness to that."

"I'll tell you what bothers me in this story," Brendan intervened. "It's that Lily didn't wait to speak to Violet whenever she came in from the barn. Wasn't she just dyin' of curiosity? She knew it wasn't Kevin, once she'd got the phone call."

"Well, they don't . . ." Kevin hesitated, conscious he was about to say too much about the family that employed him. He tossed the bag of fertilizer over his shoulder, preparing to leave. "I'll tell you this," he added, red in the face, and not from exertion. "I don't know how people live in this blasted village. What goes on behind their own front door is nobody's business . . ."

"Naiveté doesn't suit you, Kevin," O'Dwyer cut in.

"All right. I'll just finish this. Things aren't what they seem . . ."

"Humph!" exclaimed Brendan, and then coughed to cover it.

"Miss Violet and Miss Lily, they're not as thick as we'd all like to think, if you take my meaning?"

"Are you telling us that Lily wouldn't have asked Violet what she was doing talking to a man in the barn at twelve-thirty at night?" said Sinclair.

"Well, at least not straight away."

Mr. O'Dwyer moved to the door and held it open for Kevin to carry out the sacks. "It's all right, Kevin," he said, defusing the tension. "We believe you, when thousands wouldn't."

"I'll tell you this," said Kevin, still striving to have the last word. "They all carry on exactly as before. Miss Violet, now, she's gone a bit thin and grim-faced. But other than that, I see the three of them at morning coffee. And when I take my dinner in the kitchen, they chat or not, as the case may be, exactly as before. Rose and Violet were loading the truck this morning 'cause Paddy's boy was sick and it was business as usual." And with that, Kevin escaped through the door.

As those neighbors chatted and gossiped, Violet at that moment was seated at the fire, alone in her sitting room. It was true. She had striven very hard to maintain a semblance of normalcy. But inwardly she was tired. Very tired. She glanced across at Lily, seated at the desk, running up the weekly milk bills to be delivered with the milk early the next morning. Neither had yet spoken of the extraordinary information Lily had freely offered O'Shea.

"The Feeneys haven't paid their bill in six weeks," Lily said from the corner.

"I hear there's a new baby in that house," replied Violet.

"Shall I leave it awhile, then . . ."

"Mmm, they're old customers. I should think we could carry them a bit, don't you?"

"Have you decided about the fete?" murmured Lily, still busy at her books.

"I think we should leave it . . . for this year." Violet's voice held a sigh. Ever since her father's time there had been a summer fete on the grounds of the Moore farm, barring the year her mother died. They had always raised a goodly sum for the Church restoration fund.

"I think that's a mistake," said Lily matter-of-factly. "It will only give rise to even more talk."

"But people will merely come to peep and pry . . ."

"I think you underestimate your neighbors. It's a month away yet. Talk is dying down already, I suspect. No one coming to the fete will be ignorant of the situation. It's not as though we draw crowds from far and wide . . ." Lily's voice held an unspoken question.

"All right, don't cancel it yet. I'll think about it a little longer."

Violet surprised herself. It was seldom that she was so indecisive. Perhaps the situation was exacting its toll on her after all, sapping her energies.

She was almost glad Fleming had called, even if it had only been a lightning visit. Arrogant and impertinent though he was, at least he was trying to help, more robustly than it was likely Gerald Fitzgerald would have done. He probably wouldn't have had the time nor the inclination. Wedded to his law books, she thought bitterly. Always the same. Drawn to the big city, the bright lights and the theatre of the law. He'd be as much at sea here in Wexford now as the smart-aleck Dubliner. She had been right all those years ago. Fitzgerald's heart never lay with the land. She could remember the resentment in every line of his body when he was put to the haying each summer on his father's farm. Those had been good days. She had loved going to the local farms to help with the haying. Turn and turn about. The young people would come to Moore's to help as well. It was a shame the way all these modern machines had killed off those happy times. Now a tenth of that number could accomplish the haying, and in half the time. The dances had been good too. Fitzgerald was always there, but he seemed then to have eyes only for Lily. Maiden spinster Lily. That would never have worked. And she had been proved right about Fitzgerald when he sold the farm after his father's death, despite the fact that there had been a depression and prices were bad. She remembered that Lily had not been pleased when she had beat him down and bought half his fields for next to nothing. But it had been important to expand the farm at that time.

Typical Fitzgerald. Couldn't be bothered to come back to Kilmartin himself, so he had sent his protégé. Young Mr. Fleming—wet behind the ears. And now he was off to visit the Walshes. She hadn't seen any of them in years. All that nonsense was in the past, buried in the past.

She rested her head in her hands and sighed. Then she felt Lily's eyes on her and straightened her back. It wouldn't do to give way in front of Lily. Not now.

The Walshes. It wasn't to their advantage either— to speak of that ancient business. And what could it have to do with this present mare's nest? Fleming certainly seemed pleased as punch with that theory of his. But it was preposterous. The enthusiasm of an amateur and a fool. She stirred restlessly. Perhaps it would have been better to discourage him. But then she was certain that would whet his curiosity further. She shivered. She seemed to hear the rattling of old bones in the closet.

James had devised a plan of sorts while he drove, but as he approached the long lane to the Walsh's farm, he grew apprehensive.

Now, four short, wiry men the color of acorns, and all remarkably resembling each other, watched him approach. He had had difficulty finding them. There had been no answer to his ring at the bell, and he had had to clamber through the muck in the yard, ruining his black wingtips in the process. They stood silently, staring not too inquisitively as he walked toward them.

James felt a chill up his spine. The sun had sunk behind the outbuildings, and although there was light in the pale blue and orange sky, there was no warmth in the air. He glanced at their faces and realized if his hunch was right, he could be looking at the face of a ruthless murderer. But which face? Which of these four stern faces held a secret from the others? Or were they all involved? His thoughts were fragmented as he introduced himself.

"Fleming. James Fleming. I'm Miss Violet Moore's solicitor. Would you mind if I ask you a few questions?" James offered his hand, but when no one took it, he dropped it to his side.

"Concernin' what?" said one of the four nut-brown men. James had difficulty understanding a much thicker Wexford accent than he had encountered up till now.

"Well, I think you probably heard about the death —rather, the murder—of Jack Walsh."

Four heads nodded almost imperceptibly.

"I was wondering if you might have any information to give me," said James simply. He found he could no more be subtle with these men than he could plough a straight furrow.

The one who seemed to be the eldest waved James into the barn. With trepidation James followed them, and like them, took a seat on a bale of straw.

"You'll find no sympathy here, Mistur Fleming. Jack Moore was a dead man to this family for more than twenty-five year'. There's nothin' that any of us can tell ya."

"If you'll just permit me to ask a few questions, then. About the past . . ." The four men glanced at each other and then gave the slightest of nods. The eldest, for that was how James perceived him, spoke for them all.

"It depends," he said laconically.

"Depends?" murmured James.

"On the question."

"I need to know a little about Jack's, em . . . Jack's friendship with your sister. In fact I'd like to speak with her if I could."

There was a long silence as the eldest Walsh brushed the straw off his striped navy wool jacket. For a few moments James thought that he hadn't been heard.

"Mr. Fleming, Jack Moore came damn near to ruinin' our Kathleen's life. If it hadn't been for him, the darlin' girl would be with us still . . ." He smiled slightly at James's look of alarm. "Our sister is in London."

Another brother spoke with some bitterness. "Aye. And she's married to some pommie bastard too. To my mind that Jack Moore did ruin her life. She was so embarrassed when he took off, without a word to her. One day he was here filling her head with grand promises of her life with him, how they'd be livin' up at the big house, how she'd never have to dirty her pretty little hands again. As if waitin' on him was a privilege compared to lookin' after us. One day he was

73

here, and the next day he was gone. No girl could put up with that, what with the neighbors whisperin' and all."

"And you've no idea why he just picked up and left, in the middle of things, so to speak?" asked James, puzzled by this bit of new information. Somehow the pieces weren't falling into place as he had hoped. "Surely they kept in touch? He must have come back at some time, or written to her?"

"We had our suspicions all right," offered the eldest brother. "We knew she'd gone up the big house to see the sisters, but Violet Moore told her some story or other. And then one day she too was gone. She left us a letter that she'd gone to London with a girlfriend and not to worry. There was nothin' to do about it. We accepted she was gone."

"Can you tell me, is this the source of the bad blood between yourselves and the Moores?"

"You might say that."

"Do you know if Jack and your sister got together again in London?"

"Not likely. About two years later she wrote to say she was getting married to some medical student and asked if any of us would come over for the weddin'. But there was too much to do here at the farm . . ."

"And has she been back?"

"Not a'tall. She's a family of her own. She sends the odd card and photo but . . . ah, she's dead to us now."

James felt suddenly, oddly depressed. He was tired of these stories of departure, of partings that weren't really partings but escapes, flight from one type of loneliness to another.

The brothers stood up with one accord, and James followed them lethargically out of the barn.

"You wouldn't by any chance still have her address, would you?"

"It's in the kitchen drawer," said the eldest brother. "Billy will get it for you."

James was surprised. Were they simply trying to get

rid of him? He copied the address from the crumpled piece of paper, thanked them with a nod, and returned through the muddy yard to his car.

Human warmth and the sound of animated voices, food for his belly and pints for his soul—that's what was needed now, James decided. He turned his car into the car park of the Drooping Well. He shook off the chill of the day and of his unfruitful conversation with the Walshes and seated himself in a cozy corner. The sausage rolls, heated for a minute in the microwave at the bar, seemed like a full-course meal to his hunger. He was just ordering another when Mr. Sinclair slithered to his side.

"A word, Mr. Fleming?"

"By all means, Mr. Sinclair. I've been meaning to speak to you." He was amused at the beam that lit up Sinclair's face.

James listened attentively and sipped his pint in comfort as Sinclair told him in minute detail of what he had witnessed the morning of the discovery of the body, including a detailed description of the hearse, its silver filigree and its unusual opaque windows.

Satisfied with the information, James turned the conversation to other things. He had recognized in Sinclair the gossip of the most useful sort. Willing to talk but not to embroider.

"Tell me, Mr. Sinclair, if you can, the meaning of the extraordinary name of this pub?"

Sinclair smiled and launched into his story.

"It's a short story, really, but most amusing. The pub used to simply be called Murphy, after the owner and his son after him. But Tom Murphy decided not only to improve the interior—the evidence of that eclectic style you see before you—he also decided to improve the exterior and give it a more memorable name than the name it was known by. He came up with the name of the Dropping Well on account of the well out back, but his wife, who had a sense of humor and was a bit piqued at her husband's recent performance after a few pints, altered the name on the order docket for the sign makers. The sign makers, who, let's face it, must have had a sense of humor also, never questioned Murphy. And the damage was done! But the name caused such an amount of fun here in the pub and in the vicinity that Murphy had the good grace to let it stand. As he said, as a warning to all the other husbands who came in to the pub for a drink!"

James and Sinclair had a good laugh together, and the mood was comfortable. James sipped his pint and stored the tale in his memory. It would bear repeating.

"I'm just amazed that the Walshes talked to you." Sinclair's voice broke in on his thoughts.

"Why is that?"

"Surely you've heard that story?" His voice rose with enthusiasm.

"I know that Jack Moore left Kathleen standing at the altar, so to speak. And that she went to go and live in London, and she married there." James smiled. "The Walsh brothers certainly seemed put out by the fact she abandoned them to look after themselves."

"Is that all you know?"

"Mmmm." James watched silently as the barman put up the shutters and lowered the lights. He checked his watch. Damn, he thought, closing time. And yet he observed that nobody moved. The barman locked the door. After a few minutes the pub's patrons started ordering their pints in earnest. James leaned back and relaxed. It would be a good long night's drinking for the locals now.

Sinclair settled comfortably to his second hot whiskey. He virtually licked his lips as he launched into his story.

"Ah, now we all remember the night Jack left Kilmartin. But the Walshes remember it most of all. There'd been trouble brewing for a long time, as I told you. This night it was very crowded here in the pub. It was old Tom Murphy's place then. It was a very warm night. Virtually everyone here had been at the haying all day, and the rest of us had been at the horse trials. People were tired but in great form. The sun had been splitting the stones for days.

"There had been a bit of singing, a lot of chat, and more than a lot of drinking. Jack was at the bar, full of himself, tellin' one and all who'd listen how he and Kathleen were gettin' married soon, and that Violet and the Walshes would just have to get used to the idea.

"Remembering back, I'm sure now that he knew Mike Walsh was within hearing. Suddenly, like a pot coming to boil, voices were raised. Mike—he was the second brother—went for Jack. He was pretty tipsy, and wild in any case. As I say, he went for Jack. People pulled him off Jack. Old Tom had got the stick ready, but he didn't need it. He and the barboy dragged Mike out, but everyone heard him."

"Heard him?" said James anxiously.

"We, all of us, heard him say he would get Jack. That no snot-nosed Protestant would marry his sister. That he'd kill him first."

"We all knew that it was the drink talking. Jack was shaken a bit at first, but then laughed it off. Or so we thought. I clearly remember that Jack stayed on for a few more pints and then rolled off home, as merry as ever."

"As it turned out, the next day the Walshes came to the pub. They were looking for Mike. They said he hadn't been home all night and they assumed he returned to the pub. You could drink all night in those days—much as we're doing now."

James took the hint and ordered another round, but he drank slowly, concentrating on Sinclair's remarkable story.

"Mike Walsh was missing all that day. In the end, one of the hired help found his body out in a field that had already been cut. It was in a narrow stream that divides two of the Moores' fields. Lying there at the bottom, the body couldn't be seen from the lane. The chap who found him had been cutting across the field to another where they were working. He was a young lad and he got an awful shock. Apparently Mike was lying as he had fallen, face forward, his arms spread out on either side. There were bruises on his head and face, and he had died from a blow to his head. There was some talk that he had really drowned, that lying unconscious in the water, he had swallowed water and drowned there." Sinclair shook his head sadly.

"There was a lot of drinking at the wake and a lot of speculation as to why Mike was in the Moores' field at all. I was there for part of the wake, but it went on all day and night. The Walsh boys got plastered and went looking for Jack Moore. They swore it had to have been him that did it. The police had found a rock covered with blood, near the body. But they still had ruled it an accident: that Mike had been cutting across the field in the dark, intent on carrying out his threat to kill Jack. And with drink taken, he must have lost his footing and fallen into the stream, hitting his head as he fell. Almost everyone except the Walshes seemed to accept that. The Walshes believed that Jack had fought with Mike and pushed him in the stream and left him there to die.

"A few of us followed the Walsh boys up to the Moores'. We knew that Violet and the sisters were alone there.

"There was a powerful scene on the front steps. The Walshes demanded to see Jack, but Violet wasn't having it. A lot of words were said in the heat of the moment, but she finally demanded they leave or she'd get the police. Then Danny, who was a farmhand there at the time, came to the front door with a shotgun. They never did get to see Jack . . . I must say Violet looked magnificent that day. She was in her full health and youth, her eyes flashing and her hair blowing in the wind. Facing down those wild Walsh boys, she was a woman to be reckoned with, and there's no mistake."

Sinclair paused, saving his best till last. He ordered

another whiskey and James a pint of stout while James fidgeted. At last the drinks came.

"It transpired that . . . Jack had left Kilmartin. In fact, he had left Ireland. None of us knew what to think. The Walshes, of course, swore that it was a sure sign that Jack had murdered Mike and fled the country. But the police had questioned Violet, and she had told them that Jack had come directly home that night from the pub. They had been able to check the times Mike left and when Jack had left. Jack had been at home with Violet at the time the doctor said that Mike had died. There were no other signs of a fight and no witnesses.

"Violet brassed it out. She said that Jack had not gone that night, but rather the next day. That he'd heard about Mike's death and he didn't want to cause the Walshes any more grief. She claimed he'd said that if he hadn't been joking about Kathleen in the pub, Mike wouldn't have lost his temper.

"Violet explained that obviously Mike had been on his way to confront Jack, and being drunk, had fallen into the stream. But that Jack felt so bad, he wanted no more to do with the family. She went on about how he was just a young lad, that he'd never really been serious about Kathleen . . . which of course served to enrage the Walshes even more. At the time, she seemed to make sense. Jack was young, and wild. We even thought that perhaps he had got in over his head with Kathleen, and that he had seen a way out of the marriage and tying up with a family where there'd always be bad blood."

James sat back, astonished at what he'd just heard. "And was that it?"

"Pretty much. At the time, we all supposed that Jack would come back in six months, or a year at most. That he'd wait until things died down and then return to the farm. And in the way of things, we all gradually forgot about him. Except the Walshes. They continued to claim that Jack Moore had killed their brother. When Kathleen went off, it just cemented

their bitterness. They keep to themselves and . . .
well, you've seen them for yourself."

James was glad of Sinclair's invitation to spend the
night. The local bed and breakfast was in darkness,
and he knew he couldn't drive to Riders, having drunk
over the legal limit. He walked with Sinclair the mile
to the house, and as he walked, he considered what he
had just heard. He realized that the Walshes might
indeed have been willing to give him Kathleen's
address in London—just to distract him, to get him
off their trail.

His heart lifted as he looked out over the somnolent
fields. He glanced up the hills and wondered in which
field Mike Walsh had died. This was a major break-
through. Here at last was a tie-in, a motive for
someone to have killed Jack Moore on his return to
Ireland after twenty-seven years. A believable motive.
For James knew that in Ireland there was seldom a
more powerful motive for murder than revenge.

Chapter Five

"At first I thought that this Walsh story was a bit farfetched," commented Gerald, getting up from his desk and stretching his arms to meet behind his back. "But I'm growing more intrigued as you talk!"

He turned abruptly and faced James. "I suppose you've heard the office gossip?" Gerald indicated his chest with the stem of his pipe. "There is no call for alarm, and I don't want our clients getting wind of it."

"To be honest, Gerald, I've heard two or three versions from the staff already. What did happen when I was in Wexford?"

"A turn, as they say. Even I thought it was the end. But Dr. Barry at St. Vincent's assured me it was a terrific attack of indigestion. The old ticker will be fine. I just have to watch the angina."

James returned Gerald's smile and, with him, shrugged off the news of his attack. But privately he wondered at Gerald's gray color and his lack of animation. He looked older today than his fifty-five years. As if he had read his thoughts, Gerald came around from behind the desk, sat in the easy chair beside James and rested his head on the chair back.

"I'll tell you this, James. The attack scared me. When I was lying at home in bed—couldn't sleep of course—I had some time for reflection. Scenes from my childhood in Kilmartin came back to me as vividly as this conversation. Rural Ireland is a very different kind of environment in which to grow to manhood. I imagine you've picked up on some of that difference even in your short stay in Wexford? It's not that values are so very different. But aspirations are. The sense of pride is stronger. The land is full of contradictions. The people hold on to their privacy to the point of obsession. Yet at the same time they are always self-conscious in the real sense of the word . . . always aware of living their lives out in a public arena, a theatre where all the players are known by name, where the actors and the audience constantly change places with one another. Oh, the scrutiny!" Gerald stared out the window, as the faint noise of traffic in Merrion Square reached them.

James considered Gerald's words. Although he had traveled to apparently exotic places which had served to point up the larger contrasts between Ireland and other countries, he had never looked at Ireland in this way. Chagrined, he realized that he had adhered to the stale generalizations that people applied to his own country. He knew the timetables of trains in Italy. He knew the timetables of trains in Ireland. But what of it? Had he seen the people and had he come to know them?

"I'm not sure what you're driving at, Gerald," he said at last.

"It was your mention of the Walshes. Believe it or not, the name triggered off the strangest memory. But I see that it is just of a piece. Confined to bed as I was, I had time to cast my mind back to those early days in Kilmartin. And the Walshes now are fresh in my mind. I used to play handball with one of the Walsh boys."

"Then can you also remember when Mike Walsh died?" James asked, astonished at this coming together of apparently diverse connections.

"Yes, actually, I do now. There was a tremendous amount of speculation. I was a student at Trinity when the whole incident took place. But on weekends at home—the odd time I returned—there was still talk."

"Did you believe that Jack Moore had killed Walsh?"

"No, not for a minute. But I do remember that there were a lot of questions as to what Mike Walsh had been doing in that field."

James was insistent. "Don't you see? The significant feature is what the Walshes believed and might still believe about Jack Moore. The location of the body in that field on Moore's Farm may have served to convince the Walshes that Jack did indeed kill their brother, despite the fact you say that the police considered his death an accident. It strengthens my theory that they held a grudge—for years—awaiting an opportunity to strike back at Jack."

Gerald caught some of James's enthusiasm. "I see your point, and I'm glad of it. Sheridan may be able to use the implications of what you're saying to throw some doubt on Violet's motives—by shifting attention to the motives of the Walsh family. It could be enough to plant the idea in a jury's mind. I'll put through a call to Sheridan now and give him what we've got. He was on to me yesterday. It seems that the Director of Prosecutions has nearly completed the Book of Evidence. He will be approaching the High Court this week, looking for the case to be put on the docket for June. You see, my boy, we only have the months of April and May to gather as much evidence as we can for Sheridan. I want you to give this case top priority. Let's have a look at your calendar and see what we can do to clear the decks."

* * *

James let himself in to his own spacious and comfortably decorated flat. Switching on the gas fire he poured himself a brandy and sat heavily in his swing leather chair.

He couldn't shake his present mood, nor did he want to. He sat back letting the myriad images of the past few days rush into his mind, seeking for the key to his depression. He had grown almost used to these moods—if not black then certainly dark brown—overtaking him, ever since his breakup with Teresa. But this time the mood took on a different aspect, and he sensed it was because the source was different.

Sinclair. Was it Sinclair? James had been surprised at the evidence of prosperity in his home, although the man's taste was most definitely austere. Sinclair had inherited money. And by investing it safely and wisely, he had made money. He could satisfy all his wants, and with each passing year, as James guessed, his eccentricities had intensified.

And Gerald. Gerald depressed him as well. He had seemed so negative about his early years in Kilmartin. And now a widower with no children. Empty houses full of empty rooms.

Silence filled his own sitting room. Was he going down the same road? he wondered as he opened his briefcase. The question remained unanswered as he finally settled down to his work.

James's mood was markedly different when, at eight A.M. exactly, the 737 lifted off the runway in a perfect takeoff. He smiled as he leaned back in his seat and accepted a drink from the Aer Lingus hostess. The last few days at the office had been productive. He had freed up some of his billable time and concurred with Gerald that a personal visit to Kathleen Walsh Banks was certainly in order. And now London, one of his favorite cities, lay ahead, holding the answer, he believed, to the questions surrounding Jack Moore's life and death. Surely it must be Kathleen who could establish for him once and for all the fatal connection between her brothers and Jack Moore.

At Heathrow Airport James indulged himself by renting a Jaguar, and was in the outskirts of London in record time. He checked into the small, comfortable hotel and as he quickly unpacked, wondering yet again at the Walsh brothers' willingness to give him their sister's address. But for all that suspicion, he was grateful. Tracking her down under her married name after more than twenty years would have taken more time than they could afford, now that the trial date had been fixed for June fifteenth.

The day was still young, only eleven A.M. James sat on his bed, took out his notes and checked Kathleen's address. He knew London well, and her home was a mere half hour's drive in traffic. He had already decided not to phone her. The element of surprise was too important.

And suddenly James knew he could not justify putting off the evil hour any longer. If he was to see Kathleen alone, it made sense to try to visit her during the day.

Driving south, out toward Wimbledon, he tried to organize his thoughts. But his incipient dread of this meeting only increased as he approached the intersection that his map indicated would lead him to Buttonwood Road. His palms were sweating as he parked the car at the corner of the street. Eyes peering from behind curtains did not need to see a stranger emerge from a Jaguar at Mrs. Banks's very door. He walked slowly down the road, glancing surreptitiously at the numbers on the doors of the neat, prosperous brick-fronted terraced houses. As number 89 neared, he tried to compose himself in the manner of an insurance agent. He was sorry he didn't have a case of samples to disguise his approach. Wildly he thought that perhaps she wouldn't be home, perhaps she worked, perhaps he wouldn't have to fulfill what he now realized was a rather unpleasant mission.

Kathleen Banks opened the door at the first ring. James would have known her for a Walsh—she was small and wiry, fit and brown, with a strong look of her brothers. But she was also meticulously dressed and groomed, her dark hair gleaming in the watery London sunshine.

"Mrs. Banks?" James asked after a brief hesitation.

"Yes?" she replied, suspicion in her voice, her eyes swiftly glancing to see if he carried a sample case or a bible or copies of the *Watchtower*. She closed the door slightly, shielding herself.

"My name is James Fleming. I am a solicitor with the Dublin firm of Fitzgerald's." James spoke quickly as he observed her expression grow guarded. "Please, Mrs. Banks, your brothers in Kilmartin gave me your address. I must speak to you."

Suddenly she became conscious of how long he had been on the step. She glanced up and down the road, and then through clenched teeth said, "I will allow you to step into the hall, but you must show me some identification."

In the small, bare foyer she glanced at James's business card and at his driver's license and even scrutinized his passport.

"This way," she said finally, and walked stiffly into the sitting room. "Please sit down. I can only give you a very few minutes. I have another appointment." With this she glanced through the white curtains that draped the large picture window.

"This is rather awkward, Mrs. Banks, and may well take more than a few minutes." He turned aside from the anger and fear in Kathleen Walsh's face. Taking out his notebook, for want of something to do with his hands, he glanced unnecessarily at a few pages. Still she didn't sit, but stood as if holding herself together with her tightly folded arms.

"I am representing a Miss Violet Moore in a legal matter." James watched her reaction, trying to gauge his next step, but she looked toward the window.

"Go on," she said finally.

"Believe me, Mrs. Banks, I wouldn't have troubled you except for the fact that this truly is a matter of life and death."

"Whose life? Whose death?" Kathleen hissed, gathering herself together as if coiling to spring.

"Violet Moore's life. Jack Moore's death."

He waited, but she didn't speak, didn't question his extraordinary statement.

He tried again. "Mrs. Banks, I understand that your connection with Ireland is long broken. But the events I need to ask you about happened many years ago, before you left Kilmartin. I believe that if you could answer some questions for me, you may well help us build a case that would serve to clear my client's name."

"Violet Moore's name?" Kathleen smirked and stopped herself. "I haven't heard her name in twenty-seven years." Her face reddened. "Yes, I can tell you she was proud of her name. But surely you know that by now."

James was surprised at the vehemence in her voice. She stared down at her fingers, pushing the cuticles back fiercely but absentmindedly.

"You said just now, something about her life and Jack Moore's death?" she asked. James nodded. "I take it then that Jack . . . Jack Moore is . . . dead?"

"Yes, he is."

"Does this have something to do with his will, then?" Alarm filled her face. "Does it? Is there something in his will that . . . relates to me or someone else?"

"I'm not at liberty to discuss the will at this time," James said, trying to keep her interest. But he failed.

"Mr. Fleming, I know that as a solicitor what is said to you in confidence is nearly as sacred as what a doctor might hear . . . therefore I tell you I do not want my husband or children to know anything of your visit or our conversation. This issue is closed." She moved abruptly toward the door.

"Mrs. Banks. Believe me"—a certain sympathy

filled James's face and voice—"I would never harm you. What I need to know are the details of the night that your brother Michael died."

Kathleen's face was blank, as though she hadn't heard him.

"Mike, your brother. Do you remember that there was talk that Jack Moore was involved?"

"Jack Moore, is it? He was nothing, nothing but a boyo, that's what we called them then. One of the lads . . . He left Kilmartin at that time. Went off to make his fortune in the big wide world. And did he?" She looked sharply at James. "Did he make his fortune and go back to the big house and live it up in fine style with his county friends and his county relatives?"

"Well, he made a great deal of money."

"And Violet? You said she was your client. Trying to break the will, is she, trying to do his children out of their money?" Bitterness welled up in her, overpowering her. She closed her eyes then, shaking her head.

"I can't help you, Mr. Fleming. Mike died. Jack left. Violet stayed. That's all I know—and you, no doubt, know all that already."

Disappointed, James stood up and walked with her to the doorway. "Jack Moore is dead. Yes. But he was murdered . . ."

"Sacred heart of Jesus . . . leave me, leave me alone." Kathleen covered her face with both hands.

He saw his chance and took it.

"Kathleen. Listen to me." He spoke rapidly, urgently. "There are no children. Jack Moore never married. Never had family. His corpse was found in a pauper's coffin dumped on his sister Violet's doorstep. Listen to me! He'd only been back in Ireland a few days. That is why I'm here. To discover who wanted Jack Moore dead."

It was some time before she composed herself. At last she sat down and indicated to James to do likewise.

"Mr. Fleming," she said finally, "first I want you to

tell me about Jack Moore's will. Am I mentioned? Or anyone I might know?" Kathleen's face was hard again, and the line of her jaw tightened, making her look less the English housefrau and more the Irish harridan.

James was surprised by the question, but he answered it. "I can't reveal the contents to you, but I think I can tell you that you were not," he lied smoothly.

"Then I say again, I cannot help you."

"But Mrs. Banks, Violet Moore is my client. She is being charged with murder. You must see how unlikely that is. A woman such as she—"

"Hah! A woman such as she indeed. That's my point exactly. I wouldn't lift a finger to help her, even if it were in my power—which I assure you it is not."

"But surely . . ." James paused at a loss, "you wouldn't want an innocent woman to be punished. More than that, surely you would want Jack Moore's murderer to be caught."

"Let me be straight with you. I loved Jack Moore. And I foolishly thought he loved me. But he didn't. He left me, well, virtually at the altar."

"You were to be married?"

"Well, we would have married, I was fairly certain of that at the time, but . . . he left Kilmartin and circumstances changed."

"Mrs. Banks, that's precisely what I need you to tell me about. I know there was some talk that Jack had quarreled with your brother . . . talk that he had perhaps even caused his death—accidentally or intentionally. Didn't you feel anything then or since? Didn't you wonder that Mike might have been killed by your . . . fiancé?"

"No! No, no, no. How could I think that, for Jesus' sake? I never believed Jack had anything to do with poor Mick's death. I just figured that he fell in his drunken state. It wouldn't have been the first time. But I think you're driving at something. I would prefer you to be straight with me." She waited, calmer now.

"It seems to me that you have someone on your mind—someone who might have wanted to kill Jack. Tell me—who?"

"It has occurred to me, Kathleen, that your own brothers might have believed that Jack killed Mike that night in the field. They . . . indicated to me that they blamed Jack for your leaving Ireland . . ."

"For my leaving them, more like," she interposed.

"Well, yes. They feel he ruined your life and possibly killed their brother. Surely there is a reason that Jack Moore was killed in Kilmartin, where he was born and bred—and not in Dublin or America. It stands to reason that it was someone in Kilmartin who hated Jack."

"Mr. Fleming, you're more naive than you look. Are you seriously asking me to clear Violet Moore of this charge of murder by shifting the blame to my own brothers? That is what you're trying to say, isn't it? That my brothers bore a grudge against Jack for twenty-odd years. For Mick's death and my leaving them. And that the moment his feet touched Irish soil, they murdered him? Do you seriously think that even if they were guilty as hell, I would trade their lives for Violet Moore's worthless existence?"

"With or without your help, I will find the person who killed Jack Moore."

"Let it go."

"No, Kathleen, I will find the truth. No matter how much digging, no matter how much raking up of the ancient past."

"Is the past never to be dead and buried?" Kathleen's voice was now almost pleading.

"No!" James wondered at his own obsession. Not until now had he realized how committed he was to this pursuit. And not because he believed in Violet Moore's innocence. Or now even in her worthiness.

"Violet Moore is innocent."

"Innocent, is it? Ah, Mr. Fleming, it's all in how you define that word!"

"If she didn't kill Jack—and I believe that she

90

didn't, although she'll say nothing in her own defense —then she's innocent."

"Oh, she's guilty all right!" Kathleen said, her voice hissing. "And I can tell you that she'll say nothing to defend herself because she knows her own guilt. She lives with it every day, and has for twenty-seven years."

"Kathleen." James turned and faced her. "If you know Violet is guilty, then tell me that at least. This truly is in confidence. It would help me to know if she killed Jack, even though I am committed to her defense. Perhaps . . . perhaps there were extenuating circumstances. I don't know. But I will know the truth."

They sat in silence for what seemed hours.

At last Kathleen turned toward him. "Before I speak to you, you must swear, professionally and as an honorable man, that you will not reveal to a soul what I am going to tell you."

Desperate, James swore to her satisfaction. But he was uneasy.

"I am only telling you this now because I realize that in your determination to find the truth, you may come upon a fact that could destroy many lives." She paused and then continued. "Jack Moore and I were very much in love. In love the way seventeen-year-olds can be, passionately and foolishly. I was foolish, and I found that I was expecting our baby. It was early on, and I told Jack straight away. It took the wind out of his sails for a few days, but he came around. We had talked of marrying all along in that idle way, ignoring the differences in our background, and our religion." She stopped and peered at James. "Have things changed at all . . . in Ireland I mean?"

James shook his head.

"Not in two decades?"

"No," said James simply.

"No," she said sadly, "I suppose not."

"Go on," James urged.

"What he said was that he would speak to Violet.

He knew she'd go mad, but he was the real boyo, and the farm was one quarter his, as he always told me. Ah, he was full of talk, but I was willing to believe in it then, and in him.

"There was terrible trouble that morning when Mick hadn't come home and then when he was found dead. The house was in an awful state. The brothers were crazy with grief. Outsiders wouldn't have seen it, but we were a close family then and it was . . . it was a terrible shock."

"It must have been," James murmured.

"There were the police, of course, and then the arrangements for the wake and the funeral. I didn't see Jack at all. I was at home the whole time cooking and cleaning and sitting with the body. And there was no one sympathetic to my knowing Jack. No one brought me news of him in that house. Jack didn't come, but I didn't expect him to. He wasn't welcome in my home at the best of times. I heard the talk that he was involved, but I never believed it. I figured he was keeping out of the way. But then after the funeral, I heard talk that he had left home . . . I waited for word of him and got none. Finally I was so desperate for news, I went up to the manor to speak with Violet Moore."

Kathleen stopped and looked away.

"To be brief, Mr. Fleming, she told me that she knew about the baby. And that Jack was gone to London, that he had run away from his responsibilities, as she put it. I was only seventeen, and I panicked. My brothers would never have me if they knew about the baby. My mother was dead, God rest her soul, and Jack was gone to London. Violet said she'd help me. And she did, as I thought at the time. She made all the arrangements, told me what to say. Just before I started to show, she took me to a convent down in the country, where the nuns looked after bad girls like me. And when the time came, the nuns— with her encouragement, no doubt—arranged for a family to adopt my baby . . . my baby girl." Tears rolled down Kathleen's face and she didn't brush them away. "I wasn't allowed to meet them. I wasn't allowed to know any details. I wasn't even allowed to say good-bye . . ."

"Did you ever . . . ?"

"No, I never saw her again. I never had word of her. I left as soon as it was all over, and I came here, to London, and here I am still. Violet had told me to go to Australia and had even given me the fare. But I didn't have the courage . . . it was too far, too far from all I'd ever known."

"It must have been very lonely for you."

"Save your pity. I have a good marriage. And two fine sons. Which is why, Mr. Fleming, I swore you to secrecy. No one except Violet Moore knew this story. And Jack. Not my husband, not my sons. Not even my brothers. And no one must ever know. It would destroy the peace and happiness I've worked so hard for . . ." She stared at James. "I was afraid that if you pressed Violet Moore for details, she'd reveal all this to you. But now, even if she does, I have your solemn oath that you will never use it."

"Yes, you do," said James reluctantly. "May I ask you this? When you questioned me so closely about the will, were you . . . ?"

"Oh, God, it wasn't for myself, if that's what you mean. I wondered for a few moments if maybe Jack had mentioned our child in his will. I thought perhaps, perhaps . . ."

"That he had remembered her, thought of her during all those years?" said James.

She nodded. "One more thing. Mr. Fleming, if . . . if in your pursuit of truth you learn anything of my little girl, would you please let me know somehow, someday. And on your oath promise me that if you do, you will never betray me to her? I've been betrayed too often in my life."

"Are you sure, Kathleen? Don't you want to . . . ?"

"No!" Kathleen interrupted emphatically. "Never! I assure you. Let me be dead to her. But she will never be dead to me, please God." She shivered.

"Then I promise."

For the first and only time, she smiled at him. A lovely, warm smile that lit her face from within and showed him what perhaps the real Kathleen was like—with her husband, her sons, her own friends. He wondered at himself as they parted on the steps that he had not had the sense to place Kathleen in his imagination as a woman with a full life, and not merely a factor in a situation that was long dead if not buried. Once again he felt like the specter at the feast.

The afternoon flight back to Dublin had been dreary. As James sought out his car in the long-term car park, a fine, heavy drizzle began to fall, drenching his hair and shoulders even as he stood unlocking the car. There was nothing more dismal than Dublin Airport in the rain, he thought crankily, unless it was Shannon Airport in the rain. Why tourists didn't turn and run at such a climatic greeting he never knew.

The highway was empty and equally dreary. James's thoughts turned to Kathleen as he drove. Had he really learned anything or was he just fooling himself?

He turned down Dorset Street and into the top of O'Connell Street. The mass of wet shoppers bustling at the Henry Street crossing looked dowdy and drawn after the glamor of London. Grim faces bent into the rain and wind. Suddenly he wanted out. Out of Ireland, out of his job, out of the messy situation that he saw brewing ahead like the storm clouds that brooded over the Dublin Mountains.

Chapter Six

"Shocking! Absolutely disgraceful!" Sinclair addressed the air, thinking he was alone outside the forlorn-looking shop.

"Talking to yourself again, Sinclair?" A wry voice startled him, and he jumped lightly off the step and onto the gravel.

"Don't you agree then, Kevin?"

"Agree that it's a disgrace you can't get your tobacco whenever you want it, Sinclair?"

"Is that what you think?" squawked Sinclair. "Then what are you doing here yourself?"

"Just checking to see if the shop is open—like yourself," Kevin said amicably. "But I agree, it's a shocker. I don't know anyone who hasn't taken it to heart. I am not sure whether to go up to their house. You know . . ." he finished lamely.

"Mmm, I agree. It wouldn't be seemly, but still . . ."

"Come on, let's have a word with Eileen, she'll know what's new, if anyone does."

"Are you mad? It's not yet seven, man, we can't go knocking on her door, close as it is."

Kevin glanced down the row of sleeping cottages, all of their front curtains still tightly drawn, the morning sun just slanting across the tops of their gray slate roofs.

Then the door of number 10 opened and Eileen stepped out, complete with head scarf and bag clutched under her elbow. She walked determinedly toward them without seeing them, her head bent into the wind.

"Good morning, Eileen," both men said together. She looked up and smiled.

"My first customers, is it?" She took a key from her pocket.

"I say," said Sinclair, bemused.

"And what do you say? A tin of tobacco, Mr. Sinclair?"

The men followed Eileen into the shop as she unlocked and turned on the lights.

"God, it's damp in here. Three days makes a terrible difference."

"There's an old paraffin heater in the back," said Kevin. "I can light it for you, if you like."

"Ah, none of that smelly paraffin for me, thanks all the same. Mr. Sweeney said I would be able to use the bar heater."

"That's a concession, knowing him."

"Well," said Eileen kindly, "he's in a bad way yet, and I think he's glad of my help."

"Help?" Sinclair quivered with curiosity.

"Mmm, I'm going to help run the shop as best I can. He thought half days to start. As soon as I heard the awful news, I offered to do whatever I could. Mr. Sweeney thought since I lived so close by and knew most of the customers, that it might work out."

"And the post office?" asked Kevin.

"Sacred Heart, are you serious?"

"I guess that was a silly question."

"No, no, dear, it's just the thought of it. I'm not

96

qualified. The post office wouldn't allow it. But I swear it would scare the wits clean out of me, I'm sure, after the terrible things that's gone on here!"

Eileen had started checking a handwritten list.

"They'll be no papers today, of course, nor milk, but I can get them going tomorrow. And then there's, mmm, the bakery's deliveries and the eggs. God, I don't know how those two manage." She sighed and looked around. "I think for today if I can just manage the dry goods . . . and the prices. Lord, are the prices marked?" She read over the list again and then located a master price list crumpled and faded, lying under the long counter.

"Definitely half days to start. Actually, Brendan is none too bad. He's still got a terrific headache from the concussion, and that's affecting his eyes. But he said that he thought he'd be in, in a few days, if the doctor says it's all right."

"And poor Mr. Sweeney?" asked Kevin, plugging in the bar heater and positioning it near Eileen's feet, but safely away from the shelves and goods.

"Oh, he's very shaky. Of course he claims he's grand. The doctor says he must rest. He got a terrible blow to the chest, you know."

"No, we didn't know, Eileen, for heaven's sake! Everyone has a different story," Kevin said impatiently. "For God's sake don't keep us in suspense."

"I'm not, I'm sure," Eileen said huffily. "You're like two old cats around a plate of gizzards!"

"Then take pity on us, ma'am," wheedled Sinclair. Eileen shot him a look.

"He got a blow to his chest when those gurriers shoved him with the end of one of their guns. He made a rush at them, you see!" she said triumphantly.

"So the papers got it right. What a foolish man," said Kevin soberly.

"Foolish, maybe," said Sinclair, "but true to form. He's a tough old bird. And he hates this kind of thing with a passion." Sinclair was strident. "He took his job with the post office very seriously indeed."

"Well, he didn't take this here glass cage seriously enough," Eileen added, annoyed. "If he'd been in it—"

"If he'd been in it, he'd be dead now, and that's the truth!" a fourth voice added.

"Ah, it's yourself, Mr. O'Dwyer," Eileen said smoothly. "Can I help you?"

"I think it's you that's needing the help, but if you will, I'll take a tin of cat food. The old moggie's off her food, and I thought I'd give her a treat."

He counted out the thirty-seven pence, which in turn Eileen counted out into her hand and then threw in the till.

"If you don't keep a running account," imposed Sinclair, "you won't know where you're at, at the end of the day."

"Mr. Sinclair, *can* I help you?"

"A tin of Three Nuns please, four ounces," he said, and paid, noting with satisfaction that Eileen wrote down the transaction.

"He could be dead . . ." said O'Dwyer. "With the door open to the cage the way Sweeney always kept it, they could have shot him in the cage like fish in a barrel. God knows why they didn't anyway."

"I agree," said Kevin, "it was a miracle that they chose to knock them both out, instead of using their guns."

Eileen shivered. "Oh, dear God, it could have been so much worse. Yes, they could have been dead here on the floor." She looked at the floor and crossed herself.

"And was it the IRA, like they suggested on the papers?"

"Well, my sister's son's wife's brother in the police told the family that they were fairly certain. Even though the IRA haven't claimed it. From the description of the way they were dressed . . ."

"And the manner in which it was done," added O'Dwyer. "It had all the earmarks. Brutal, brutal."

"Do we know what they got?"

"Oh, they got it all. You know it was Tuesday. They got the old-age pension, they got the children's allowance, they got all the cash. Begod, they even took the stock of stamps."

"You seem to know a lot about it, O'Dwyer," said Sinclair.

"Aye, that's because I read the papers I buy."

"Sure, what would those reporters know, they only talked to the police in the town."

"Enough, enough of this palaver," interrupted Eileen. "Scat, the crowd of you! I've got to think, and I can't with this gossipin'. Have you no homes to go to?"

"Right, then, we're off," Kevin said amiably, and held the door quite pointedly for the other two men to leave. "And good luck to you for taking this on."

"I can't believe this," exclaimed James. "Why didn't you tell me straight away!"

Gerald was startled at James's reaction. "Well, I'm telling you now. What's the matter? It has no bearing on our case."

"Well, I . . . well, we don't know that yet."

"Do you mean the IRA?" Gerald snorted.

"We just can't dismiss it!" James tried to cover it, but he failed. He was shaken by the news that Mr. Sweeney and Brendan had been brutally attacked in Kilmartin the day he flew out to London. And by the terrorist Irish Republican Army, from all accounts.

"And you say they're all right, yes?"

"Yes, they're not dead or dying, if that's what you mean. But I think the reports indicated they were badly injured, head wounds or chest wounds . . ."

"Christ!"

"You'd think you knew them well." Gerald's tone was annoyed. "I knew Sweeney before you were born . . . but on the other hand . . ."

"On the other hand, you wouldn't know him if you fell over him."

"No," said Gerald, taken aback. "Nor the son."

"I do know them; I feel as though I know them. If there's nothing doing here, Gerald, I'd like to go down to see them."

"There's nothing on, but I wanted you to take over the Molloy case. The family home is being auctioned, and as their solicitors, one of us should be there. The money from the sale is to be divided four ways, and there's sure to be murder over it." Gerald smirked. "They're a greedy bunch."

"Gerald, can't Bill Carey look after that one? And allow us to concentrate on this situation? We can't leave any avenue unexplored. Who's to say there isn't a tie-in? Nothing happens in Kilmartin for donkeys years, and then within a matter of weeks there are two major crimes." James's voice rose. Even as he talked, he convinced himself of a connection. "Maybe it was the IRA. Maybe it was someone copying their modus operandi."

"Maybe. But there hasn't been any IRA activity in Wexford for some time. However, check it out if you must. You cleared your desk before you went to London. And speaking of London—was it worth the trip?"

"Yes and no. The Walsh sister—Kathleen—absolutely does not believe that her brothers were capable of killing Jack Moore. She believes that Mike fell because he was drunk. She said it wasn't the first time that kind of thing had happened."

"Well, doesn't it disprove your theory of a long-standing grudge?"

"Perhaps. But she struck me as a kindly person, incapable of believing the worst about her brothers. And she did admit, in a roundabout way, that they had been angry at Jack for leaving Kilmartin and for leaving her—they were sweethearts, remember? And they were annoyed that she chose to emigrate after Jack had gone. Naturally they would hold Jack accountable for their sister leaving Ireland." James fudged, trying to avoid mentioning Kathleen's pregnancy, as she had requested. "I still feel there's life in this theory, Gerald," he added weakly.

"Okay, maybe. We just need enough to sow doubt in a jury's mind that Violet was the only one who might have wanted to kill Jack. You've worked hard at this case, and it's paying off. You have found somebody who had a motive—revenge. Our side does not have to prove that the Walshes did it! Listen, I'll set up a meeting with Sheridan and he can talk to you, if that will help?"

"After I get back from Kilmartin?"

Gerald shrugged. "If you insist."

"I do."

James returned to his office. He gathered his briefcase and buzzed Maggie to book him into Riders Inn.

She buzzed back. "Would that be a single or a double?"

The hues of a hearth fire tinted the road and the fields as they fell away on either side. The sun had sunk behind the hills on his right as James drove fast into the village of Kilmartin. He slowed the car outside Sweeney's shop and was heartened to see a light burning inside.

"Mr. Sweeney," he called robustly as he burst in the door.

"Mr. Fleming—you put my heart crossways in my chest, barging in that way!" Eileen primped her hair and straightened the apron she wore over her clothes.

"Is he here, or Brendan?"

"No, I'm sorry. Hadn't you heard?"

"Yes, yes," James cried impatiently, unbuttoning his Crombie overcoat. "But when I saw the light . . ."

"I see. No, they're both still laid up I'm afraid, but I was speaking to Brendan only this afternoon over the telephone there, and he says he'll be in to work for a few hours in the morning. Thanks be to God," she muttered under her breath.

"Can they see people, visitors, I mean?"

"Now *that* I can't say, Mr. Fleming."

"No, of course not. Right! I'll be staying at Riders and, well, I'll ring them from there. Blast! It's so late now, I imagine it'll have to wait until morning. Just tell me—are they both all right?"

"As far as anyone can tell. Brendan was concussed, but I think he's okay. Mr. Sweeney, now, it's hard to say. Oh, Mr. Fleming, he's not a young man to be takin' such a beating."

"Beating?" James shook his head. "Those bloody bastards!"

"They were that and more. The mothers who bore them should fall down on their knees."

"Take care of yourself, Eileen. Perhaps I'll drop in on you tomorrow." James waited by the door until she had locked up and started back to her cottage.

He was getting to be a sentimental fool, he thought ruefully as he put the car in gear and headed for Riders. He wondered how he would while away the evening now, pent-up energy cramping his limbs.

He needn't have troubled himself on that score, he realized later, as Captain Rider's widow forced him around the gardens in virtual darkness on a "turn before dinner."

"And have you made any progress on the case?" she asked after their pleasantries were exchanged.

"It's difficult to say if it's progress. I'm down here now to learn more about the attack on Sweeney's shop."

"Dreadful business. I assume you're making a connection between the murder and the attack."

"Well, yes, I hope to."

"You're not alone in that. Many of us have been thinking along those lines. I hear a lot, you know," she said in answer to James's look of surprise. "Tending behind the bar. Local people have been speculating too—like yourself."

"And what have they been coming up with?" said James, knowing that he was grasping at straws.

"The gist of it is this. They're saying that the way in which Jack Moore's body was, well, disposed of—at dawn, on the steps of his ancestral home—had all the signs about it of the IRA. On the other hand, the IRA don't usually use knives. If we can say 'usually' in this distressing circumstance.

"This village and its surrounding lands have been quiet for many years. Suddenly, within a matter of weeks, there are these two atrocious happenings! And since it seems that it was the IRA who robbed the post office, people are thinking that perhaps it was some sort of revenge against the village itself, as Jack Moore's home. But perhaps you'd like to discuss it with Inspector O'Shea?"

James stopped in his tracks. "O'Shea? Here?"

"Why yes, he's staying overnight, like yourself. Although he arrived early this morning."

"Do you know why?"

"I know he was making inquiries in the neighborhood."

"The usual stock answer, in other words."

"I'm afraid so," said Mrs. Rider as they turned back toward the inn. "I'll seat you at his table if you like. I do that sort of thing very smoothly."

"I have no doubt," said James, laughing, "but I couldn't stomach a meal sitting opposite O'Shea. Let me enjoy your fine cuisine in peace."

And it was indeed an exquisite meal. The salmon cutlet had been perfectly prepared, the chicken consommé equally superb. A generous slab of apple tart swimming in cream made James feel like a boy again. And what's more, he had enjoyed every morsel despite the knowledge that O'Shea was seated a few tables behind him. It was when coffee was served that he saw the inspector approach, and glanced up with what he hoped was a disinterested expression.

"Fleming!" boomed O'Shea. Certainly all the diners would now know who he was, James thought wryly.

"O'Shea, no less." James laid it on thick.

"How did you find this little bijou?"

"I might ask you the same," and with more justification, thought James, annoyed.

"Oh, knew it for years."

"A likely story . . ."

"And you?"

"Oh, the same story." Checkmate, O'Shea, James added silently.

"I see. Well, will you join me in the bar?"

Together they walked in.

"Two pints of stout, there, Mrs. Rider," O'Shea ordered lustily. Mrs. Rider caught James's eye and smiled demurely.

"By all means, Inspector. I'll bring them to your table."

When they were seated, James got to the point. "Let's eliminate the cut and thrust, shall we, O'Shea?"

"I thought I was doing all the parrying."

"Glad to hear you admit it." James smiled. "Seriously, you're down here because of the post office business, aren't you?"

"A related affair, certainly."

"O'Shea?"

"All right, all right. Yes. I am."

"But you're murder squad."

"Last I heard." O'Shea was facetious.

"In other words, O'Shea, you're down here to establish a connection between Moore's death and the hit on the post office. Yes?"

"If there was a connection, yes, I would establish it."

"But . . ."

"Who's to say?"

They leaned apart as Mrs. Rider placed two pints on the table before them. Other patrons gradually filled the small room, until smoke and the press of bodies raised a canopy of privacy over their heads.

O'Shea settled back and contributed the smoke of his untipped cigarette to the general fug.

"O'Shea, can you share what you've found out?" James was blunt.

"Well, I don't see why not. You seem to think I take sides in this kind of endeavor. I assure you, I do not. I do my job. I let the barristers do theirs."

"But that's nonsense. You work, in effect, for the Attorney General, who prosecutes. And you can keep me and the likes of me in the dark or not, as you choose."

"But I choose not to keep you in the dark, Fleming, you or anyone else, insofar as it does not interfere with the A.G.'s functioning in a case."

"Can you tell me anything? You see, I believe there's a connection between the two events. The murder and the hit on the post office in Sweeney's shop. Perhaps revenge is the common denominator. In that case, it puts my client well out of it. The two events are 'political,' as they say. Unless you're about to suggest Violet Moore is an agent of the IRA." James laughed mirthlessly.

"Stranger things have happened, believe me, Fleming. But no . . . to be fair, I would not think that of Miss Moore."

"Thank you," James said, signaling for another two pints from the bar.

"The trouble with you, Fleming, is that you sit there smugly assured that there's no way Violet Moore nor the likes of Violet Moore would dirty her hands with the IRA. And what do you base that assumption on?" O'Shea jabbed his cigarette offensively in James's direction. "I'll tell you. It's based on nothing more than the fact that you're a Prod." He smiled as James jumped and looked around to see who had heard.

"That's right. Because you're a Prod and grew up with them, because you've been in your secure little nest of prosperous businessmen and successful professional men and charitable ladies who look on the Queen of England as one of their own and who endow the arts and run homes for indigent Masonic spinsters, you think to yourself: 'Ah, no upstanding, prosperous, landed Anglo-Irish gentry or jackeen would dirty their hands with the IRA . . .'"

James felt his face redden both at the description of his kind and the fact that O'Shea had read him so well. "And I'd be right," he said defensively.

"And that's where you're wrong. Why man, have you forgotten your own history? If it weren't for the Prod patriots over the centuries, we wouldn't even be having this conversation."

"That was then—"

"And this is now."

"Is this a personal attack or what, O'Shea? Because I don't intend—" James was rising from his seat as he spoke.

"Hush, man, hush." O'Shea motioned with his hand for James to sit down. "It's just those self-assured airs of yours that riled me. Look, have another pint on me and I'll give you a little modern history lesson." James was slightly mollified.

"Don't fool yourself that these IRA Provos are all a bunch of hotheaded youths, adopting guerrilla-style tactics and running around with Russian-made weapons. Man, these bastards are training in the Middle East, they're on speaking terms with the likes of Gadaffi. They're single-minded, they're arrogant, most of them are dirt poor, most of them are Catholic or were . . . and what does that mean? That's a discussion for another day. I tell you, Fleming, this isn't my scene, as you know. I've never been in the Special Branch, and I don't want to be. But I read between the lines, as you should. And hear the talk. Man, these people are politicized. They have education. Some of them are Marxist, some of them are a new breed. But are you aware of that? And if you don't bother your arse to know what's going on under your very nose, do you think those fools that give them money know more than you?"

"Hold on, O'Shea. Hold on. I don't need a lecture from you. You don't know the first thing about me.

There's something more to this, something more than the drink talking. What the hell is this all about?"

"Sorry. Sorry. It's true. Fleming, I was taking it out on you. I've had some information from the States. The FBI was tipped by the IRS—that's the Internal Revenue Service, if you didn't know—and they followed up the lead. In fact it was an obvious route to go. We had asked them to look into it ourselves."

"Look into what?"

"Moore's politics. Prosperous Irish-American, very low profile, no family, etcetera. Anyway, they think they've turned up a connection with NortHelp."

"The Northern Irish aid group?"

"That's it. The American CIA have to take it from there because the FBI sources only take it as far as that side of the Atlantic."

"Is it true?" James's face showed his astonishment.

"Well, let's say I've seen the faxes of his tax returns. They seem to show in outline form that he may have been making large—very large—contributions to the 'movement,' in the shape of NortHelp. The dates, however, are sporadic, with long periods of time where there was no activity."

"Major money?"

"Perhaps."

"And recently?"

"Within the last twelve months."

"I can't believe it."

"Why? Because he was a Prod like yourself?"

"Frankly, yes. What a route to go!"

"Listen, neither of us knew the man. Who have we met yet who knew him?"

"True, but we know—I think we know—that he belonged to no typical Irish-American organizations. I've seen Sheridan's research. He didn't even subscribe to an Irish-American paper, for God's sake."

"True but they're on every newsstand in Boston, I can tell you."

"And you're saying that he could have been getting

his picture from such sources—about what's been going on here in the last twenty years? It's bizarre. I'm sorry, O'Shea. I don't buy it."

"Don't. It's no skin off my nose. But I don't see why you're holding on to your self-generated picture of the victim. Listen. He goes to London or wherever. And then he lands up in Boston. There's an Irish mafia there, just as in New York. Our version of the old boy's network, I suppose. Your old emigrants' network." O'Shea laughed at his own wit. "So let's say he gets his feet on the ground. Works hard, keeps his nose clean, makes progress in a career and branches out with investments and stockbrokering. Ends up owning his own firm. Meanwhile he's willingly lost all contact with home, but that's not to say that he isn't like millions, man, millions of Irish in Canada and Australia, in London and the States. They get nostalgic for the oul' country. They wear green on Paddy's day. They read in the papers about the struggle of the oppressed. They look in their wallet and they say: I can be part of that great historic struggle. I can make myself a part of history, I can cover myself with the glory that shines on the likes of Emmet and Wolfe Tone and Parnell—all Prods by the way. And all they have to do is lift a pen or a phone."

"So you are describing Jack Moore: no family, few friends, just acquaintances—if we believe the reports —no church affiliation."

"Exactly . . . when you have nothing, you search for something. You buy into a dream and become part of it—with money."

"Well!" James sounded relieved. But he was anxious for additional proof of a direct connection between Jack Moore and the IRA. "Then tell me this, then. Did he make large contributions to anything else?"

"Yes. The United Fund, a hospital for children, some local campaign funds. Those contributions were sporadic too."

"In other words, reflecting perhaps what was going on in his life at the time?"

"I hadn't thought of it that way, but yes, your analysis is right on the mark. He reads something, or sees something, an appeal in the papers or on TV, and he breaks out the checkbook."

"So you view the NortHelp contributions in the same light—that is, sporadic and impulsive?"

"Don't cross-examine me, Mr. Solicitor, that's the barrister's job."

"But you obviously take my point?"

"Yes, Fleming, I do . . . But I'm not saying that he couldn't have had a serious committment to the IRA."

"Then you do believe there's a connection between his death and the IRA, and between the robbery and the IRA."

"I didn't say that."

"Why else would you be here? O'Shea, how long have you known all this about Jack Moore?"

"Not long."

"But you suspected something of the sort when you came down to take charge of the Moore case."

"Yes, the manner of his death . . . well, actually, the manner in which the body was disposed of—at dawn, on the steps—it all pointed to revenge. It pointed for that reason to some political connection. And the ordinary murderer generally does not have those kinds of resources at hand."

"So, you're telling me that even though you suspected something political, as you so nicely put it, you still went ahead and charged my client? Someone with absolutely no political connections and, for God's sake, no motive to kill her own brother, whom she hadn't seen in nearly thirty years!" James's voice rose and his hands tightened around the pint glass.

"Fleming, Fleming. Everything's political." O'Shea's booming voice dropped to almost a whisper and his strong face was somber. "There was obviously the pressure from the Attorney General. You know that."

"But you know that too."

"Yes, of course, but he was under pressure from the American embassy for a quick solution."

"What!"

"Shh, man. I'm being frank with you, but please grow up. If you want to stay in this business, you can't possibly remain this naive."

"I'm not naive. I expect sworn officials of the department, including the Attorney General, to keep their oaths."

"Hold on. Do you think I could ignore the fact that the body was found on Violet Moore's front step? That the weapon was found in her barn? That the weapon was from her own kitchen, with her prints on it? For Chrissakes! Could I finally ignore that her own sister pinpointed her in conversation with an unknown man around the time of the death? The evidence was too strong not to bring a charge. The Attorney General saw that. If it kept the Americans happy, then that was a bonus."

"And why the hell were they involved?"

"Because Jack Moore is, was, an American citizen. He got his papers years ago. As an American citizen he was under the aegis of the embassy as soon as he landed here. Normally they would take no interest in one of their citizens visiting his former homeland, but they could hardly overlook the fact that he was murdered!"

"And no doubt they had some quick tip about the NortHelp connection?"

"Perhaps. We have no way of knowing that."

"I'm not as stupid as you seem to think, O'Shea. They don't want that made public. A prosperous American who has given major money to NortHelp, killed twenty-four hours after his arrival in Ireland."

"I don't think our government would want it either. Wouldn't do the Tourist Board a lot of good when they

110

were planning their ad campaign. Go home to die: visit Ireland! Send money first!"

"Your gallows humor is . . . well, gallows humor."

"Sorry. Here. How about another drink?" O'Shea was conciliatory.

"Listen, O'Shea. If Jack was giving major money to the 'cause,' why would the IRA want him dead? Surely they would be killing the golden goose."

"To be honest, I'm not sure yet. That's what we're working on. But there have been one or two precedents over the years. It runs like this.

"The donor decides, perhaps because his contributions are so large, that he wants a more direct involvement in the 'struggle.' He may want to dictate where or how the money is spent. He talks with the organizers and they get anxious. The message is relayed through the grapevine. He comes over to check it out for himself. And hey, presto!

"Alternatively, there's been one or two cases where the happy camper becomes disillusioned with the way the 'cause' is being served. He reads about the killing of an innocent family returning home from their holidays, blown to smithereens because their green van is mistaken at a distance for a British Army vehicle. The happy camper isn't happy anymore. He's got innocent blood on his hands. And because he's been a big contributor and, up till then, stroked by the powers that be in the States or wherever, he complains to them, perhaps attempts 'political' argument and high philosophical discourse. And getting nowhere, he says he'll blow the whistle on the whole thing, that he'll go public—with what little he knows, which is usually damn all. But in their case, unlike Oscar Wilde's aphorism, any publicity of that kind is bad publicity."

"So steps are taken?" James was horrified at the scenario.

"Too much to take in?"

James was silent as he stood up to leave.

"Before you go, just tell me how your trip to London prospered?" O'Shea smiled.

"Is nothing sacred?" James asked wearily.

"Very little, I'm afraid, Fleming. But you're learning."

"Good night . . ."

"Right."

James fell into bed exhausted. And it seemed a mere matter of moments when the pale morning sunshine fell across his face through the narrow window whose curtains he had left undrawn in his weariness.

After indulging in a cholesterol-laden and infinitely satisfying Irish breakfast of sausages, rashers, black and white pudding, two eggs, and beautifully grilled tomatoes, followed by white toast, brown bread and marmalade, and an enormous pot of strong tea, he felt fit and anxious to be off to visit the Sweeneys.

He arrived at their house without warning them in advance, hoping that this would strengthen his chances of actually getting in to see and talk to both Brendan and Mr. Sweeney.

It was on a low hill, and the garden and buildings were half hidden from sight by hedges of boxwood and holly. But the view from the house and from the rear of the house was magnificent, commanding the valley in which nestled the tiny village of Kilmartin, its main road meandering like a stream between the hills and fields and farms. The air was beautifully fresh and bracing. James closed his eyes for a few seconds and had the sensation of a cool, fragrant shower washing his skin and his hair. Thoughts of house hunting drifted into his mind. Yes, he wanted a house, one with cozy rooms and poky cupboards, a farmhouse kitchen and a spacious garden with, yes, potatoes growing, and onions. He sighed and opened his eyes.

He lifted the heavy brass knocker and waited for the low linteled door to open.

Brendan peered blindly through the crack that eventually appeared. "Yes?" he said questioningly.

"Brendan. It's James Fleming, Fleming, from Dublin."

"Oh, goodness, wait . . . wait . . ." Brendan fumbled in the lower pocket of his baggy cardigan and pulled out his glasses, which he placed carefully and gently on what James realized was a very bruised nose.

"James . . . James . . ." Genuine pleasure filled his voice as he led James into the small oak-beamed hallway. "Please, follow me, this way." Brendan turned first to his left and then to his right. "Here, in here." They entered a small room crowded with massive oak furniture from the twenties. Full as it was, it was still very cold.

"Da, Da! It's James Fleming from Dublin. You remember?"

"Of course I do," Mr. Sweeney said crossly, turning stiffly in his chair.

If Brendan hadn't directed his attention to the wing chair drawn up to the cold hearth, James would not have seen the tiny man who huddled there in a large, crocheted afghan of more colors than Joseph's coat. A low table with the remains of breakfast was to his side.

Brendan fussed and stewed until Mr. Sweeney snapped at him to bring up a chair closer to the hearth. Why, James could not fathom, until he sat and saw a few red embers still glowing beneath a mountain of ash.

Brendan stood rubbing his hands nervously.

"Tea, Mr. Fleming?" asked Sweeney the elder.

"No, thanks, I just had breakfast."

"Not to worry. Bring us in a fresh pot anyway, Brendan."

"Right, Right." Brendan left the room, not to return for a very very long time.

James weighed what to do, and took the bull by the horns at risk of offending the old man.

He knelt on one knee easily and swiftly and drew over the cover from the grate. Spotting the shovel and an empty coal hod, he lifted out the mass of ash that had fallen under the grate and which was choking off the fire from what little coal remained. Small flames leaped up, fed with this new breath of air. James shook down the fire a second time and loosened the ash and quickly tonged a few pieces of coal onto the heart of the fire.

"Not too much there, Fleming."

"Oh, no sir, just a few bits and pieces to keep it alive."

"Right, we wouldn't want a blaze on a warm spring day such as this." Mr. Sweeney pulled the afghan round his neck and tentatively stretched his slippered feet toward the warmth.

James smiled inwardly and felt the better for easing the old man's stiff limbs with the help of the fire.

"It's Brendan, you know, he can't see to do it properly. Humph." Sweeney stirred in the chair with irritation at his son.

"It's just the two of you, then?" James said conversationally.

"Yes, sadly, the missus died some years ago. But we manage, usually." Mr. Sweeney glared at the wall which, James assumed, the room shared with the kitchen. He was glad Brendan couldn't see that look. The sooner the two of them were back at work, the better, he realized.

"Mr. Sweeney, I was terribly sorry to hear of your trouble. How are you feeling now?"

Sweeney rubbed his chest. "I'm not a complainer, Fleming, but I can tell you, not even when I played Gaelic football did I experience such a blow nor the pain I've had from it ever since. But it lessens slightly each day. Dr. MacIntyre comes up to see me. There's little he can do. It's bruised muscle, a damned nuisance. You see, I'm fit as a fiddle otherwise, but if I go

114

to lift my arms, it pulls the muscle, and here I am rabbiting on . . ."

"No, no, no. I'm interested. Please finish what you were saying."

"Well, as far as I can remember, the burly young gurrier hit me with the butt end of his gun—I'd hardly call it a rifle—a big, mean-looking yoke, it was. I was making a rush at him, and he caught me full in the chest. It knocked the wind completely out of my body and, well, MacIntyre said I fainted."

"And a good thing too, in a way."

"Not a'tall. If I had taken the blow, perhaps I could have tackled him."

James looked at the wizened, determined face and held his tongue.

"What do you think yourself?" he said after a silence.

"About what?"

"About the robbery?"

"No doubt in my mind it was the IRA boys, the Provos. They wore balaclavas. There were two of them, you see. Youngish, from the quick way they moved. Dark jackets, those jeans everyone wears nowadays, and black balaclavas."

"Did they speak?"

"Oh, indeed. They rushed in the door. It was before five-thirty that morning. I was waiting on the papers to arrive, and of course they hadn't. On the other hand, it was the bus driver who found us. Few others would have been about at that time. Unless it was Sinclair." He laughed at his own little joke and winced with the pain the laughter brought.

"Could you tell anything from their voices?"

"Well now, there's a thought. No one has had the sense to ask me that. But now that you do, it reminds me. I would've said the accent was Sligo."

"Sligo?" Brendan's voice squawked from the doorway as he balanced a tray of tea and cookies with one hand and shut the door behind him with the other. He placed the tray on the small round table near the heavily curtained east window.

"Sligo?" He repeated. "Are you saying that their accents were Sligo? Not a bit of it."

"And why not?" Mr. Sweeney bristled.

"I'll tell you. It was Donegal and no mistake, and I'll ring the station today and tell them to put it in my statement."

Mr. Sweeney considered for a moment. "Brendan, I have to agree."

"Of course you do." Brendan beamed. "You see, James, I was little help to the police. When one of the men leaped over the counter, he pushed me out of the way and knocked my glasses off. I couldn't see a thing after that, but I went toward their shapes. I heard them call to each other just before I was struck in the face.

"And that was it. But accents are a bit of a hobby of mine. Because the old eyes aren't so good and I often can't make out peoples' dress or appearance, I take a little bit of pride in placing their voices and their accents. And I do believe that these two thugs were from Donegal. But, yes, Da, close enough to the Sligo border to put you in mind of Sligo."

"Well, that certainly would seem to lend credence to the Provo theory. Donegal is a county known for spawning and then hiding these political types, being as it were, next door to Northern Ireland," James said.

"Political types!" Sweeney's voice rose toward a shriek. "Don't grace them with such a word. Politics is *not* their game."

"I apologize, Mr. Sweeney, of course you're right." James sipped his tea and somehow found an appetite for the ginger-nut biscuits piled on his plate.

"There's no doubt in either of your minds it was the IRA, then?" James asked as he ate.

"None whatsoever. They were experienced. They moved like lightning. They were familiar with the glass cage. I admit the door of it was open. I had been counting the money to get ready for the various payouts. It was the first Tuesday, you know," Mr. Sweeney added a bit sadly. "I've always done it that way, you see."

"And it's been a very efficient system, Da," Brendan said gently, and caught James's eye.

"He's afraid now that Dublin will take away the post office from us."

"Oh, 'twould be a blessin'. I'd be glad to see the back of the old thing. Bloomin' cage and endless work. You agree, Brendan, don't you? You'd hardly miss sorting the mail every day?" Sweeney peered at his son.

James knew immediately how very much Brendan would miss that, but said nothing. Inadvertently, a sigh escaped his lips.

"It's a dreadful business . . ."

"The post office?" squawked Brendan.

"No, no, I mean, this attack on you both. I'm just very glad you're well, that you're here to tell the tale."

"Indeed. But the police will never catch them. They're in Donegal as we speak. Playing at war games amongst the rocks," Sweeney added with some bitterness.

"How's it going with Miss Moore?" Brendan asked, changing the subject.

"Well, Brendan, I'm hoping to tie this attack on the post office in with the murder. It's a bit complicated, but I thank you for being so frank with me about your experiences, both of you. I'll go now, I don't want to tire you."

"Man, we're both tired with the inactivity. Next time I see you, I hope it's across the counter of me shop." Sweeney's grip was surprisingly strong as he shook hands with James. Brendan went ahead and unlatched the old plank door. "It was nice of you to come, James." Brendan beamed at him. "Sure, we'll be all right. I expect to be in the shop tomorrow, if you'll be coming by?"

"You never know, Brendan."

James climbed back into his car, sad, in a way, that he wouldn't be dropping into the shop on the morrow. His home, such as it was, was elsewhere. He breathed a little good-bye to the village of Kilmartin and turned the fast car on the road to Dublin.

—— *Chapter Seven* ——

In the end James was astonished how easy it all was.

There, for anyone who might be interested, was the information that Kathleen Walsh was so desperately trying to conceal. It had been a simple matter of patient reading at the Central Office for the Registration of Births, Marriages, and Deaths. He knew the birth had taken place at the end of the year in which Jack Moore had left Ireland, twenty-seven years ago. And he also felt that the convent where Kathleen had gone would most likely have been in one of the less populated counties; in other words, far from Dublin and its environs, and also far enough away from Wexford. Consequently, he had started on the western counties first, and by the end of the afternoon had found the listing.

As he folded up the bit of paper on which he had copied the date and place of birth, all kinds of thoughts raced through his mind. It struck him forcibly that Baby Girl Walsh might know—if she were alive—that she was illegitimate, and would know the names of her parents, for Kathleen had named John Stuart Moore as the putative father. Their two names were linked at least in one legal record, if not on a marriage certificate.

Did Baby Girl Walsh ever wonder about that young mother listed on the record as living at home, or about the young father listed as farm manager, both living in the county of Wexford? Did she even know that their names were there for her to see? Did she wonder why she had been born in a convent in Tipperary? If she hadn't applied for a passport or for a driver's license, then she might not.

The nun with whom he had spoken over the telephone had been less than helpful. He had said simply that he wished to locate a child born at the convent. She had stated categorically that it was impossible. But as James well knew, in Ireland nothing is impossible. But no amount of wheedling and persuasion had helped. Just seconds before she rang off in a huff, he requested she inform the Mother Superior that he was coming to the convent anyway.

The drive to Tipperary was extremely pleasant, but finding the convent at the farthest reaches of the town of Thurles was less pleasant. He took three wrong turnings, the third into a winding country road that crossed and recrossed a river, only to deteriorate to a boreen and then end in a rutted field. He knew he had scratched the car. His temper rose. For all he knew, he had followed the River Suir back to its rise in the Slieve Bloom Mountains. A heavy rain began to fall, further obscuring his vision. He saw not a soul in the surrounding mountain fields, and he drove back to the so-called main road. Then he began all over again, this time ignoring the signposts that had misled him. Finally, as his exasperation reached exploding point, he made a turn, and through the dripping windshield and the dripping trees which intensified the torrent of rain, he spotted a gray stone building, grim and foreboding. Not even the stone cross that surmounted its perfectly rectangular construction would distinguish it from a prison or a reformatory or, for that matter, an orphanage.

The flat windows showed no light, and looked for that reason as though no glass shielded them. In vain James tried to read the small brass plaque on the right side of the double entrance doors. Bent against the rain, he threw his raincoat over his head and ran lightly up the steps. The Convent of Our Lady of Perpetual Help.

"Oh my!" he mused aloud. Nothing could have looked more austere or been so misnamed, at least to the outside observer. He started to turn back in order to lock up his car, but glancing at the bleak and deserted landscape, he decided not to bother. He pulled the old-fashioned brass-handled bell and waited. And waited. Undecided whether to ring again or just stand there like a fool, he was startled to turn and see that the door had been opened a crack. He bent down to see a tiny, wizened white face.

"I am here to see Mother Superior," he shouted against the wind, feeling foolish as he mouthed the words. Mother of what? he was wondering. And superior to what? A small stream of water suddenly dribbled into his collar. Then the door closed on him. They were refusing to let him in! His fist was just on the point of pounding it when the door opened a second time.

"Your name?"

"Fleming, Fleming!" James shouted, half in anger, half in embarrassment.

"No need to shout. I have perfect hearing despite my age," she announced, finally admitting him into the lobby. In James's haste to shed the dripping coat and wipe his damp neck, he failed to notice at first the splendor of this large entrance hall.

The parquet floor gleamed as if newly laid. On one side of the hall stood a long table, its polished mahogany catching the light from the brass hanging lamp that shed a softness and an illusion of warmth. The little nun took James's coat into a tiny room off

121

the lobby where a crackling fire burned in a small grate. She swiftly hung the coat and spread its skirts wide for it to dry. An antique umbrella stand stood at the ready, and James, without an umbrella, suddenly felt that he wasn't quite the well-dressed man in this little nun's eyes.

To the rear of the vestibule facing him was a wide wooden staircase, uncarpeted and gleaming like the mahogany table. He noticed then the small door tucked beneath the stairwell and the larger, more imposing carved wooden doors opening off either side of the lobby. The nun turned the ornate handle on one of them and said briskly, "Walk this way please, Mr. Fleming."

He entered a surprisingly beautiful room, with pleasing proportions, despite the height of its ceiling. Another fire lit the room with its welcome warmth. A rich Persian carpet, slightly worn in places, was laid in the center of the wooden floor. Two overstuffed couches stood facing each other, and a low round table between them held current news magazines. On either side of the fireplace were two half tables, companions, with bowls of daffodils that were sisters to the ones James had seen in the hallway. Their yellow trumpets were so bright, interspersed with others of such a delicate hue as to be almost ivory, that they made him smile. A simple painting of the Madonna and child hung over the fireplace, and James gazed at it. Always wary of the Catholic penchant for overstatement, he was surprised at the beauty of the painting. Not an old master certainly, but striking in its portrayal and its lack of garishness. He glanced around. An equally simple statue of the Virgin stood discreetly on a table in the corner by the window which fronted the drive, and where he could see his car standing in the torrential downpour.

Suddenly the car and the world outside seemed very distant. He was unaccountably warm and peaceful. He shook himself. He could hear . . . nothing, nothing but his own breath. He strained and still could hear nothing. "Quieter than a church," he said to himself, smiling. "And more welcoming."

A fire burned on the hearth, and he spread his hands to the warmth. He did not hear the handle of the door turn, nor did he hear the footfalls of the tall woman who approached. He sensed rather than saw her, and turned quickly. She seemed to glide across the floor.

"Mr. Fleming." It wasn't a question. She extended a cool, thin hand and grasped his firmly. "Please, sit down."

James did as he was bid, trying to evaluate what manner of woman was in front of him. "Mother Superior?"

"Yes," she said simply.

He waited, assuming she would ask him to call her something more reasonable. Even "Sister" would be more amenable to him at this point. He waited in vain.

The silence lengthened. She didn't offer to assist the conversation with the usual platitudes such as "How may I help?" James became tongue-tied.

"My card," he said at last.

"Thank you. I shall take it for my records, but I have already ascertained your credentials through a friend in Dublin."

"A friend?"

"A clerical friend."

"I see," said James, taken aback. "And you know why I am here?"

"Yes. I know what you want. That's why your first request was refused. But since you insisted on coming in person, I will certainly talk to you. But I can only refuse you again."

"But you don't know which child's adoption I am concerned with . . ."

"I assure you it makes no difference. The policy applies to every child—without exception."

"Mother . . . Superior, I am involved in a case

where my client is accused of murder. She is a Miss Violet Moore, who arranged for a young mother to come here. I believe my client is completely innocent. That means someone else committed this terrible crime and may well go free."

"How can this possibly be connected with an adoption? From the note I have here, it was an adoption that took place many many years ago. You must take my point."

"No, Mother, you must see my point. The murdered man was the father of the baby girl born at this convent twenty-seven years ago!"

The nun's facial muscles twitched ever so slightly. Curiosity widened her pale blue eyes, but only fleetingly. Years of self-discipline reasserted themselves.

"Please, don't tell me any of the details. I shall make an effort now to forget what you have already very ill-advisedly told me. You see, nothing you can say will alter the fact that our adoption records are sealed. Don't you think over the years we haven't had other similar requests from solicitors, from erstwhile family members, from people who have gone abroad? Regardless of the cases these various people could and did make, our policy remained and must still remain sacrosanct and in force. You know that as well as I do, Mr. Fleming."

Her tone and manner were implacable. James wondered why he had bothered to come.

"As you must understand, Mr. Fleming, it is not a case of my changing my mind. The policy is there to govern those of us who have been chosen to govern. I merely abide by that policy. I might add, I believe in that policy. It has served the children, their parents, and their adoptive parents very well for many many years. Our function here is very delicate. We deal with people at their most vulnerable moments. We deal with the young mother at that emotional time of giving birth, we deal with her when she gives up that baby she has borne. And we deal with those anxious, childless couples whose lives are changed forever by an act of physical love between two people months before, people they will never know. A few seconds of, let us say, biology?—and four or five or more lives are changed forever. It is a sacred trust, and I won't be the one to break it."

The Mother Superior stood up gracefully and her austere expression softened for a moment. "I wish you and your client well, Mr. Fleming. Good-bye."

James, chastened and stymied, took her hand briefly and walked ahead of her to open the door.

Mother Superior touched a small silver bell that stood on the hall table. "Sister Benedicta will see you out," she said as she glided soundlessly from the lobby and disappeared in the shadows behind the staircase.

James stood waiting, a picture of discouragement. The sense of peace the convent had brought to him on his arrival was shattered, but he glanced kindly at the little old nun who had admitted him.

"Your coat, Mr. Fleming," she said, bustling as a tiny house martin might have bustled if encumbered by a long black habit and white coif. James followed her into the small "drying room."

"The rain has stopped, Mr. Fleming. Merely an April shower. I was just going out to the garden."

"I'd love to see it," said James.

"By all means," she said, delighted. "The scents after a rain such as this are heady, as though the flowers and herbs are giddy from their long drink." She pulled on a rain cape and led him from the lobby, down the granite steps, past his car to a wide garden James hadn't noticed in his dash through the torrential rain. She was correct, he thought. The intermingled scents rose up and were wafted toward them on a brisk spring breeze. He followed Sister Benedicta down the narrow little paths of paving stones and listened attentively as she explained her goals and aspirations, for this garden was now in her care in her retirement from years of active service in the convent.

"This is my herb garden. The comfrey's doing well, but of course it loves rain. The chives are flourishing too. But the parsley, now, and the rosemary—they're a bit slow. Now see this lemon verbena, delicious." She handed him a tiny leaf to rub between his fingers. The scent of lemon was powerful. "You are an exceptionally good listener," the little nun chirruped up at him. James had been stooping for some time to catch the words of the ancient nun.

"Well, I must tell you, my mother keeps a fine garden, as do many of her friends in Dublin. I've often visited them, and this is one of the nicest I've ever seen."

Sister Benedicta glowed with pride. "Oh, it is a dear occupation of mine. No matter what the irritations or sorrows of the day, they are soon forgotten working in a garden. And they are soon replaced by a sense of tranquility that I find sometimes even more potent than the tranquility of the chapel. But don't tell Mother I said that!" Her birdlike voice sent a peal of tinkling laughter through the quiet garden. In a separate bed were the flowers. She bent to pick a nosegay, among them the daffodils with the pale trumpets he had noticed inside. As she worked, James chatted and she listened, hungry for news of the outside world.

"I am working on a case now," he said, his voice neutral, "most interesting. In fact it might interest you, Sister."

"Indeed?"

"Yes, it involves a lovely girl, a girl who was born here, in fact, about twenty-seven years ago. I work on wills, you see, that's my main job at the solicitors firm I am with." James fudged the truth unmercifully.

"And might this girl stand to inherit?" Sister asked, intrigued now.

"Indeed, she might. A considerable fortune. I . . . well . . . perhaps I shouldn't . . ."

"Oh, but Mr. Fleming, look around you. Who would I be tellin', except the flowers and the fields?"

She beamed up at him. As an afterthought she added, almost to encourage his confidence, "I may well know her. I was a midwife in those days, you see. I knew all the girls and their wee ones. And I've followed many of them over the years."

"The mother was from Wexford, and her surname was Walsh." James thought of Kathleen's tragic face, and told her mentally that telling this little nun was no betrayal in the sense she meant it. Especially since this little nun might well have delivered her daughter.

"Oh, indeed and I do remember her, so well. That was one of the most successful adoptions we ever had, but of course you know that yourself?" She looked questioningly at him.

He jumped. "Oh, yes, yes I agree. Her parents are exceptional people . . ." he hazarded.

"Oh, yes indeed. They weren't young, of course, but so . . . let me say, loving. I knew that morning when they took Baby Walsh away that it was a dream come true for them and that she would have a beautiful life. And to think she is so successful now. I remember her mother, she wasn't more than a child herself, but she never struck me as musical. Strange, isn't it?"

"Indeed, it is. But who knows how these talents arise—musical ability, artistic ability. Sometimes there is no correlation . . ." James waffled on.

"Well, then it's a gift in the true sense of the word. And she has the gift of music, that is sure. So young and already making a name for herself. And now you say she may have wealth too?"

"Ahh . . . she might indeed."

By now they had walked to the boundary of the garden, and here he made his farewell. He was sorry to leave the peaceful garden and the sweet-voiced old woman with the ageless face. As he started the engine, he cringed to hear it roar and sully the silence, however briefly. Nevertheless, he tooted his horn, waved, and was pleased to see Sister Benedicta give him a return wave.

James's heart soared. He could barely enjoy the drive back to Dublin, anxious as he was to pursue the leads that Sister Benedicta in all her innocence had given him. A girl with a career, music; in the public eye; and parents who lived in Dublin and who would be just that bit older than most parents of a daughter of twenty-seven. "God bless you, Sister Benedicta, your name truly suits you," murmured James as he hit the highway and let his car fly.

"Flanagan!" James stood on the pavement hailing his friend. A short, stout, bearded man threaded his way through the traffic stalled at the long light at the corner of Stephen's Green.

"Fleming," said Matt, slightly out of breath. "It's good to see you, you old bastard!"

"Likewise I'm sure. Come on, we'll be late . . ."

"As usual." Laughing, the friends took the steps two at a time and entered the imposing cold hall of the College Club.

"This is a bit extravagant, isn't it, Fleming?" said Matt as they were seated at one of the white linen-covered tables near the impossibly high Georgian windows that fronted the building.

"Not a'tall. I'll put it on my tab."

"And put it down as a business expense for one of your poor, ignorant clients?" Matt laughed.

"Perhaps, perhaps . . ."

"I must admit, James, I've always wanted to see the inside of this place. Ever since school, passing by on the pavement looking up at the white heads in the window with cigars or pipes sticking out of their gobs. What are the fees again?"

"You don't want to know."

"Come on?"

"Well, I think they went up, maybe fifteen hundred pounds a year, around there."

"Lord. And for that you get . . ."

"Well, we can eat here like this."

"And pay?"

"Of course. And there are private rooms at our disposal—for parties or perhaps business matters, or just for a place to come and read the papers in peace."

"God, you're a snot!" Matt said, smiling.

"So what else is new?"

"You and your type have to get your peace and quiet. Not like the working stiffs like me. I have my staff room for that—but so do the other twenty faculty members. Not much peace and quiet in there, I can tell you."

"Don't give me that. I've been in your staff room. And I clearly remember cozy broken-down armchairs and tea always brewing and fireplaces burning brightly."

"Ah yes, but that was at my old school. You haven't bothered your arse to visit me at the tech. All shiny bright and spanking new. The staff room has walls made of cinder block—you can't hang a bloody thing on them unless you use tape, and then it dries up from the central heating and falls off. I assure you we have color-coordinated red plastic chairs and Formica tables, God, it's awful."

"Flanagan, these things take time. The likes of you will soon introduce civilized living to the staff room."

"Impossible. For that you need drafty windows, creaking wooden floorboards, and a fireplace that doesn't draw. But I'm not discouraged, the staff are suitably crazy. If that changes, then I'll give up and go become a tree farmer."

"That's no sacrifice. You never saw yourself as a vice-principal anyway. You'd probably love tree farming."

"I might, but I doubt Dorothy would."

An ancient stooped waiter approached. James ordered and then resumed their conversation over a glass of sherry each.

"So how is Dorothy? And my godson and his three brothers?"

"Two brothers, don't get ahead of yourself there, Fleming!"

"Sorry. Everyone I know has so many children, I lose track sometimes," James said sheepishly.

"Don't worry, your day will come." Matt attacked his beef and vegetables. Through his cabbage he assured James that he would succumb to marriage sooner or later, but as his oldest friend, he advised him to make it sooner.

"And why is that?" asked James.

"Because, my good man, you are getting bloody set in your ways." He waved his fork to indicate their surroundings, and bits of cabbage flew in a small arc around them.

"Bachelor life—that's what this is. Fast cars, indifferent food, good clothes, and not a good woman in sight. How do you stand it?" Matt laughed.

"I don't really," James said seriously.

"I know that," said Matt, "that's why I can chance saying all this to you . . . I saw Teresa last week."

"And?"

"And she looks great. She still has those great knockers, in spite of the two kids."

"Two?"

"Mmm, one within this last year. She's in the same badminton club as Dorothy. You know they're cousins ten times removed, or some female nonsense like that. They went for a vodka and lime, and when I collected Dorothy, we spoke for a few minutes."

"Two?"

"Yes, two. Now, what about it? Any woman on the horizon?"

After this news, James attempted to divert the conversation, but Matt persisted.

"For God's sake, James, you were with me the first time I met Dorothy, that night at the dance . . ."

"And you were with me the night I met Teresa . . ."

"Jesus! Fleming, let it go. No one else is telling you, so I will. Let it go. Get on with your life. Let me tell you, a few snot-gobblers rubbing mashed banana

130

down your suit will give you a whole new perspective on your life!"

"Are you trying to put me off?" They laughed together and moved on to other subjects. This was the start of Matt's midterm break, which lasted ten days, so they made arrangements to meet again.

"Great dinner, Fleming. I won't thank you, since you can afford it and I can't," said Matt as they crossed to the Green, walking toward James's office.

"Tell me, Matt, have you heard of a young musician who's been making a splash in the papers in the last year or so?"

"Look who you're askin'! Is it your memory's going as well as your mind?"

"Right. Okay. But ask Dorothy, would you? She was civilized when she married you, unless you've rubbed off on her. She might know."

"I will, since I see you're serious. What's it about? A case? Or an affair of the heart?"

"Oh, it's a case. I'll tell you a bit about it on Friday night." They parted and James returned to the unwelcome news that his mother had phoned.

"What did you tell her?" James groaned into the intercom.

"I told her exactly what time I expected you in the office," Maggie's voice crackled with irony through the receiver. A faint buzz reached his ears. "If I'm not mistaken, that should be your mother now." Maggie was laughing as she switched off and then put the call through.

"James." His mother's voice was icy and James shivered.

"Mother, dear, how are you?"

"'Mother dear' my foot. Do you realize how long it's been since—"

"But of course, it's been ages. You have no idea . . ." James listened with half an ear to his mother's complaints as an idea—a brilliant idea, he felt—formed in his mind.

"Mother, I must see you."

"But that's just what I've been saying."

"No, seriously, I must see you . . . tonight."

"Tonight, but that's ridiculous. You know perfectly well that tonight's my bridge night. You're just like your father. He always expected me to drop everything and join him. He never did like bridge either—"

"Mother!" James's voice was stern.

"Yes," she said sweetly.

She always did like it when I'm bossy, thought James. "I'll be over around half-eight."

"Yes, dear, and where are we going?"

"No, I said I'd be over at half-eight."

"I heard you, dear."

"I see. Right, Mother." James sighed. His mother never stayed home. "You pick the place, just be ready, please." James said it without hope. His mother was infamous for never being ready.

And this time she wasn't ready either. James lounged in the love seat by the dwindling fire. No need to feed it if we're going out, had been her excuse. He'd heard it all before. He glanced around the room. Every available surface was covered with memorabilia of one sort or another. Photos of Donald and himself in their prep school uniforms, all shiny hair and crooked teeth. Photos marking every step of their mutual careers in medicine and law. There was even a framed press release of when he became a member of Fitzgerald's firm.

He wondered idly why his father had never branched out on his own, always preferring the security of being a partner in a large firm of solicitors. He wondered too how he himself had ever lived in this house. Few memories attached themselves to the items in the downstairs reception rooms. No, his haven had been his own room, but he was reluctant to go up to it now. He knew his mother hadn't touched it since he'd moved out. And not because she kept it as a shrine to her eldest son, but merely because she hadn't got around to it. She had cleared out Dad's things fairly quickly, James recalled, but without a doubt she had loved her husband, and he knew that she cherished his memory deeply and privately. As his mother entered the room he looked at her with more compassion than he had for a long time.

"The Park House," he suggested hopefully as he helped her on with her coat and untangled her scarf from her sleeve.

"No, not the Park House. The bridge club always refresh themselves there, and I did make elaborate excuses why I couldn't play tonight. No, I think O'Byrnes would be better."

James groaned inwardly. The same old place. He would know half the clientele, since half the clientele lived in his mother's immediate neighborhood. And then he realized that that was exactly it. His mother wanted her friends and neighbors to see him with her. In his present mood, it was a small concession.

As he'd anticipated, the O'Neills were there—husband and wife greeting him with enthusiasm. And so too were the Connollys, who grilled him—not only about himself, but about what little information he had on his brother Donald. They were accompanied by Mrs. Greene, a lovely old widow, whom they often brought out for a drink. She patted James's hand as if he were still ten, and smiled benignly as he sat and chatted briefly.

At last James and his mother settled in a quiet corner. As they sipped their tonics and nibbled a few dry-roasted nuts, James listened patiently while his mother caught him up on the various births, marriages, and deaths that had occurred in the last six weeks in her large circle of associates. Having depleted her store of information, she was persuaded to take a small sherry, and James broached the purpose of his visit.

"Mother, I know how very up-to-date you are on the music scene in Dublin . . ."

"More than you are, certainly, James, and more's

the pity. When I think of the money we threw away on your piano lessons . . . And Mrs. Kehoe swore you had promise."

James laughed. "She swore every one of her students had promise."

"Yes, well now that she says it about your mother, I think you had better keep your levity to yourself. You know I've told you I'm taking lessons. I've told you more than once, James!"

"As I was saying—"

"That I know the music scene, yes, dear?"

"Do you know, I mean, have you heard of a young Irish woman who's been doing rather well lately? I'm sorry to admit I don't even know what instrument she plays, but I've heard in a roundabout way that she's, ahh, making a name for herself. Does any of that ring a bell?"

"But James, you can be talking about only one person, Sarah Gallagher!" He looked blank. "Humph, you are impossible, James, I can't bear it when you are so thick. Sarah Gallagher, the violinist. She's been the talk of the town since last season. How can you have escaped hearing about her? Don't you read the paper?"

"Of course, but—"

"But nothing, my dear. And what kind of people do you associate with that they haven't even mentioned her in conversation? Train enthusiasts." She spoke the last two words as though these innocent buffs carried the black plague from one train station to another.

"Allowing for my own thickness and the ignorance of my friends, could you perhaps deign to enlighten me about this person?" James's tone was lightly teasing.

Vivienne Fleming drained her sherry, and was forced to add that at least James's father had shared her interest in classical music! She sighed heavily, and James quickly signaled for another small sherry.

"All right, James, I just felt I had to clear the air."

Obviously, thought James to himself.

"Sarah Gallagher is from Monkstown. Really, no one knew of her until last season when she made her Dublin debut. Serious musicians, of course, had heard of her through reviews of her Italian debut two years ago. She's about twenty-three, perhaps twenty-five. Perfectly lovely, if you can judge from her photographs in the paper. I unfortunately did not get to hear her play last year. She performed twice with the RTE symphony at the National Concert Hall. In no time all the tickets had been sold out, and that was the first year I let my season ticket lapse since your father died. Very stupid of me."

"And she plays the violin?"

"Yes, and apparently she is extremely gifted. They speak of her as being one in a line with the likes of John O'Connor or James Galway."

"In other words?"

"In other words, you with the tin ear, an artist of international repute, an artist of serious potential, someone who will be recognized outside this wretched little island of ours!"

"Is that it?"

"Of course that's it, what more do you want?" His mother's voice grew suspicious. "Why are you pumping me, anyway?"

"I can't tell you that, at least not yet." James smiled his most charming smile to deflect his mother's intense curiosity.

"James, you are insufferable. You are, at least in this, exactly like your father. I can still hear him saying those exact words . . ."

"Yes, Mother, and so can I . . . and you know why?"

"Yes, I suppose so. This must be one of your so-called 'cases'—you've inherited your father's secretive ways." Mrs. Fleming was rankled, and the sherry had made her cheeks glow.

"Secretive ways! I think if anything, I inherited his

disposition to be not only discreet, but to keep professional confidences confidential!" James stressed the last word. "I mean it, Mother, this is strictly between you and me. You have been a big help to me, but I can't tell you about it all yet." His voice held the promise he would tell her at some future date, which seemed to satisfy her.

"I can help you further, perhaps, James. I have a ticket for one of the two concerts Sarah Gallagher will be giving this month. They're as scarce as hen's teeth. I was lucky to get the one I got."

"But surely we could attend together."

"Gladly, but I truly was able to purchase only one ticket. You take it, James. Apart from all your subterfuge, you might actually enjoy the splendid music."

"Thank you. I'll make it up to you. By the way, do you know the family?" His mother's circle of acquaintances was so large that James felt anything was possible.

"No, I don't. But Mrs. O'Hara's cousin has relations in Carlow on her husband's side who are second cousins to the family. That's how I know they're in Monkstown. An old Catholic family, I believe." James's mother said this with a tinge of disbelief that a Catholic family could produce an artist of such stature, and she bore it with a personal sense of long-suffering tolerance for such aberrations. "Though of course Mr. Joyce was a Catholic," she added, apropos of nothing.

James smiled and held his tongue. He had learned long ago that it was impossible to make a dent in his mother's fixed beliefs. Though immensely popular, and with friends of every persuasion, the experience had done nothing to alter certain of her inherited ideas. She "drew lines," as she was fond of telling him in his youth. These invisible lines were indeed invisible, except to those who knew her best. And James, after battling his way through five years at Trinity and a liberal education, finally gave up. He had realized that if important real-life experiences had failed to change her ways, then nothing theoretical or even merely logical would shake them.

He drove his mother home and collected the ticket. She exacted her price, however—he wasn't to get off lightly—for he found himself committed to escort her to a wine-and-cheese affair for the Dog and Cats Home on Grand Canal Street. Nonetheless he felt mean-spirited when he refused her offer of coffee and biscuits which he knew from long experience would be stale. As it was, she happily shut the door on him before he had reached his car. He could just see her through the hall window haphazardly piling her bad-minton racket into yet another capacious tote bag, looking forward to her match and morning coffee— on the morrow, as she had said.

The feeling of excitement in the concert hall was almost palpable. And James caught the anticipatory buzz as he moved from the lobby, where champagne was flowing freely, and toward his seat. He mentally thanked his mother again for the superb third-row-center seat—despite the price she would extract. He was virtually in line with the low dais on which Sarah Gallagher would stand, just to the left of the conductor.

In the intervening days, James had read articles and reviews on Sarah Gallagher in past issues of various papers. He was embarrassed after the fact to realize just how much coverage had been afforded this violin-ist, and that he had blithely missed all of it. Dorothy Flanagan had phoned him one night, confirming all his mother had told him but adding little else. And she hadn't mentioned Teresa. James didn't know whether he was glad or not, but he didn't inquire.

A few very discreet calls around town to various solicitors he knew and trusted had yielded more information. The Gallaghers were extremely comfort-able. It was old money and very low profile. The father was now in semiretirement, and as a family, they had led extremely quiet lives with their only child, Sarah. He had learned too that there was a strong connection with the Church. Mr. Gallagher was an all-but-anonymous and very large contributor to the archbishop's personal favorite charities. Although James hadn't established a connection with the Convent of Perpetual Help he'd so recently visited, he felt at this point he didn't need to make one. Ireland was, after all, Ireland.

James read the program and learned that Sarah Gallagher had studied with private teachers in Ireland as a young girl and at the National Academy of Music. At an early age she had won a scholarship for a summer to Florence and, while studying in a classroom environment, was spotted by a maestro who had since taken control and direction of her studies and her public career. Excerpts of reviews from various continental papers were all in agreement. Sarah was a violinist of exceptional precocity, brilliance, and potential. Maturity could only bring more.

A whisper over the front rows like a breeze over a field of barley. Head leaned to head, and mouth was placed to ear, up and down the rows to James's left and right. And James followed with his eyes as programs were discreetly pointed in the direction of an elderly man and his younger wife, who moved slowly and shyly down the right-hand aisle to two end seats in the first row.

James was bemused. These two surely were Sarah's parents. Why, then, didn't they sit to the left, where they would have had an unobstructed view? But as James observed their quiet demeanor—the lowered eyes, the slight discomfiture, their awareness that too many eyes were on them—he realized they hadn't wanted to be even in a minimally more exposed spot than they were already. The audience shifted and cleared its collective throat as the orchestra and then the conductor took their places. A hush fell as Sarah

Gallagher came to the front of the stage and the first notes of the Paganini and Fritz Kreisler set pieces were struck. The music was magnificent and, to James's ears, turbulent, emotional, stirring. He was no judge of her technical brilliance, but the music and Sarah's persona quickly melded into the one experience. He was thunderstruck. Thunderstruck simultaneously by the power of the music and the beauty of the violinist. It was only during the intermission that James regained his presence of mind in time enough to glance over at the Gallaghers and see them beaming with pride, shaking hands discreetly with people who seemed to be close friends, and shaking their heads in unison at what James took to be invitations to withdraw to the lobby or one of the various bars. They resumed their seats as the well-wishers moved away to refresh themselves, and James followed suit.

He indulged in a Gauloise in the lobby, one of the few occasions when he permitted himself to smoke, and he listened attentively to the fragments of conversations that flowed around him in the crush of the crowd. The mood was ebullient, not a murmur contradicted it. James returned to his seat at the first bell, anxious for the remainder of the concert.

The second half rivaled the first. The music held fewer fireworks, yet somehow carried one a step further. Her violin sang and wept, lifting his heart along with it. Haunting melodies hung in his ears, filled his head just as the applause filled the hall. For an Irish audience, it was unusually demonstrative. James's eyes held the figure of the slender young woman in the simple blue scoop-necked dress. Her mahogany hair swept up at the back, her throat and the line of her chin were indelibly printed on his memory. The sway of her body, the lift of her elbow, the movement of her wrist, these too were etched on his mind. James stood on the steps of the Hall as the crowd broke up and people hurried to their cars. He could hardly distinguish between the impression Sarah Gallagher had made on him and the impression the music had left behind. The only thing certain was that thoughts of murder and illegitimacy were very far from his mind this night.

Chapter Eight

"What is it?" Mrs. Fleming's cross and groggy voice whispered faintly into the receiver.

"Mother, it's James!"

"James?"

"Your son!" James fairly shouted.

"How could you possibly disturb your mother at this hour? What time is it?"

"It's eight o'clock in the morning, for God's sake!"

"Are you ill, James? You seem so overexcited. Perhaps you have a fever."

"Mother, wake up for God's sake! I need to ask you a few questions."

"All right. I'm sitting up now. Hold on while I plug in the Teasmaid."

James listened impatiently at his end to the sounds of his mother fiddling ineffectually with the silliest gadget yet conceived by modern man: a device that heated water and brewed horrendous tea at one's bedside. They were a favorite of the older generation, and James had duly given one to his mother one

Christmas past. After a few muttered but mild curses, his mother returned to the phone, her voice a bit stronger.

"Such a nuisance . . ."

"The tea maker or me?"

"Both, if you must know. Your brother Donald never wakes me up at this hour. All right now, what on earth's the matter?"

"Mother, I went to Sarah Gallagher's concert last night. It was everything you said it would be. I need to meet her, and I wanted to know what you could do for me."

"Most extraordinary, James. However, since, as you know, I'll do anything for my eldest son, I'll see what I can manage. I'll ring Mrs. Smythe after breakfast, she's with the Dublin Musical Society. I think I heard her talking the other night at the Mother's Union—something about young Sarah Gallagher. But please, James, let me get back to you . . . now, good-bye!"

His mother rang off firmly, but her words set James's mind racing. He had to meet Sarah, and as soon as possible. He hoped it could further his case, but underneath he knew that he was smitten, captivated, at least from afar.

True to her word, Mrs. Fleming phoned back by noon, having maneuvered an invitation for James to accompany her to a small reception which the Musical Society was giving in Sarah's honor following her second and final concert at the National Concert Hall.

The venue at the Baptist Hall on Leeson Park seemed a most unlikely place to hold such an event, but James kept his criticism to himself as he entered the modern but rather bleak building. A long table was set with urns of tea and coffee and trays and plates of fairy cakes, Madeira cake, and currant buns. James cringed. It had all the trappings of a church fete. Surely this was not the arena in which Sarah should be shining. However, he quickly noticed that although the crowd was not as glittering as that at the concert, it seemed to be a crowd of true enthusiasts. Soberly dressed for the most part, the guests, he soon learned from his mother's adept introductions, were the heart and soul of the classical music community. Many teachers of music were there, members of the Academy, the music critics from all the papers and magazines—all mingling and speaking knowledgeably about music in general and Sarah Gallagher's talent in particular. He spotted her immediately, dressed in a simple two-piece sea-green knit dress, the soft cowl neck falling gracefully around her throat. She moved easily from one cluster of attentive listeners to another, laughing gaily or listening intently. Confident, self-assured. And not in the least as James had fantasized. At last she approached the small circle where he and his mother stood. James was embarrassed to find himself moving slightly behind his mother as introductions were made, like a small boy at a wedding finally meeting the glowing bride. But his mother, as usual, was superb.

"Miss Gallagher," she said, her voice rising with enthusiasm and forcefulness. "This is my son James. He has, I am afraid to admit, a tin ear. But after hearing you play last night—after I so nobly sacrificed my own ticket to him—he has become an admirer. In fact he threatened me with loss of sleep if I didn't arrange for him to attend this evening and have the pleasure of meeting you. James!" His mother tugged at his sleeve, and James's face grew crimson.

"I assure you that there is a kernel of truth in what my mother says, Miss Gallagher. I did indeed enjoy your performance very much. And yes indeed"—James nodded at his impossible mother—"Mrs. Fleming here did indeed give me her ticket, much to her own loss, I'm sorry to admit."

"Well, perhaps you shall both hear me play when I perform in Dublin next season." Sarah was distant but polite. James sensed her slipping away, and tried desperately to hold her attention.

"Miss Gallagher, have you ever ridden on a steam train?"

"Pardon me?" she said, and smiled at last.

"James!" Mrs. Fleming interrupted, and James stepped on her toe. No matter. "Miss Gallagher, please excuse my son. He is a solicitor, but he insists on taking an absurd interest in trains. Trains of any kind. I hardly think that Miss Gallagher travels by public transportation, James."

"Indeed. But you might enjoy this, Miss Gallagher —an annual event organized by the Irish Steam Train Society. The ride is worth the price of a ticket, believe me. You see the coast line of the whole city—from Bray to Howth—in a most pleasurable way, going back to a more gracious era."

"It sounds delightful." Sarah nodded.

"The line runs along the sea. It's a rare treat now. A steam train, I mean."

"And do you travel often by train?"

"Ah, no, not here in Dublin at least, not often, but I've traveled abroad on trains. I am a true buff, as my mother mentioned." James smiled at his mother's back as she moved discreetly away.

"And where exactly have you traveled?"

"Most recently in Russia, but really all over the world. My next trip will be Peru, I hope, if I ever finish this—" The words froze in his mouth and a look of horror flickered over his face. Sarah was startled.

"Is there anything . . . ?"

"No, not. I just wondered . . . I mean . . . I have yet to travel the trains in Italy. In fact all I know at present is that Mussolini's single greatest achievement was making them run on time . . ." James blundered.

Sarah looked at him quizzically. "That's an unfortunate memory. I assure you Italy has more to offer than worn-out stereotypes."

"As does Ireland. Ireland has improved in the years you've been away."

"Quite." Sarah moved off ever so subtly, ever so firmly. "Good night, Mister . . . er?"

"Fleming. James. James Fleming." James Fleming inadvertently followed her for a few steps, fairy cake in hand, looking as gormless as he felt.

He was subdued as he drove his mother home, but she read his thoughts.

"Not a success, I take it, James."

"Unmitigated disaster."

"I agree. I've rarely seen you so charmless."

"Thanks." His tone was bitter.

"Honestly, there you were. The best-looking, certainly the best-dressed. Smooth as silk under all kinds of circumstances, and there you were, behaving like a schoolboy, wet behind the ears."

"Don't you want to add that I had egg on my face?"

"And currant buns in your hands . . . honestly, James. I did my best."

"Well, you'll have to do more. I . . . I wasn't myself tonight. I have a great deal on my mind . . ."

"I realize that James. It's this case you're working on. I've never seen you quite so preoccupied with work before." She paused. "She was interested, you know."

"Pardon?"

"Miss Gallagher. She was interested in whatever that was you were saying about the excursion."

"Are you trying to make me feel better?" said James desperately.

"Not in the least. You know that. No, I could tell that for one brief shining moment you had caught her attention. Pursue it," said his mother.

"Honestly?"

"Yes."

"Will you help me?"

"If I must," Mrs. Fleming laughed gaily. "Tell me what you want."

"You tell me. What would be appropriate? Do you think . . . do you think you could have some get-together at the house?"

"That's a possibility."

"Catered?"

"Catered, of course not."

"Catered." James repeated, brooking no argument.

"If you pay," said Mrs. Fleming sweetly.

"Certainly. But get somebody good. Not one of your dowdy . . ."

"Dowdy friends, James dear?"

"Sorry. Don't tease me, Mother. This is important."

"So I see, dear. Will you come in and discuss it, then?"

"Sorry, Mother, must dash."

James sped away from his mother's house and slowed down at the intersection. He wished, excited as he was, that he had some place to dash to. But, as usual, there was not.

The next morning, when he entered his office, a message from his mother lay on his desk. He returned her call.

"It's all set," she announced triumphantly.

"I can't believe it!" exclaimed James. "You are a wonder!"

"I'd love to take all the credit, darling, but actually it was a stroke of luck. Mrs. Smythe—you remember her from last night—rang quite early. She knew that Miss Gallagher had been hoping to meet Chris Reardon, the young Irish composer. He couldn't make the party last night, but Mrs. Smythe has got hold of him—he's free on Saturday night—and Miss Gallagher has agreed to come along after a dinner with some family friends. It will be quite an honor to have two people of such renown to the house, James!"

"You really are terrific, Mother," said James appreciatively. "Now, what's the plan?"

The party on Saturday night was a success, in everyone's judgment. The caterer had chosen well, and the platters of hors d'oeuvres kept coming, conversation flowed like wine, and the mood was not merely jovial, but ebullient. James as the male, as his mother so delicately put it, played host to his mother's hostess, and the early years of boredom and adolescent resentment paid off. James was witty. James was entertaining. Best of all, thought James, James was intriguing.

Sarah arrived fashionably late and was swept into the mood. James nodded and served her but kept his distance for some considerable time. She was not there, after all, to meet him, but to be introduced to Reardon, who had yet to show up. Timing was all, as his mother noted, and since looks and youth were definitely on his side in this company, only his ineptness could bungle it. He felt Sarah's eyes following him occasionally, and he let his wit and charm shine most evidently whenever she was near. Choosing his moment, he approached bearing champagne in fluted Waterford glasses.

"Share a loving cup with me," he whispered, and felt a sense of achievement when she took the glass from his hand and smiled at him.

"You are James, the James I met the other evening?"

"The very one," returned James, laughing, "but in my true colors this time."

"Were you flying false colors then?" said Sarah.

"Hardly false, only the motley of a complete idiot!"

"Hardly an idiot, sir, since you were praising me," returned Sarah lightly.

"Seriously, Sarah—may I call you Sarah?" James went on without waiting for an answer. "I wasn't myself and I apologize. I'm seldom intimidated, but you see, it's true what my mother told you. I know so very little about music, I was truly tongue-tied . . ."

"But you know a great deal about trains?"

"Oh, please, spare me my blushes!"

"And a great deal about the law, I take it?" said Sarah more seriously.

"That I leave for business hours," James said hurriedly. "Trains, and other things, occupy my off hours."

"What you said about them did actually interest me. I was even considering . . ."

"Being my traveling companion?"

"Perhaps . . ." Sarah laughed.

"I am at your service. If you're free tomorrow, I'll get tickets for the excursion and prepare a picnic, Madam, or is it Ms.?"

"Perhaps it's Mrs. . . ." Sarah said coyly, and laughed at the expression on his face.

"You jest?"

"Yes, all the time." She smiled. "But I'm free tomorrow afternoon. I'll attend Mass with my parents at the Pro-Cathedral, and after that I'll be free until tea time."

"That's good, because the train leaves at noon. I'll collect you."

"No need. I'll meet you on the platform at Bray— say a quarter to twelve?"

"That's music to my ears . . ."

"Oh, dear, James, please . . ." Sarah turned lightly and walked off to meet the composer, who had arrived at last.

"I have a tin ear," called James to her retreating back, "not a tin heart!"

"That remains to be seen," she answered without turning.

James hummed off-key as he helped his mother clear away the debris of a roaring success.

"She's nothing what I expected," said his mother as from a great distance.

"Mmm?"

"She's not what I thought. James, are you listening to me?"

"No, Mother, I'm not. Did you say you were expecting?"

"James!"

"Sorry. No, she's not what I expected either. Although I'm not sure how I'd explain it."

"I'll tell you, you dim-witted male. She's as independent as hell."

"Mother!"

"It's true. She's—how would you say it? Yes, you think she 'goes against type.'"

"Not that exactly, Mother. It's just that I had expected that she would be terribly airy-fairy, head in the clouds. She appeared to be so ethereal on stage, so transmuted in time and place. You know yourself her features are so . . . so . . ." James ended awkwardly.

"How appearances can deceive, then, James," said his mother. "She's spunky and feisty and independent. For heaven's sake, child, she's lived abroad for years, she's traveled extensively. She's not a little convent girl from Monkstown."

"I know that! And I wasn't picturing her that way. It was more that I thought she was, well, more like her music, if you grasp my meaning."

"Yes. Yet again you have projected a personality on to a girl that has nothing to do with the reality. And so yet again you have to go back to square one and try to find out what she's really like."

"I know you'll laugh at this Mother, but we, Sarah and I, are taking the steam train excursion tomorrow afternoon—from Bray to Howth . . ."

"And back again, I assume? Well, at least for once your enthusiasm for trains and for young women have not been mutually exclusive."

"I don't get it, Fleming," Matt snorted, and wiped his mouth with a coffee-stained handkerchief. He and James were eating kebobs in pita bread in the front seat of James's car.

"What don't you get?" James mumbled through bits of lettuce and dripping sauce. He groaned as a mayonnaise-covered lump of lamb landed on his knee.

"You sound to me like a man in love."

"Do I?"

"Suspiciously so. What I want to know is exactly how many times you've gone out with her?"

James beamed. "The train ride and the picnic—of course it rained—and then the theatre, and every day since then. And last night I had her over to dinner."

"So . . . what's going on here?"

James put down his food, his appetite gone. "Did you invite me to lunch to give me a spot quiz . . . if you call this lunch?"

"Sure, this is lunch. I wanted to give you a change of pace from your club and your fancy restaurants. You need to get down with the real people!" Matt grunted through his lettuce.

"Please, Matt, next time I'll pick the place . . . and I won't let so much time pass either."

"Good, but don't change the subject. Now, what has this musical dream machine got that all the others haven't, up till now?"

"I've given that a lot of thought, believe it or not," said James to his old friend. "I think it's what you were getting at just now when you asked what she's got. She's got a life, and it has nothing to do with me. She's beautiful, of course. And sexy in a highstrung kind of way. But she's verbal and witty and bright. She doesn't seem to mind that I know next to nothing about music. Because that's her life. And it's full. Do you get my drift? I don't smell marriage a mile away when I'm with her. I don't suddenly see myself as a potential marriage partner! No, Sarah is as free as her music . . ."

James sighed like an adolescent as Matt roared. "I'll tell you, Fleming. You're attracted because she's safe. She's not looking to get married. And perhaps she is unattainable. You know what I think?"

"Do I have a choice?"

"No. I think this is just another in a long line. Sarah the unattainable. No commitment on either side. Am I right?"

"I don't know." James was glum.

"Then think about it. And rev up this car because

150

I'm going to be late—I've got to collect two geese at the Connolly Station left-luggage counter. My daft cousin sent them down from Sligo. Good layers, she claims. P'rhaps one will lay me a golden egg!"

"There's more to it than I've told you," James said quietly as they drove.

"Oh God!"

"I think I might be falling in love with Sarah. Not with the idea of her. But with *her*. And I think she may well have some feelings for me. Serious feelings. But she's tied into a case I'm involved with and I . . . I don't think ethically I should be seeing her."

"Well, this is more complicated than analyzing your love-life. What are you doing? Using her to get information?"

"For God's sake! Will you listen to me for a minute. I've got myself in a terrible jam."

Matt said nothing.

James's thoughts were grim and muddled as he longed to discuss the issue with Matt. But now he felt he had said too much. He had been very discreet with Sarah, and still they had seen a great deal of each other. After their picnic at Howth he had seen her for a part of each day or evening for over two weeks. And he had found that the more time he spent with her, the more what he knew about her background increased in importance. He had already been looking for physical resemblances between her and Kathleen in London. He had begged off meeting her adoptive parents in Monkstown because of his growing obsession with her past. Was Jack musical? The thought was ludicrous. There were times when he saw Jack's chiseled, dead gray face superimposed on Sarah's vital one. God, that way madness lies.

"Matt. Sarah's adopted."

"So? Is that a problem for you or for her?"

"No, she's very good about it. She's known since she was a child and she has no problem with it."

"She's not one of these people who want to seek out their biological parents?"

151

"No, not in the least. She loves her parents deeply, and her own life is so full I don't think she's felt that need, the need to find out . . ." James's voice faltered.

"Is there more to this, James?"

"Yes. You see, because of another situation, let's say, I happen to know who her real parents were. Who her mother is, I mean. Her father died recently. I know the whole background. But this is so silly. She was two or three days old when the Gallaghers adopted her. It's just, I can't get what I know about her background out of my mind." And how can I tell her? he thought. How can I tell her her father was murdered and her mother is married in London? How can I tell her that her uncles are four thick, bitter farmers? Or that her three aunts are shriveled spinsters with no life of their own? That her aunt is accused of murdering her natural father? God, if only I could dissociate all this from that brilliant girl.

"Look, Fleming," Matt said at last, "you've got your emotional lines and your ethical lines crossed. You'd better uncross them."

"I know, but it's tough. I never intended to get involved. I was acting the part of sleuth, enjoying myself. How could I know that she . . . Oh God!"

"There's another thing?" Matt's voice was neutral. "Is it because what you know about Sarah's natural parents doesn't live up to your, let us say, social expectations?"

"Yes! Yes! Is that so wrong? Sarah's incredible. She's everything that's gifted and lovely . . . Yes, you're right there. I am a snob, and I don't want her to know about her background . . . And I don't ever want to be the one who has to tell her either! You see, there's nothing in her that stems from her past! And she knows nothing at all about that past. All she knows is that she was adopted at birth."

"Then leave it at that. Accept it, as Sarah has."

If only I could, thought James, and a shiver ran down his spine. As soon as the case came to trial, there was a real possibility that Sarah's connection to the principals involved might become known. How would she take it? And as important, what would she think of his duplicitous role in the situation? He had to act. He had to prevent this case from seeing the light and glare of publicity, a publicity that would possibly destroy Sarah's career, in Ireland at least, and destroy the relationship he believed was developing between them.

Matt paused as he got out of the car at the station. "Dorothy's giving me a lift home. She'll be so thrilled with the geese!" He grinned, and then more seriously added, "Ring me!"

"In another lifetime," said James grimly, "when it's over."

James's voice was curt as he greeted Violet Moore when she opened the heavy front door.

"I'm surprised to see you again," Violet said conversationally, but her look was guarded.

"Really?" James commented, slightly sarcastic.

"Please, this way."

James followed her into the sitting room. "Lily and Rose? Are they joining us?" he asked.

"No."

"Good, because I have a number of things to say to you Violet . . . that are, I think you will agree, of a very personal nature."

Violet sat down, and for the first time James saw a look of strain and fear pass across her face.

"Firstly. I have been puzzled from the beginning as to the reason why Lily claims she saw you the night of the murder. You have refused to discuss this with me, but I'm afraid I have to insist. I think I should tell you that our case for the defense is going rather badly." James hoped to shock Violet, and he was pleased to see he had succeeded.

Violet was silent however.

"I need to know now, today, if you were in the barn on the night in question."

"No, I was not." Violet's voice was firm.

"Then it follows that Lily is lying?"

"Yes, it follows."

"Violet, how can you be so calm? Have you questioned her about this? Don't you see how damaging her statement is, how incredibly damaging her testimony will be—if it comes to that in court?"

Violet nodded almost imperceptibly.

"Have you discussed it with her?" James felt like shrieking, trying to shake this woman's calm demeanor.

"I can't." Violet's voice was strained and she twisted her fingers in her lap.

"You can't or you won't?" pressed James.

"Both. Don't you see there'd be no point? I know she's lying. And I know why she's lying."

"Then for God's sake, tell me! It will help your case. We must break her testimony. You live every day in this house with her. It's beyond me. It's truly beyond me. How can you live every day with this knowledge and still not confront her, challenge her? My God, I don't know how you can stay in the same room with her. You still tell me that's she's lying?"

"Yes."

"And that you know why?"

"Yes."

James waited. He began to pace the room, allowing her silence and his own anger to build.

"Why isn't Fitzgerald handling this case?" she said at last.

"He is. He's in charge of the case. He has been from the beginning."

"Then why isn't he here?"

For a moment James wondered the same thing, but he carried on. "Because, Miss Moore, as you well know, it is I who have been doing all the legwork in this case. That's my job. I report to Gerald. Believe me, he is intimately involved in all that I do."

"He knows you're here, then."

"Yes. Call him if you don't believe me." James took a chance.

"I do believe you."

"Then trust me too," James's voice was softer.

"This will do neither you nor me nor the case any good."

"Tell me anyway."

She looked him straight in the eye and spoke without flinching.

"Lily lied because she hates me. It's as simple as that."

He waited for her to elaborate, but she didn't. "Simple! Do you seriously expect me to believe this? That she is simply lying, that her lies could support a case that could send you to prison, that could destroy your life, Miss Moore!" His voice was scoffing and his disappointment great.

"It is the truth!" Violet's voice was ice cold.

"Miss Moore. I've done a lot of investigation into the background of this case. At no time have you told me the truth, or offered to tell me, or helped me in any way. What I now know to be the truth I have had to seek out for myself."

Violet stood up suddenly, angry and defiant. She pushed past James and walked to the door. "That's enough!"

"It won't work with me, Miss Moore. I'm not leaving until you help me help yourself."

"You are leaving now, Mr. Fleming. No one, no one speaks to me in that way."

"No, Miss Moore. You can't bully me. I'm not some frightened, pregnant seventeen-year-old girl." The words had the effect he had hoped for. Violet staggered as though he had struck her.

"Yes. I know. I know a lot. And I think you'd like to know what I know."

"How dare you pressure me."

"Because I want to save your life."

"Why?"

"Because I don't believe you killed your brother."

"Not good enough . . ." Violet smirked.

"Because I don't want a young woman's life destroyed. Because I don't want the sins of the father visited on the daughter. Because I don't want your dirty laundry, Miss Moore, your very dirty laundry, washed in public."

Still Violet refused to react.

"Speak, woman, do you hear me! Speak."

"You've found her!" Violet whispered. "You've found that baby girl?" Her voice rose. "You fool, you meddling, bloody fool! Don't you see what this will do to me, to the farm? How dare you interfere in my affairs like this!"

"Because, Violet, I am trying to save your life. What is the farm to you, woman, if you are incarcerated for the rest of your life—and for a crime you claim you did not commit?"

"How dare you! I did not kill my brother!"

"Then let me help you. Help me to help you. For God's sake, for your own sake, tell me the truth once and for all! Tell me why Lily hates you, tell me why you denied burial of Jack's corpse in your family plot, tell me about Kathleen . . ."

"And about their baby?"

"Yes. And about their baby."

Chapter Nine

"I suppose it all started with my own grandmother," Violet Moore said wearily as she glanced at the now roaring fire.

"My grandmother, now that's going back a bit. My grandmother was an only child, and she inherited this land from her father before her. I never knew her, but my own mother used occasionally to speak of her. I'd say she was probably a hard woman, but then she needed to be. A woman on her own, a young woman, and all this land." Violet waved her arms expansively.

"Her holdings were even more extensive than what we—what I—have now. There were fields scattered all through these parishes, some even stretching up to the Wicklow border. Good land for the most part. She was young. She sold some and she lost others, but in the end she consolidated and held fast to her property. The deeds and Land Registry documents fill a steamer trunk, I assure you. When I was a girl I used to go up to the attic and pore over them and try to make sense of it all. You see, I loved the land even then, and the buying and getting—it was all so ancient and intriguing to a young child like myself. It was romancing really . . ." She sighed.

"In any event, Grandmother married Grandfather. I never knew him either. After fathering three girls, he died. It sounds, when I put it like that, that the effort wore him out." Violet laughed mirthlessly at her own coarseness.

"From what little I know, he was a weak man. He brought only one small field into the family. He was the last in a long line of a Clare family that had lost its land over the years, for various reasons. But poor management must have been one of them, because he nearly ruined this farm. After his death it was as though my grandmother had never been married, except for the fact of the three daughters. My mother was one of those three daughters.

"A harder life you'd never meet, Mr. Fleming. You see, there was the land but no money. Land rich, cash poor. Grandmother kept a small dairy herd. They had chickens and a kitchen garden. Mother often repeated how she walked to school, three miles, barefoot. But she wasn't alone. It was like that in those days. She was the eldest and must have got the best of what was on offer because in time her two sisters died. One of TB and the other—oh, it must have been dreadful—the other of brucellosis.

"And there she was, left alone with Grandmother. It seemed as though there were nothing but women in this family as far back as time itself. Women somehow perpetuating themselves. It was as though the men were there merely to extend the line, and when their role was played, when their bolt was shot, they faded and died.

"This is how I grew up, Mr. Fleming. With stories of the women of my family going back generations. Women who had held on to this farm and this land despite the fact that they were alone almost all of their lives.

"Matriarchy, I suppose that springs to your mind?

But what else is Ireland but a matriarchy? And hasn't it always been so? Hasn't it always been Mother Ireland? And the *sean bean bocht?* And in all of her guises. Hasn't it been the Fine Old Woman with the four green fields? And haven't our images been the likes of Queen Maeve, Deirdre of the Sorrows? And hasn't she always—since before Yeats and after—been the proud, the mystical, the powerful woman, the mother and the fatal lover?

"And I ask you, Mr. Fleming—if this isn't all Greek to you—isn't that image of Ireland the right and true one? Woman as life-giver, woman as sustainer. Women have always loved the land, but they loved it with sense, good common sense. It didn't take hold of their imaginations and cause them to go mad. They loved it as they loved their children. They didn't let it get into their hearts, but into their minds. And they didn't see land as power—they saw it as life. There's a difference, Mr. Fleming, believe me.

"What monuments do you see in this country to women, to the image of woman, to the great Celtic women? One. And it's a grave. A great cairn on Cnoc na Ri in Sligo, but it's a grave nonetheless.

"What are the monuments and statues you see in Dublin—men and images of men, Celtic heroes and fallen heroes, men one and all. Oh yes, don't interrupt. I know the poor little head of the Countess in Stephen's Green. Pleasant bits of greenery grow around that sculpture and ignoramuses walk by it and idly wonder who that woman might have been.

"Oh, wait, and haven't I forgotten? Indeed and I have. There is now a great statue, isn't there, Mr. Fleming? Right in O'Connell Street for all to see. Anna Livia. Oh such a monument to womanhood. A river. A river famous for what? Named by Joyce and made famous by Joyce. Its entire meaning endowed by him. A bony Medusa-headed corpse in my opinion. Aptly named by Dublin's wit."

"Anna Rexia?" James smiled.

"The floozy in the jacuzzi . . . more like. Oh, will

that keep us quiet? Yet another sculpture by yet another man!"

James shrugged, at a loss for something to say against this tirade.

"I'll tell you where the images are. In churches. That's what Rome did for us. What pagan sculpture could be allowed to stand, what Celtic and pre-Christian image would stand before the all-consuming ocean that was Rome? Rome! That what it couldn't wash away it subsumed into its very self. And so what images of woman did we inherit from Rome? We got what they chose to give us. Maiden madonnas. Meek and mild. In every village and town, statues and shrines to the Virgin, an even less fecund image than that of the Madonna. And then what does Catholicism give us? Hey presto! A miracle at Knock. And why wasn't it in the heart of Dublin instead of Knock? Because it was the most depressed area of the country at the time. Mayo. Who was in Mayo but ignorant, poor, suffering farmers—who would question such a wondrous thing? It gave them hope and the strength to go on in the blackest of the black times.

"And ever since, hasn't our little island had its fair share of reported sightings? And what does Rome say now, in the modern world? Well, it says neither one thing nor another. And now what do we have, in the middle of this Kerry babies scandal, with unwed mothers murdering their babies or throwing them into the sea—we have the moving statue at Ballinaspittle."

"And hundreds saw it move!" James added.

"And in the dark and in the night two men come and smash the poor plaster statue and smash its head and break off its folded hands. Ah, that was an act that spoke louder than words, Mr. Fleming."

Violet stood up suddenly and walked to the side-board, where she poured two brandies. James watched as she stood there, quieting herself.

"I seem to have digressed. But in this long and perhaps tiresome digression, I think you will finally follow the thread of my thoughts. You must understand. I haven't talked about these events for a very long time.

"My mother was a very strong woman. Physically as well as emotionally. She ran the farm and increased the herd successfully. She had learned much already from growing up on the land, but she had no formal schooling in agriculture. So she read and she studied and she gleaned all she could from the farmers hereabouts and from the auctioneers, from the financial pages of *The Irish Times*. She had an acute mind. People used to say she had a head on her shoulders like a man's. It drove her mad. She raised three of us girls and my brother Jack with no help. Because there was none. No relatives. No friendly uncles to take us on outings. I tell you we worked hard and we saw her work hard. She instilled in me—perhaps because I was the eldest, perhaps because I was most like her—such a love for this land that whenever I had to leave it I became physically sick. Homesickness, you see, is a real and not an imagined ill.

"Mind you, she wasn't affectionate herself. I think perhaps Rose minded that, of the four of us. Perhaps Jack too. When we were mere gossoons, she'd take each of us in turn and tell us that the time for kissing and holding was at an end. And so it was. But Rose, Rose never accepted it. She'd hang on mother's skirts until even she wearied of it, and then she hung onto Lily's skirts. It suited them both. It still does."

Violet glanced up at the door almost as if seeing those two young children, clinging to each other, come tumbling into the room. Suddenly James had a sense of the history of this house in which he sat. It was, for a brief moment, as though all the many personalities that Violet had sketched out for him were crowding into the room. Stern-faced women and sickly men, dying children and children dying for affection. He saw a long line of a family that had seemingly passed on its strengths in the only form it recognized as strength—a hardness of heart and an obsession with the land.

"History repeated itself in my family, Mr. Fleming, in a bizarre pattern. Mother married Father and they had three daughters and a son. Father was the only child of an old Kildare family who'd gone into trade, seed and grain I think. He had a bit of family money and took an interest in this farm, I was told. But he died a year or two after Jack was born. I didn't know him. Or should I say, I cannot remember him.

"I was coming up to my majority when Mother fell ill. She never told me or any one of us. The girls and Jack were still in short skirts and short pants, for God's sakes . . . 'teenagers,' as they say now—foolish term. I had done well at school. Mother had insisted I get an education. And despite my homesickness at the boarding school, I did very well. But I lived for the day I could return home, and home I came. It was as Mother intended—but how could I know that then? She had cancer. She had seen a doctor, and he told her out straight, as was the way. And she told no one, as was the way. She sickened before our ignorant eyes.

"The morning of the day she died, she milked half the herd by hand. I ask you . . ." Violet looked away for some few seconds, but her face was impassive. The burden of her story weighed down on James like a heavy blanket. He didn't speak, for he knew to some extent that Violet was talking to herself.

"That afternoon, after taking a very small midday meal, she said to us all that she wanted to lie down for a rest. This was so unusual that we were speechless, but we never questioned Mother . . . I know"—she glanced at James—"it's almost impossible to make outsiders understand. But she went upstairs . . ."

A chill of recognition ran through James as he heard in Violet's words a faint echo of the lines of an old ballad he'd sung as a child: "She went upstairs to go to bed/And calling to her family said/Bring me a chair till I sit down/And pen and ink till I write down . . ."

"She went upstairs and took up her pen and wrote down that she'd left her will all properly drawn and told where it was kept, what solicitor to contact, that

162

sort of thing. All very efficient. She laid it on her desk with her watch beside it. Oh, I forgot the main item she left—a short letter.

"However it was, I noticed she hadn't come down from her rest, but I didn't want to disturb her. She was a cantankerous woman at the best of times. But Rose was mooning around. She had wanted to make dumplings for tea—a dreadful cook she was—and she just had to know if Mother would like a bit of dumpling with her beef. She trotted up to Mother's room—of course it had to be Rose. It would be Rose.

"She opened the door, and it was dark, the curtains were drawn." James felt the recognition again, and the melancholy ballad ran through his mind: "They found her hanging from a rope . . ."

James shook his head and thought of Rose, poor poor Rose. He felt sorrow for Rose the living person that he knew, and not for the unknown woman who took her life in the face of a debilitating illness.

"The letter—the letter told us—told us about the cancer. She didn't offer an explanation. It wasn't lack of courage . . . I think it was pride, perhaps, and now that I'm closer to her age at the time of her death, I think also it was the awful thought of weakening and losing, of being dependent on anyone else but herself.

"Looking back I don't know which was worse. Reading her letter or hearing the will read. She said, in the letter . . . let me put it this way. She said no word of farewell to any one of us. It was a difficult time. Lily, Rose, Jack. I think if she had died in the normal course of an illness, it would have given us some time, time perhaps to grow up, to take on what seemed anyway to be our preordained roles in life. Then again she could have dropped down dead of a heart attack. We could have found her cold in a field somewhere, as cold as a sheep that fell down dead, perishing of the cold."

James was yet again astonished at the hardness of these people and their language.

Violet looked at him suddenly. "You no doubt

know some of this," she said with an edge of bitterness.

Startled, James had to think to what was she referring. At last he fathomed her meaning.

"Violet, I can say to you honestly that not one person—and I have talked to many in this village and its surroundings—has mentioned one word to me about your mother." A look of surprise flickered across her drawn, pinched face, and she leaned back against the chintz cushion of her chair.

"Another brandy?" he inquired pleasantly.

"Yes, Mr. Fleming, please help yourself."

He did so, and poured Violet a generous measure.

"Surprisingly, at least to me, her will divided the property equally among the four of us. But I, being the eldest, was to come into my share very shortly, as she knew. And therefore I was to have control over the property as a whole until each of the others came to majority. As it transpired, the others didn't care in the early years. Somehow we slipped easily into roles that mimicked our previous life. I stood in Mother's place. And they reacted to me in much the same way as they had to her. Life went on as before. But I gradually began to extend myself. I grew in confidence after the shock had worn off. It was as though . . . as though I had been waiting all my life, as though everything that had gone before had prepared me for this. I began to study and learn, to modernize my thinking, introducing improvements on the farm and with the herds.

"Time passed, and it was as though not a ripple had interrupted our lives. Lily became twenty-one and then Rose. Rose had never been strong—you know what I mean—and Mother's death, the manner of her death, had nearly unhinged her. She led a quiet life, and Lily managed her well. Rose never looked beyond the farm for any sort of life, and that was how it should be. At least I thought so. It wasn't that I said to myself, 'Now what would Mother want?' I simply did it." She sighed again at the gargantuan task of explaining her life for the first time. James nodded to indicate that he understood, that he was on her side.

"Lily, on the other hand, Lily did look beyond the farm. She had never been physically strong or robust. She was never a huntswoman, for example. She didn't like to ride, she didn't like to garden, I'm not sure what she liked. She seemed always to be preparing for a life that was completely unavailable to her. Almost ignoring the fact that she was reared on a farm and not in some suburb of Dublin. She liked to read, she liked theatre. She'd take herself off to Dublin to see a few plays or concerts. She drew or sketched or some such nonsense. Yet she hadn't much time for these pursuits because she had a role to play here on the farm, and to give her her due, she did it and did it well. Apart from looking after the hens, her real job has been the management of our accounts. And she has a fine head for money! But her heart was elsewhere—in the city, I suppose. And then she had hopes, as we used to say. Hopes of marriage, I mean. Ridiculous, really. There were one or two young men that took an interest for a while. She'd go to the occasional local dance, especially at harvest time. She got on well with some of the men who came and went here at the farm. There was a dreadful commercial traveler who actually began to court her, but I sent him packing. Totally unsuitable. Probably was married for all we could tell. Lily cried for days and then we never spoke of it again.

"Shortly after that time, though, she started to ask about her share of the farm, saying it was equal to my own and that I had no right or rule over her. She even began to hint that she would want to take her share in another form. Money, I suppose she meant. Of course that was out of the question. It would have meant selling off to get her fair market value of one fourth of the estate. If she had insisted, it would have ruined my long-term plans for the farm.

"Meanwhile Rose stood by me. Although she loved Lily, she'd never go against me when it came to the farm and all its concerns. I'd merely explain to her, Mother wouldn't have liked it, and she'd trot off and tell Lily to be a good girl. I think now if Lily had married, I would have been better off. I doubt in her married bliss she would have bothered to seek her quarter share of the estate in any form but an inheritance. But imagine Lily bearing children. She always struck me as being so frail and fearful, not in the least hardy. It would have killed her, and then there'd be a widower and some offspring and endless battles about the inheritance. But it was always in her mind, at least in those days. She had one more romance." Violet paused and sipped her drink before continuing. "A certain local man who had gone up to Dublin and done extremely well for himself. It seems he had a 'gra,' as they say, for Lily. He was on the point of settling down with a Dublin girl, but this thing he'd had for Lily was getting in the way. Imagine! He wanted it settled once and for all. He wanted Lily to marry him."

The obvious question sprang to James's lips. What did all of this mean now? With no one to inherit. What did all of Violet's hard work, what did generation after generation of slaving and drudgery and suffering to keep the farm, to hold the farm and increase it, preserve it and defend it, mean? Three spinsters, with no offspring. Three wizened trees with no fruit, with no seed. Pointless. Fruitless.

He drank his brandy as she continued. He was not going to interrupt her flow.

"So you see, I had Rose on my side, and I'd pretty much got Lily settled into my ways. When she'd get very restless, she'd take a holiday with some local lady from the church, or with a group. France. She was fond of France. But she always returned home. I used to think if she'd had any gumption she'd have stayed there, or wherever she happened to fall on her feet. But oh no, despite what she'd tell you now, she always came willingly back, back to the farm.

"But Jack . . . I hadn't reckoned on Jack. He was a mere boy when Mother died. I should have paid more attention. But you see, I knew nothing of men or boys. I never knew any very well. I was indifferent to them. I wanted to be strong like my mother and her mother and her mother before her. I had no time for men. To me they were weak. Well, our history shows us that and more.

"But Jack was growing up, and I didn't pay sufficient heed. I had not ken enough to see what was coming, on any score, for that matter.

"He was a big lad, robust and broad. Very strong. And he worked like a horse. Big head of hair, big broad grin. Energy that outmatched the three of us sisters. And he was cheerful, all the day long. He seemed to enjoy what he was doing. He loved the land, and it was growing inside him like a passion. And finally it began to show. As he grew older, that passion grew stronger. All unasked, he would mention plans he had for the farm, long-term plans. Out of the blue, at the supper table. The fact that I never responded never disheartened him. At first I thought it was idle, boyish talk, silly male dreaming. You know the way, 'Some day I'll do this and then some day I'll do that.' But it was all to do with the farm. It finally penetrated my brain. He never talked of going off to seek his fortune—don't ask me why I thought he would do so.

"There were now these conversations about what he wanted for his children. His children! And he a child himself! We never really got on. I simply had taken over from Mother, and he looked at me in that way. I probably seemed as old as Mother. He did willingly what he was bid. It was all Mother had expected. She had got good results from Jack, and I continued to get good results. And that was all I expected.

"I never anticipated that he would see his life as taking shape on the farm, that he would think of taking an active role, a leading role! But that's exactly what he started doing—introducing new ideas, different methods, buying machinery without so much as even consulting me.

"Then I heard talk around the farm that Jack was a real lad for the girls. I thought, if I thought at all, that that was just as well. Let him see lots of girls. Later I learned he was seeing that Walsh one. He started to talk about her at table. Rose would get all giggly. It annoyed me! Lily—I don't remember much of what Lily had to say. If I had to, I'd say she encouraged him. God knows why. She knew as well as I did that a match there was entirely out of the question. So much so, that that is perhaps why I didn't pay it any heed."

"Out of the question?" James asked quietly.

"Of course. Firstly, she, well, she 'dug with the other foot.' A Catholic. There hadn't been a mixed marriage in the family since the dawn of time. But it was more than that. Those Walsh brothers would have been over the moon to link up with us. They would have seized it as an opportunity to join the two estates, the two farms, possibly the two herds! It was unthinkable. After all the work my family—me, me, sir—had put into keeping this herd the purest in five counties!

"To make a painful story short, Jack got it into his head that he was in love and wished to marry the Walsh girl. He was very determined about it. And that determination seemed to fire him up—he was starting to argue with me over the management of the farm. And now I saw that Lily was siding with him against me. And Rose. Of course, Rose was mesmerized by Jack. There was an air of excitement about the three of them. I'd catch them whispering and giggling; they'd stop talking when I came into meals and there'd be the nod and wink sort of thing. They were excluding me!" A look of astonishment passed across her face briefly.

"Rose was the silliest. Going around humming little nursery rhymes. Telling Jack which room would make a good nursery and which room these 'children' would sleep in, and actually saying that Mother's room could be done up for Jack and his wife. And then she'd remember why we'd locked it and she'd have a fit of crying. It was intolerable.

"And then suddenly it all came to an end." Violet was silent for a long time, as though deciding whether to continue.

"You've told me so much, Miss Moore . . . Please, if you will, finish the story for me." James's tone was gentle but not pleading. He knew pleading was useless with Violet Moore.

"Yes, yes. It feels good to talk to someone after all this time. Jack's death has made it all very present to my mind. I had succeeded, truly succeeded, in forgetting about this ancient past. But now I can't seem to put it from me.

"The night that Jack went drinking at the pub, I had no idea where he was. I didn't see myself as his keeper and I never did keep track of him in his free time. I had been working here in this room. It was very very late, and Rose and Lily were upstairs in bed, asleep, I assume. They were never involved in what transpired, then or since. I heard a noise from the direction of the kitchen and I went out there. I knew quickly that someone was in the back hall and I threw open the door, never expecting to see Jack, I assure you. He cowered for a moment and then came into the light. He was in a terrible state. He was covered with sweat and mud, and yet he was shivering with cold—with shock, now I realize.

"He blurted out almost immediately that he had killed Mike Walsh. Walsh had been waiting for him, and leapt out at him in the dark as Jack was cutting across the field, drunk, of course. They were both drunk, I'm certain of that. He pushed Walsh and Walsh went down heavily and struck his head. When Jack couldn't rouse him, he panicked and ran home—to me.

"I admit it. I instantly saw my opportunity. I had always been quick, you see, to see a chance and take it.

That's how I prospered so well in the business of the farm.

"He was ranting and crying. The drink was still on him, yet he was sober enough to know what he'd done. He knew he'd taken another man's life, and he fell to weeping, alternating between wanting to run to the police to confess and run to hide behind my skirts. I told him they'd never believe him, that he'd be sent to prison or worse. Oh, I painted a picture, bleak and black. It was then he told me that the Walsh girl was expecting his child. Mr. Fleming, it was a worse shock to me to hear that news than to hear he'd killed Mike Walsh. I saw instantly that that unborn child stood to inherit, to take away from me everything I had worked for, everything that I would work for. I couldn't allow it, but I had to be careful. And in the end it was easy because Jack was still merely a boy, and a very frightened boy.

"I sent him off to wash himself, and I went upstairs quietly and packed his bag. I put together all the cash I had in the house, which was considerable, and stuffed it in a valise. While I was packing I thought of my plan. It came into my head full formed, like Venus springing from Zeus' head: a beautiful plan.

"I explained it to him in words of one syllable. His eyes focused on my mouth, like a drowning man, like a dying animal. It was horrible, really. I never saw before or since such an expression on a man's face. He was horribly white and shaking. I told him that he would leave the country that night, that he should go through the north and from there to Scotland. I swore to him that I would cover for him. But he said he didn't give a damn about that. His concern wasn't whether he lived or died. It was all Kathleen and the baby. And then I swore that I would care for her and for the child. But that he had to promise me something in return because this for me was such a serious undertaking. He knew that. He knew I hated the Walshes, and he knew that I would hate that child. I asked him to give up his share in the farm. I dictated a piece of writing to that effect. I still don't know if it would have held up legally. I never had to test it.

"He took it so seriously, you see. He was that kind of boy. I think that was the first and the last time I saw what manner of man he might have become.

"All he wanted was that the girl and the child be cared for. I even assured him that he might be able to return someday, but that he had to go, and to go immediately. I imagine the whole scene only took an hour or less. And then he was gone.

"I was stunned. Stunned. In a matter of moments our lives had changed forever. I could hardly take it in. I didn't sleep that night, because the enormity of what I had promised finally came home to me.

"I didn't know if I could provide an alibi for Jack. But the police, when the time came, took down my statement in good faith. I had told them that Jack had come straight home from the pub and had been helping me with a sick calf. I suppose because it was already clear to them that Mike Walsh had fallen and hit his head, rather than been hit on it, the police had pretty much decided that his death was an accident. Anyway, they accepted my statement.

"I also told them, and whoever else asked, that Jack had decided to leave the farm after he'd heard about Mike's death. That he felt bad that his teasing in the pub had led to such a terrible result. I implied that he'd gone off to London to work, and that I expected him to return in six months or a year. Because he was so young and known to be headstrong, people seemed to accept my explanation."

"And Lily? And Rose?" James questioned her sharply.

"They were puzzled. And saddened, of course, that he hadn't seen fit to bid them good-bye. But at no time did it ever enter either of their minds that Jack could have killed the Walsh boy. It was unthinkable to them. He was their baby brother.

"Initially I kept the hope alive that he'd return soon. That he was young, just wanted to see a bit of life before he settled down to marriage and responsibility. That too rang true, and they believed me, because, as I say, I had come to believe in the whole fabrication myself. I actually came to believe that Jack had merely gone off on a flit. Days passed. The three of us adjusted. We'd look for the mail at first, and we trusted he'd be back within a year or so. The talk in the village didn't reach us. After all, who was going to relate to Rose, for example, or myself, the low gossip about Jack killing Mike Walsh?

"So when Kathleen Walsh came to call on me, I was completely unprepared. It was as though she no longer existed. And yet there she was, in the sitting room, here where we are talking now." She closed her eyes as if to see that young girl more clearly.

"She reminded me immediately of Jack. She was deathly white. I thought she would faint on me, and I actually asked her to sit down. She spoke simply and directly. She asked me where Jack was, and I told her I didn't know, that I hadn't heard from him. At that point it was the truth. Her eyes filled with tears, but I give her credit—she didn't cry. She told me frankly that she was expecting Jack's baby. That she needed to get in touch with him so that they could marry as planned. She didn't have to tell me what her brothers would do, or what the talk would be, if she started to show before she married.

"She was seventeen, with no money, and in this situation virtually friendless. It was so simple. I was kindness itself. I could see the surprise in her eyes, but she accepted my kindness like a child. I told her that I would take responsibility for her and the baby in Jack's absence. That I would take care of everything. That no doubt Jack would be in contact soon, and just to give me a little time to figure things out.

"In that week I laid my plans. It was essential that she be got away from the village. I believed her when

172

she told me that no one else knew about the child. She had far too much to lose to gossip with her girlfriends. I knew, as we all did, that there were convents dotted 'round the country who took care of this kind of thing. I contacted a girl I had been to boarding school with, who had had a sister with a similar problem. She was reluctant at first, but I got the information. I contacted the convent in Tipperary and made the arrangements.

"Then I fed Kathleen her story, that she was fed up looking after her brothers and the farm, and now that Jack had done a bunk, she too was going off to London to seek her fortune. She left home, having packed and prepared as she would have if indeed she had been going off to London. Her brothers were livid, but she told them she was determined and that there was nothing they could do about it. They made no move to stop her. I met her in Dublin and escorted her myself to the convent in Tipperary.

"I brought her down on the train and took a local taxi service out to the convent. I could tell from the driver's discreet reaction it wasn't the first time. Kathleen was very weepy, and perhaps resentful too. We had had a few angry words and there was, needless to say, very little friendliness on either side. I installed her with the nuns. They impressed me as competent, and more worldly than I had expected. I have had few dealings with nuns . . ."

Violet paused at last and stood up slowly, as though to stretch her legs. She walked to the window and parted the drapes, looking out blankly. James was relieved to have a few minutes' respite, although in truth he was hanging on every word. He went over to the sideboard and poured two more brandies, bringing ice and ginger ale on a tray back to the low coffee table. He pondered that Violet was perhaps a mere ten years older than Kathleen at the time of these events. He wondered at the coldness, the detachment she had felt toward that young unhappy girl, carrying a baby and alone in the world because of it.

Violet resumed her seat, straightening her back and leaning forward. This time she watered her brandy with ginger ale and sipped slowly.

"And what of Jack?" James prompted, virtually reminding her of his presence in the room.

Violet sighed. "I am about to tell you. Jack did escape the country, and in a matter of weeks the furor here had diminished. He had no way of knowing that, of course. He had gone to London and had landed a job very quickly on one of the big building sites. There was a tremendous amount of construction going on then, after the war. There were thousands of Irishmen in London doing exactly the same thing, and no one paid any attention to yet another one earning good money by the sweat of his back. As I recall, he seemed to make good pay, for shortly after he settled he began writing to Kathleen, in care of me here at the farm, and enclosing money for her. I knew because I opened the letters . . ." She paused as James shifted in his chair.

"Yes, I opened them and I scanned them briefly. What he said to her was much the same as what he also wrote to me. He was sending the money for Kathleen and the baby. He thought they were here at the farm. I led him to believe that was the case. I told him not to write too often. I was afraid that the Sweeneys or the postman, and of course Rose or Lily, might intercept one of the letters. But I guess no one had the same audacity as myself." She smiled weakly at the irony.

"To be fair, I used Jack's money to pay for Kathleen's needs, supplementing it with my own, of course. It did make me feel better. But my scruples soon faded. Jack had plans to bring Kathleen and the baby over to London. He believed they could get a bedsit or flat and that they could live there until a time came when perhaps he could return to Ireland. I told him the police were still actively looking for him and that it could be years. But he was so young, even the thought of a ten-year absence didn't discourage him!

"Meanwhile I mentioned to Kathleen in one of my few visits to the convent that Jack had written from London to tell me that he was about to emigrate. I was vague about it. I hadn't needed to embroider the story because she believed it immediately and was devastated. She felt completely rejected and, for a young girl, became very bitter very quickly. That was just as well. The nuns and I thought we might have had trouble persuading her to put the baby—if it lived—up for adoption. She did weaken a bit in her resolve, I understand, at the time of the birth. The nuns had rung me and I went down the same day.

"I remember seeing her in her room. She looked so young and fit and well. It was hard to believe she had given birth just hours before.

"I told her the baby would have a better life with a secure family. That she herself would have no life at all if she kept the child. She was a practical girl and knew that herself. I told her then that I would help, since Jack had not. That we might have been sisters-in-law but for Jack's immature behavior. That was a hard one to force out of my mouth. She was wary of me, but believed at least enough to allow herself to take my money. I told her to go to Australia. She knew girls from her school that had already gone out there. It didn't seem such a farfetched idea. She knew better than I that her life in Ireland was over. I gave her the passage to Australia and money for clothes and a bit of a start. And she took it. That was the last I saw of her."

"Did you see the baby? Your brother's daughter? Your own niece?" James thought wildly of Sarah's striking face and her graceful hands, the music of her violin and the strength of her nature.

Violet looked up suddenly. "No, of course not." She spat out the words. "She was as nothing to me. A scrap of a thing. I never for a moment thought of her as part of Jack or part of the Moore family. She was an unfortunate accident."

James reddened with instant fury at the words. He

was very close to losing his control with this heartless woman. He would have to leave the room if the conversation didn't change quickly.

"I see you think I've a heart of stone. I admit that I do, but please remember this: I freely took on responsibility for Kathleen and the baby. I discharged my duty. I believed, then and now, that what I did was best for all them, for all of us.

"I made sure through the nuns that the adoptive parents were highly respectable, educated—that they had money went without saying. I specifically didn't want a farming family. The family who took her were all that I asked and more. There was just one problem. They were Catholic. I would have preferred . . . But then, so was Kathleen. The child had been baptized a Catholic right there in the convent, so there were no difficulties in the adoption process. When I learned the family was Catholic and that all was taken care of . . . yes, I admit it, I lost interest. It was a closed chapter to me."

"And for Jack also?" James tried to conceal his tone of distaste at her atrocious callousness.

"Jack? Oh, that was fairly simple. Or so I thought. He knew when the baby was due, of course, and his letters at that time were beginning to be more frequent. As soon as the confinement was over, I wrote and told him that the baby, a girl, had died at birth. It wasn't a lie!" She glared at James, to stop him from speaking, if he attempted. "That child was dead to him. I told him Kathleen was shattered and, in order to put all this sorrow behind her, she was going out to Australia. And he believed it. He believed it because she hadn't written to him in all those months, and now what they had had between them was all over."

"Because she never did write . . . because she believed he had abandoned her as you had told her?" James's voice was bitter.

"I told her I wrote to him. Of course, when she didn't hear from him herself, she grew discouraged, especially in the latter months of her pregnancy. She felt that only I and the nuns cared for her. She felt Jack had run out on her, and I did not discourage that idea."

James stood up. Pacing the floor, he tried to confront the reality of Violet's story. A young couple completely manipulated by the woman who sat in front of him. A baby deprived of its parents because of this woman, a woman totally without remorse. He glanced at her with loathing. She seemed neither to notice nor to care, and resumed talking.

"I didn't hear from Jack for months. I assumed he was getting on with his life. One night . . . one night months later . . . I went out to the back barn to check on a cow that was in a bad way. Suddenly Jack was in front of me." Violet looked up. "I couldn't believe my eyes. He looked older, much older than when he had gone away. And he was sober. He had put on weight and, well, it's hard to describe . . . he was different. Older, bigger, more threatening. He had come on a mail boat into the port of Wexford that very night and had made his way on foot to the farm. He told me straight out he hadn't believed me, that he knew Kathleen had loved him. He said he knew that even though the baby had died, she would have come to London, at least to talk, to settle things between them. He had begun to suspect, when he thought about it, that I had prevented her from writing, from seeing him or finding him in London.

"I was truly frightened of him. He was ranting at me, telling me that he should never have trusted me. That his child would be alive if it hadn't been for me. If he had been there with Kathleen when the child was born, if he had married her and taken her off to London with him . . . He was moving toward me, screaming at me. I thought then—foolishly—that if I told him at least that the baby was alive, he'd calm down. He seemed so caught up with this baby's death, you see. His dead child. I thought . . . I thought he'd be pleased to know the truth at least about that. So I told him that the baby had lived. He stopped in his

177

tracks. It was like stunning a beast, like knocking it on the forehead with a great blow. He stood swaying, his eyes glazing over. I tried to get his attention. I poured out that the baby was well, a little girl, that a wealthy, established family had adopted her and that she would have a wonderful life. When I said adoption, he turned his wild eyes on me. I thought he would kill me—the look that passed through his eyes. And then he began to rave . . ."

Violet's chest heaved at this, the only sign of emotion she had shown. James felt the sweat starting up on his face and neck as he saw the scene through her eyes. And he saw a man going through a hell of his own making.

"He screamed at me. He told me I had killed him more surely than if I had shot him, more certainly than if I had handed him over to the police and told them outright that he had killed Mike Walsh, more cruelly than if I had put the noose around his neck with my own hands!

"I thought he would kill me then and there. He saw, as if in a flash of lightning, that I had taken his share of the farm, that I would take away his alibi from him if he tried to return. He spat out the words in a wild jumble. He shook me till my brains rattled and his spittle and his sweat covered my face. He told me I had taken his baby from him, the child of his love for Kathleen and hers for him. That Kathleen was gone, the baby was gone, the farm—gone, life itself. He was crying and shouting how he had lived alone all those months in London, in fear and self-loathing, how he'd starved himself to send money to Kathleen to buy the baby fine little clothes, fine wee things of linen and lace. How he had sent money to pay for their passage to London, where they would be a family together, where they would choose a name for their baby together. He stopped talking for a moment and stared at me. And then he came for me—he lifted me up like a rag doll, he shook me, screaming in my face that word—family, family. Then he threw me to the floor of the barn with all his strength and staggered out of the door, crying and ranting ... I lay I don't know how long. Minutes, hours? I was frozen with fear and horror. Finally, I grew so cold that I dragged myself back to the house. I thought he might be there, somewhere, waiting for me. He seemed somehow so near death himself that killing me could be his only satisfaction. I searched the house, I searched the outbuildings in the morning light ... but he was gone. I never saw him again ... alive."

—— *Chapter Ten* ——

Maggie's voice crackled over James's intercom. "Mr. Daley rang five times yesterday, James, about the Hanlon will. The travel agent called in with the outline itinerary for your Peru trip. And the Big F wants to see you ASAP."

James sighed. Exhausted and uneasy after learning the whole story from Violet, he dreaded recounting it all to Gerald.

"Put him off, will you, Maggie?"

"I don't think that's wise, pet," Maggie sagely advised. "I'll tell him you'll be in in ten minutes, will that do?"

Forced into making a decision of some kind, James reluctantly chose to edit Violet's story. In the men's room he splashed some cold water on his face, and gathering his thoughts, walked briskly to Gerald's office, where his greeting was warm and cordial.

"I got your office memo, James. And I was surprised—sit down, my boy—that you'd been down to Kilmartin yet again. You didn't mention you would be going."

"Sorry, Gerald. It was a spur of the moment thing. I was beginning to feel some urgency in this case. I have the sensation . . . I feel as though time is running out on us . . ."

"And so it is, James. Sheridan spoke to me this morning, but more of that later. Tell me, how did you get on?"

"Better than I expected," James said brightly. "You see, I have been worried about Lily's story . . ."

"'Story'?" Gerald leaned back in his swivel chair and reached for his pipe.

"The story that she had seen Violet at the barn on the night in question. Violet had denied that part of the story from the beginning. And I believed her."

"Why?"

"I suppose because she was your client and, well, because you've known her for donkeys years. I didn't press her about it, and as you know, she has been less than forthcoming. But it kept eating away at me. I couldn't understand how Violet could continue to live with Lily in such close quarters if Lily had been lying. On the other hand, I couldn't grasp why Lily would lie—she has nothing to gain, obviously."

"And what have you learned?"

"This may seem unbelievable to you, sir, but somehow the whole story rings true. Violet talked rather freely, for her."

James looked up and smiled at Gerald. Gerald was nodding in agreement.

"She spoke of her family's long history, of her love for the farm—which to me sounds quite obsessional—and how she, well, in a nutshell, lived for the farm and brooked no interference. You probably are aware of most of this from dealing with her legal matters over the years?"

Again Gerald nodded.

"Well, to put it succinctly, she wanted to control the farm, and consequently, to control Lily, Rose, and

181

Jack. Regarding Lily, it seems that she interfered with Lily's own personal plans. Lily hoped to marry and leave the farm. Apparently there was at least one serious romance—in other words, a chance for Lily to marry. And Violet prevented it."

"That seems preposterous!"

"Which? That Lily had plans or that Violet interfered?"

"That in this day and age Violet could have stopped Lily."

"This happened years ago, Gerald. And I had the impression that she must have pressured her into staying for Rose's sake, and perhaps used the fact that their mother might not have approved. Now that I know Violet, I can imagine too that she undermined Lily's confidence. God, she is incredibly hard. Don't you find her so?"

"Indeed and I have, James. I've dealt with her property transactions, and she's as hard as nails in business. Fortunately we only met occasionally over the years. To be frank, although I was willing to take on this case, I have been only too happy that you've been handling it. Violet is our client and she deserves a sympathetic handling of her case. You were able to give her your unprejudiced attention and concern. I doubt I could have. She puts me off."

"Yes, she puts me off too." James's face grew somber, almost sad, and Gerald caught the change.

"Is there something else? You seem troubled."

James didn't answer.

"Well, presumably Violet believes Lily lied for revenge. That's a pretty serious accusation against Lily, James."

"That's just it. I don't know Lily at all, really." James threw up his hands. "God, I hardly know Violet. But somehow it doesn't seem possible that gentle, considerate Lily could be capable of holding such a grudge, of orchestrating a vendetta!"

"I agree, but our hands are tied. As you know, we

can't question Lily, since she's a witness for the prosecution. How about Rose?"

"Oh, God, it never crossed my mind to trouble Rose. You didn't want me to . . . ?"

"Not a'tall. Even if she had some information, she'd make a terrible witness. A cross-examination would demolish her. No. You did right. Yet, I sense that Violet convinced you . . ."

"I think she did. While I was sitting in her living room yesterday it all was completely believable, the human psychology of it rang true. Even Violet's manner and voice rang true. She's so acquiescent, so . . . almost defeated. She feels Lily's betrayal to such a degree, she will not even mention it to her. Honest to God, Gerald, this case is getting nowhere. Lily will be the most damaging witness."

"I'll reserve judgment on that, James. Now let me hear what else Violet told you."

James recounted most of the story, leaving out, as he had decided, the key fact of the survival of the child. Although he told himself that it was on account of his foolhardy promise to Kathleen in London, it was in truth because he could not yet bear for anyone to know Sarah Gallagher's true identity. And he did not want Gerald to tell him that he must instantly sever his connection with Sarah for professional and ethical reasons. He recounted Jack's last meeting with Violet, but let her original lie—that the baby had died—stand.

Gerald sighed and stood up, pacing the room for some minutes.

"I'm not sure," he said at last, "what you have achieved here, James. It seems to me that Violet's story only blackens her chances. I think what you've done is uncovered a sort of motive . . ."

"I don't see that . . ." James was heated. Here was Gerald finding a motive, and he didn't even yet know about Sarah.

"I'm sorry, James. But look. Say Violet had heard

from Jack, knew that he was coming back. That's certainly possible. Look how she managed it years before. Perhaps Jack had written, or better still, phoned her. He might have threatened her perhaps physically—that at least would give Violet a possible defense of self-defense. But that would be weak . . ." Gerald thought aloud. "Yes, weak because, on the other hand, it might leave her wide open to an accusation of premeditation. She knew he was coming, and when, and so planned to kill him. It won't matter if she feared for her life, because there's no way we can show he threatened her."

James cursed his own stupidity as Gerald continued to pace.

"And then, say he didn't threaten her, say he was phoning just to tell her that he was retiring, for example. Jack was still a youngish man. He could have been coming home for good, and would expect to resume his rightful place in the managing of the farm. Violet as much as told you she was obsessed—your word, remember, James—with that farm. She might have plotted to deal directly with the situation by killing him on his arrival, and then managed somehow this ruse of the hearse. It's messy, but with the information you've got, the prosecution would slide over little details like that and go for the jugular. They could connect her past behavior with Jack—the lying, the robbing him of his share—with her present behavior. If she lied then, why not now? If she wanted the farm for herself then, why not now?"

James groaned. Only too well he saw Gerald's point. And he alone knew that the existence of Jack's child, Sarah, would provide an even more powerful motive for Violet.

"James, James, don't blame yourself. Facts are facts. I'm only speculating. I don't necessarily believe in the story I just presented. I'm just illustrating what use could be made of this information, how it could be fitted and tailored by the prosecution."

"What should we do?"

"Frankly, nothing. By that I mean I don't think you should report any of this new knowledge to Sheridan."

"But—"

"I know, I know that is your job right now. But listen, man, we don't want the barrister on the case losing faith. No. Leave well alone . . . at least for now. Sheridan's good, and he's got his own investigators. I've already instructed him to follow up Moore's possible connection with the IRA, or should I say IRA support groups. If he learns anything more, let it come from his investigators. Or from Violet herself. They'll be meeting before the trial begins . . . No, take it from me, James. You've done enough damage for a while."

"I see your point, Gerald, but there's one more thing. Don't you think the fact that Violet can state Jack confessed to killing Mike Walsh will go in her favor. By that I mean, we now know for certain that Jack did it; even if it was an accident, we know he did it. Mightn't that strengthen the case the other way, since it gives the Walshes a motive for the revenge killing of Jack?"

"Perhaps, perhaps. But we only have Violet's word on that. And furthermore, I have reservations about letting Sheridan in on any of this. If you reveal what you know, it proves that Jack and Violet acted in collusion in the past—something that has caused bad blood between them for twenty-seven years. No, leave the Walsh angle alone. And let's hope something will come out of the investigation into Jack's involvement with the IRA boys."

James nodded reluctantly. It was his own fault. So far he'd done nothing substantial to help his client's case.

He told himself that he often drank at the Legal Eagle—a pub near the Four Courts—but it wasn't true. Sitting discreetly in the far corner, he would, if asked, have said that he was allowing fate to take its own course. The barrister, Sheridan, a prematurely graying but striking man in his forties, came in. Suave and at ease with the many legal types in the lounge bar, Sheridan spotted James at once as a less than familiar face and joined him without invitation or ceremony. Gerald could not gainsay that coincidence.

"You look glum, man," said Sheridan, smiling warmly. "Not used to this kind of case, are you?"

"I confess I'm not. I'll be glad when it's over," James blurted out.

"As bad as that, hmmm? You'll get used to it. I'm glad I bumped into you, actually. I've had news from the States. My investigator there located a small-time lawyer, as they say there. Not the man Moore usually dealt with. Just a shopfront fellow. How and ever, it's this man who is holding what seems to be Moore's most recent will. I was going to ring Gerald tomorrow to tell him, since I believe it's within your firm's venue to inform the family, and if they so instruct you, to probate the will. It's going to be very interesting to see whom Jack named as executor of his will. Or executrix!" Sheridan paused, watching James closely as he sipped his drink.

"I say, why don't you do me and yourself a favor. The will has to be brought over by hand—I don't trust it to the mails at this juncture. I could send one of my people, but it could as easily be you. You could ask a few questions of your own while you're there. I think the experience would do you good."

James was startled by Sheridan's suggestion, and didn't answer right away. The conversation moved on to the topic that most concerned them.

"How does it look?" James asked anxiously.

"Not bad, not bad." Sheridan spoke with confidence. "I was quite interested in O'Shea's nugget of information which Gerald handed on to me—about Moore's contributions to the 'cause.' Even if Jack Moore didn't have any direct connection with the

IRA—and I've got some people working on that now—I still think I can bring it in to the case to show that others might have had some reason for wanting Jack Moore dead. The absence of motive on Violet's part is very important, Fleming." Sheridan's voice grew somber. "That's why I'm rather anxious about the will. In the event there is something in it that reveals a connection with Violet about which we know nothing—"

"All right, Sheridan, I'll go. But I want you to proceed as if this meeting never happened. I think Gerald would take this suggestion better coming from you than from me. He's a stickler for form, you know, a bit—well—crusty, since Mrs. Fitzgerald passed away." The lies came easily to James's lips, and he was surprised himself how glibly they did so. Yet there was a germ of truth in what he said. He didn't want Gerald to know he had been talking to Sheridan behind his back.

"Fine. No problem." Sheridan glanced kindly at James as he moved away. "Chin up, old man, you'll get the hang of these things, in time."

James spent a second anxious day at his desk, fully occupied with a family dispute over a six-year-old will that in ordinary circumstances would have tickled his fancy. Usually he relished mediating, or better still, refereeing, convoluted battles amongst well-heeled West Brits greedy over their mother's little bits of land and gold watch chains that Daddy should have left to them and not to her when he died twenty years previously. Normally it amused him to see otherwise respectable people in their sixties fighting like children over a bag of candy. However, his interest in ancient wills was rapidly fading.

Finally Maggie buzzed him to visit Gerald's office. He approached, making his face a complete and innocent blank.

"James, my boy, I have something to take your mind off Violet's immediate problems."

"Yes," James answered doubtfully.

"Sheridan rang me this morning with real news. His man in the States has located Jack Moore's will! I suggested to him that you fly out to Boston ASAP and pick it up yourself. After all, James, wills used to be your specialty until you tried becoming an amateur sleuth."

James detected a definite tinge of annoyance in Gerald's voice, and wondered who in fact suggested he fly out to Boston.

"Now?" he asked neutrally.

"Now, James." Gerald's voice was firm. "This is exactly right. It's what you know best. See the American lawyer, collect the will, use some of that fatal Irish charm and see what you can dig up. Suss out why Jack didn't use his usual firm of lawyers. It's imperative that the defense be given any new information as soon as possible."

"When do I leave?"

"I'd say catch the Pan Am weekender flight from Shannon. Three days in Boston should be enough. I would guess the American lawyer—Solomon is his name, by the way—would be willing to see a colleague out of office hours. Here's his number. Get on to it. Now."

James crossed to his office, and by the time he reached Maggie's desk, felt the old adrenaline starting to pump—the thrill that travel virtually to any place caused to run through his veins. Within moments Maggie had Mr. Aaron Solomon of Brookline, Massachusetts, on James's line.

Solomon's broad Boston accent boomed into the receiver. He would be delighted to meet Jim on the Saturday afternoon. He would even pick him up at his hotel. Jim was to call him when he'd checked in. Had Jimboy ever been to Boston? James relished the chance of seeing an American colleague's workplace, and said so. Solomon gave Jimboy the office address and his home number—he was working on Saturday, he shouldn't be, but he was—and then hung up.

James smiled. No one yet had attempted to call him Jim, even in school. He decided to try it on for size.

As James reclined in his business-class seat, glass of complimentary champagne in hand, he debated whether to use the in-flight telephone. He pondered for a moment, wondering who of his circle would relish such a call. Sarah was out, for obvious reasons. Matt was on a school trip to Wales. And his other friends would appear to react indifferently. His mother! She would react. He hadn't even thought to ring her to tell her he was leaving.

The call was a resounding success. But when he rang off, the thought occurred to him that it was a sad day when a man of his age was reduced to phoning only his mother. And he thought fleetingly of the house on the hilltop in Kilmartin, and the nameless, faceless wife who would have answered his call with pride and delight, and the two bonny babes who would have been clinging to her, shouting "Dada" down the phone.

Unselfconsciously he pressed his nose to the window. He had spotted two icebergs below, and was now following the line of the coast from Newfoundland. He recalled what he knew about the Viking explorations of the north Atlantic, and thought then about brave, mystical St. Brendan, setting out from Ireland in a leather boat centuries before Columbus. About his description of the giant turtles that swam alongside him on his terrible journey, and of the fires in the sky that he had seen as signs from God. He smiled. It just went to prove that old truism. Wherever you went in this world, an Irishman was there before you!

His hotel in the newly redeveloped harbor-front area of downtown Boston was luxurious. Colossal bed, tasteful appointments, basket of fruit, flowers. His own refrigerator, a phone every four feet, including one by the toilet. He showered immediately, and appreciated the endless and powerful stream of hot water—when, if ever, would Ireland provide showers that worked like this! The view—he observed as he dressed—was intriguing: the bustle and hubbub of what seemed a giant arcade. But he hadn't wanted new, or even plush. He had wanted class, the kind for which Boston had been famous. The hotel, lovely as it was, could be in any major city. He had wanted age and dust, leather-covered books in oak-lined reading rooms, hotel stationery on an inlaid writing desk. He wanted obscure oils on the walls, not mere prints chosen by the interior decorator to tone with the wallpaper and bed covers. He had wanted originality and he got homogenized comfort. Yes, once this whole business was sorted out, he'd take Sarah to Riders Inn for a romantic weekend.

Having eaten a light meal, James strolled out into the mild evening and found himself nearing the harbor. Caught up in a line, he moved willy-nilly with the crowd toward a ticket booth. BOOZE CRUISE, the sign announced. Two-hour cruise of Boston Harbor, return at midnight. Lights and music from the live band beckoned, and shortly he found himself leaning on the railing of the upper deck, large paper cup of watery beer in hand.

The breeze as the boat picked up speed was stiff and became increasingly cold. He felt the salt on his lips and face and the faint, damp spray saturating his skin. He felt invigorated and refreshed after eight hours inside the airplane. The loud sounds of the lively crowd—people all in their twenties, and all dancing and drinking, and inexplicably yelling—somehow faded as the skyline of Boston took shape, rose up above them like a fairy land and then retreated, leaving only a distant promise on the horizon and a black expanse of ocean that increased with each throb of the boat's engine.

In a way, he was glad when they docked back in Boston. Music and lights beckoned from the various open-air nightclubs as he walked back toward his hotel. But he was tired, and tired of being on his own, so though half tempted, he headed back to his hotel. It was already four A.M. Dublin time.

In the morning—a glorious warm, dry morning—James phoned Solomon at his office, then took one of the trolleys on the underground platform and rode a bare fifteen minutes to Brookline, where the line surfaced and the stops were like miniature English rural railway stations, all neat and scrubbed, with a cozy little shelter on either side of the tracks. The journey was a treat for a train buff, and he wrote down the make and model number of his vintage trolley. On James's request, the driver held the trolley so he could take a quick photo.

Solomon's office was easily spotted, situated as it was on Brookline Avenue in a row containing an insurance agency, an ice cream parlor, and an undertaker. James knocked on the glass door and was instantly greeted by a tall, overweight, jolly man slightly older than himself. They passed through a small waiting room clothed in linoleum and vinyl and into an equally drab inner office. Law books lined every wall, and a commercial water cooler bubbled softly in the corner. Solomon's desk was metal with a Formica top. Jack Moore's brown manila folder was placed prominently in the center. James felt he was taking part in a grade-B movie, but within seconds found he had misjudged his man.

"I know your time is short, Jim, my boy, so we'll get straight to business. If you had more time to visit, I'd show you some of the sights, but a weekend is not much time for you to get a picture of this man Moore."

James smiled at his new monicker and at the man himself, warm, jovial, and shrewd. He appreciated his directness.

"I'll tell you what little I know. The details stand out in my mind because, A, I dealt with Moore only once, and then briefly, and B, the circumstances to my mind were extraordinary. But before I even get started on that, let me tell you, firstly, how I even came to know about his death. I think you might make something of this.

"About one month ago—I can check the date for you, as I kept the papers—I began receiving airmailed copies of your *Irish Times,* daily copies. I read them—actually, I skimmed them—thinking it was a promotion of sorts. And I do handle a lot of Irish-American clients who live in this Irish enclave here in Brookline. But they kept coming. I was curious, and phoned their business office, which kindly informed me that no, it wasn't a promotion. I had been put on a three-month subscription list. When they told me the exorbitant cost, I was knocked for a loop and asked if they could tell me who had paid for it. They said they had it on record, it was a gift subscription to me from Jack Moore. They still had the gift card, but it was penciled in that the card was not to be sent.

"Naturally, being in this business, I was curious, and began reading the paper more closely. But you see I had already thrown out the earlier papers I had received. Thinking I might have missed something, I got all the copies I had missed, and in reading them over, finally came across the small coverage that that paper had given the murder of Moore! I phoned the consulate here because I believed that I was holding Jack Moore's last will and testament!"

James was speechless as the complex ramifications of this information filtered through to him. Solomon watched his face closely.

"I see you are having the same reaction I did. Moore had the papers sent. I believe he must have been in fear of his life from the time he made the will—and that time coincides with my receiving the newspapers . . ."

"And presumably it coincides with the date he left Boston and traveled via London to Dublin . . ."

"Yes. It does."

"You see what this means?"

"Wait, there's more. I couldn't understand it, that day Jack Moore walked into the office, no appointment, no previous recommendation of me by a friend. I do believe he literally saw the sign in the window and walked in off the street."

"Did he live locally?"

"Yes, about a ten-minute walk from here. A good building some fifteen years old—turns out he built it. That was his line . . . well, one of them. He walked in and sat down where you are now. He said he wanted to make a very simple will, and he showed me a bit of paper. And it *was* simple. He merely wanted to leave everything in his possession at the time of his death to his closest blood relative. And that was it. No names. Well, you'll see that for yourself. I have the will here for you to take back to Ireland."

James scanned the simple document, becoming increasingly anxious. Apart from Kathleen and Violet, and only recently himself, who else could know that Jack's nearest blood relative was his daughter Sarah? Motive, motive, motive. He was holding it now in his hand.

"Is it bad news?" Solomon's curiosity was palpable.

"Well, you could say that," James admitted cautiously. "A lot would depend on what Mr. Moore had to leave his surviving relative."

Solomon nodded. "That I can't tell you. But if you look at the attached letter, you'll see why I think it was considerable."

James looked closely at the notation on the second page.

"Do you recognize what you're reading?" Solomon laughed. "It's a Swiss bank-account number!"

After a few pleasantries, including a check for Solomon's consultation fee, Jimbo thanked him and returned to his hotel, this time by taxi. He immediately phoned Sheridan's man in Boston, one Joe Sorvetti, and identified himself as Sheridan had instructed.

"I've been expecting your call, Fleming."

"What can you tell me about Moore's financial situation? We know his holdings were considerable."

" 'Were' is the operative word, Mr. Fleming. I can tell you what I just phoned through to Sheridan. As far as we've gotten in our investigations, it seems that Moore systematically and over about three months liquidated every holding we've been able to locate: property, bonds, IRA's, stocks and shares, bank accounts, annuities, term insurance. He even took some small losses to enable him to do the thing quickly. He was a careful businessman, took no risks, as far as we can establish. We've been working from information from the feds—the IRS to you. I doubt there's anything we've missed. I don't think there were any secret holdings, 'offshore' stuff. I don't think it was his way. It's as though he was just going along as usual and then, one day, abruptly decided to convert everything into cash."

"Do you know where it is, this cash?"

"Indications are that it's now residing in Switzerland."

"I see. And was what he did with the cash hard to maneuver?" James was careful.

"Yes indeed. American law on transporting funds out of the country is strict and complicated. So far we can't find anyone who assisted him in doing it."

"So you're saying to do it himself would have taken time and some planning."

"Most definitely."

"Can you give me a figure, an amount, so I know what we're talking about here?" James asked hesitantly, dreading the answer.

"If you'll take a ball-park figure—about three million."

"And legally, I mean, is it okay now? You know—can there be any consequences?"

"He seems to have done it 'right,' if you take my meaning."

"Thank you, Mr. Sorvetti. I'll tell Sheridan how much help you've been."

"Wait! There's someone I think you should talk to while you're here. Moore's doctor. I couldn't get anywhere with him. Close-mouthed bastard. You might try your luck, though. Dr. Vincent. His office is just off Brookline Avenue—do you know the street?"

"I do now . . ."

James barely noticed the passage of time on his return flight to Ireland. The information he was carrying in his head was of far greater moment than the simple document that now lay in the briefcase on his lap.

Certainly Solomon's information about Jack Moore and about the mysterious arrival of the newspapers had been significant. And the contents of the will were a potential bombshell. And for now only he knew how great an explosion it could cause. Sorvetti's verifiable documentation regarding the amount of Jack Moore's financial worth—three million dollars!—would contribute to the nature of that bombshell. No one, not even Gerald, had had an inkling of Jack Moore's wealth. But the real coup had been his astonishing conversation with Dr. Vincent.

James smiled to himself as he leaned back and surveyed the night sky, seeing and yet not seeing the play of light on the darkening cloud banks seemingly gliding beneath the plane.

He didn't need to read over the notes he had taken after his amiable dinner at the Ritz Hotel with the eminent Boston physician. One single fact stood out amongst all the others, one of overriding significance. Jack Moore had had terminal cancer—and he had known it.

—— *Chapter Eleven* ——

James, back at his flat, showered in the all too familiar lukewarm water and changed. The elation he had experienced on the plane had not abated. He felt a burgeoning of confidence—in himself and in his sense that a solution of some kind was near at hand.

The information that he had gained in Boston was more than significant. Now he had real insight into Jack Moore. And, to his thinking, he had learned something else. Namely, the level of secrecy that Jack had maintained. Jack had had a definite purpose in mind in the weeks and months before his arrival in Ireland. And he kept that purpose, that intention, secret! Equally important, he seemed to have kept his illness a secret too, perhaps even denying it to himself.

Before his departure from the States, Jack Moore had systematically tied up every loose end. He had consolidated his large financial resources into one lump sum and had, in a sense, "stored" it, so he could have access to it any time, anywhere. Here was evidence of complex advance planning. Secret planning. Why put everything into a Swiss account if Jack were merely retiring to live out his years in his homeland? Perhaps Dublin had only been a stopping-off point. But on his way to where? Why dissolve everything, why leave nothing in place in the States? It was obvious from this alone that Jack had not planned to return to Boston.

What else was new? James shivered as he threw on his overcoat. What was new was the large amount of Jack's wealth. It was more than anyone involved in the case had guessed at.

And that large amount worried him. He knew that on the face of it money and greed would provide a very powerful motive for murder. And Violet, with Lily and Rose under her thumb, stood to inherit those millions. That's how the world would see it. That's how Gerald and Sheridan and the prosecution would see it. Gerald's earlier conversation echoed in his mind—that James had done nothing but provide the prosecution with a motive. And here he was again, seeming to do just that—only in trumps.

But that was because no one except Kathleen and Violet and himself knew of the existence of Jack Moore's actual nearest blood relative, Sarah Gallagher. That it was she who stood to inherit Jack's money.

Sarah. Sarah! If she were the one who was to inherit, then in the best fictional—and factual—tradition, she was the first who should be suspected of murdering Jack. James pushed the thought aside, but it remained a nagging presence in the back of his mind.

He checked his answering machine and was relieved. Sarah was in London taking care of a scheduled recording session for a forthcoming CD. His office hadn't phoned. And Mother was on a bridge weekend in Cork. James suddenly felt a free man in more ways than one. Throwing a few items in a small bag, he locked up the flat and headed in his car for Kilmartin. He sped through the mist cloaking the coastline.

Yes, it was evident from Jack's management of his estate that he had had a plan. It was evident that he knew he was dying and his time was short. He had returned to Ireland, to Kilmartin, his childhood home, the scene of all the gravest events of his life. That, too, must have been part of his strategy. And it was in Kilmartin that he had been murdered.

Questions formed in his mind of their own volition. Jack presumably knew that Mike Walsh's death had never been resolved. Yet he took the chance of returning. Perhaps that accounted for his putting his money in a cache? Jack would know that a great deal of money would be of help to him—either in eluding the consequences of his past actions in his youth or perhaps in facing them. James wondered if he had returned home to Kilmartin to confess, to cleanse himself in some way of the sin of Mike Walsh's death before he himself died. Had he in mind to confess to the police in Kilmartin? Or perhaps to deal with the Walshes directly, perhaps even compensating them financially? All he had to do was write a very substantial check, and he could still leave millions as an inheritance.

Or had he decided to confront Violet and settle the past with her? Only Violet, himself, and Kathleen would have known of Sarah's existence. He and Violet may have dismissed Kathleen, believing that she had been living all this time in Australia.

Was it then possible that Violet *had* killed Jack? Had he told Violet that it was to Sarah that he was leaving his fortune? Could Violet have figured that no one but the two of them would ever know about the survival of the baby daughter? Jack could have explained the terms of the will, and Violet might have struck him down, knowing that if she weren't caught, she would inherit Jack's money. Knowing that although Rose and Lily would also inherit, she was powerful enough to control them and, through them, their share of the money.

Somehow that didn't ring true for James, despite, or perhaps because of, the amount of money involved. Violet had not yet impressed him as a woman greedy for cash. She didn't need millions to preserve her farm or increase its agricultural value. And would she have killed to prevent Jack's money from leaving her control to go to some girl in her twenties with a life of her own? And if Jack didn't tell her he was dying, she wouldn't have seen even this as an imminent threat.

James's head was throbbing. He needed a better picture of Violet Moore than he now had. He needed to flesh out the image. Something was missing, and he believed that the whole story was still in Kilmartin. And he had decided on who best to ask.

"Mr. Sweeney. It's Fleming, James Fleming . . ." James hesitated, not sure if Sweeney recognized him as he peered up distractedly from his ledger book. James was relieved to see that he looked fit and spry and none the worse for his ordeal with the IRA.

"Fleming? Do you want a paper . . . Oh my goodness! James Fleming. Of course! Very nice to see you again."

They shook hands warmly.

"Can I help you with something?"

"I think that you might, Mr. Sweeney. If you could spare me a little time, I'd like to ask you a few questions about the old days?" James was conscious that a customer had entered the shop.

Sweeney grew momentarily flustered. "Oh dear, let me see. Yes, you go through to the back, yes, just go around there between the meat slicer and the phone booth, then through that doorway. I'll be with you shortly."

James took the liberty of putting on the kettle, so when Mr. Sweeney entered the small, cheerful room he was able to sit down to a big mug of tea. Sweeney inquired carefully as to how the case was going, and James let the conversation take its own course, listening as Sweeney spoke of Violet and how, in recent weeks, she seemed to be fading before their eyes, those few of the locals who had even glimpsed her.

"Eileen tells me that she's sure she's lost at least a stone in weight. That's never a good sign, my boy. And Brendan made a delivery up at the house recently—something unheard of since my father's day. And now that the mail doesn't come through here any longer, we can't keep track, er . . . have another cup of tea?"

James realized abruptly that he had noticed a change in the shop as he had passed through. The glass and steel cage was gone. He understood the sadness that Sweeney felt. He knew the old man could only see such a decision by the postal authorities as a reflection on himself, instead of laying the blame on the bastards who had committed the crime.

"I will," James said quickly, and moved on to the subject of Violet. "I'm interested in knowing more about Violet Moore as a young woman, and about Jack too. I suppose Eileen would be the one I should talk to, do you think?" James said casually, but he was watching closely for a desired effect.

True to James's expectations, Sweeney bristled, then bustled around the little room with more energy. He fairly slammed the mug in front of James.

"You must do what you think best, of course. But if you're asking me, then I would tell you that Eileen O'Grady wouldn't know as much about those days as she might let on—if you take my meaning?"

"Indeed?"

Encouraged, Sweeney expanded. "Not a'tall! You see, Eileen, for one thing, she wasn't in our parish. She attends chapel. And for another, she was younger than our general set. And for another"—Sweeney was becoming animated—"she wasn't even *in* our set. Do you read me now?" He peered intently at James, and James saw a humorous image of Brendan peering in just such a manner.

"I do indeed, and I thank you for steering me rightly. But then . . ." James paused. Sweeney smiled into his mug. "Perhaps you could help me?" said James.

"Well, that depends."

"On what?" James said, truly puzzled.

"On what you'd like to know," Sweeney said pleasantly, at ease now that he had the reins back in his own hands.

"I just want a—let's say—a picture of those times, that year before Jack Moore went away from Kilmartin, for example."

"You know, Fleming," said Sweeney, taking yet another Ginger Nut biscuit and a second banana to slice onto his small side plate, *"that* I can do, because it's a funny thing, but I can remember that time better than I could tell you what happened in the shop yesterday. They were good times in many ways. Although I mightn't have said that then.

"I had just returned to the village to take over the shop. I missed Dublin very much at first, but by that year we're speaking of, I had begun to settle down. I had married, and Brendan was a very bonny baby on his mother's knee. The shop was doing a roaring trade, and I had bought the house where you visited me. Mrs. Sweeney and I were very happy and got out and about quite a bit. Not to the pub, you understand, but to all the socials and the barn dances and the bonfires. Traveling dinners were all the rage then too."

He smiled at James's blank face. "They were great fun. It all had to be worked out beforehand amongst the people in a certain crowd. One home would host cocktails, another would host the first course—you know, soup and bread rolls—another would do the main course, and another the pudding and coffee. We'd all go together in cars, on tractors, on horses even, rushing around from one house to another. I see you think it sounds a bit mad, but I assure you it was fun, at least to us. The world wasn't so sophisticated then, if that's what you'd call it.

"Violet used to do her bit, though never the main course. But she'd often have the coffee and pudding

201

stage of the event. People tended to linger over that one since it marked the end of the evening. She didn't seem to mind, now that I think of it. Although she was not terribly social then or now. She was polite but always kept her distance. Rose thoroughly enjoyed these things. She used to go with Lily to the barn dances too. Now, that's something Violet would never do. Poor Rose. There were many nights I'd leave Mrs. Sweeney and give Rose a dance out of kindness. A good few of the married chaps used to do that . . . oh, pardon me!"

Mr. Sweeney bustled out to the front of the shop to attend to the two customers who had been discreetly coughing and clearing their throats. James smiled at the simplicity and courtesy of life in Kilmartin, and stretched out in the dilapidated armchair. His thoughts drifted. He liked listening to Sweeney, and somehow the urgency of his quest became lessened. He leaned back and assured his conscience that he was acquiring background material.

"Having a bit of a snooze then, Fleming?"

James heard Sweeney's voice from afar and stirred himself.

"Not to worry. I've made you another mug of tea. Dear me, now where was I?"

James realized that Sweeney was enjoying talking about the past as much as he enjoyed listening. "Barn dances, I think . . ." said James.

"Indeed. But we were more active than that too, during those years. We used to go beagling. Ever done it? Great fun. All of us clad in our boots, running through fields after those yipping dogs, miles ahead of us, of course. Chasing some poor fox or rabbit. We never let them attack. They'd tree their prey or run it to ground, depending on what it was, you see. But we never liked blood sports in our set. None of us rode to hounds for example. Although of course we all knew how to ride.

"You know who was a great rider? Gerald Fitzgerald. We used to say he was born on a horse. He's younger than I, but I quite clearly remember him as a young lad, riding without a saddle up here to the shop to pick up something for his mother. Of course in those days this wasn't the racetrack of a road that it is now.

"Yes, all through his boyhood he was a great rider. Did well at the gymkhanas too. And every weekend that he was down from Trinity, and even after he'd passed the bar, he'd always go for a ride, first thing in the morning, last thing before the daylight faded. He had great natural strength—ran in the family."

James smiled, trying to picture the present Gerald Fitzgerald on a horse.

"I haven't seen Gerald in years. Of course, I always knew when he'd come down to the manor to handle Violet's legal business. And I often wondered why he never called in here to the shop." He reached for another Ginger Nut. "Tell me, Fleming, why has Gerald been so absent during all this excitement with Violet and her family? I must admit I'm curious."

"Curious?" James glanced up quickly.

"Well, considering how close he and Lily were in those days."

"Close?"

"Mmm . . ." Sweeney hesitated. "Now that Mrs. Fitzgerald is gone, I suppose it's all right to speak of it. Yes, Lily and he were very thick at one time. Virtually engaged. She was the only reason he'd visit Kilmartin after he'd become established in Dublin. We all could see that. He came down frequently, and it wasn't only to see his family. He and Lily were great at the barn dances—both fine dancers. A pleasure to watch. As was watching Lily blossom. She was quite pretty in those days, in a delicate way, and she fairly bloomed then. We were all waiting for the banns to be read out at church—we were that sure!"

"Except for Violet?" said James, hardly believing his ears.

"Indeed. We could also see that she wasn't exactly urging on the match. She'd snub Gerald whenever they met. I think I remember that she was violently rude to him at the house and he stopped going there. That made it a bit awkward for Lily. It wasn't the done thing for her to go off in his car—when he got his fine new car. But they'd walk the lanes and the fields. We'd all see them of a summer night. And they'd meet at other people's houses. She didn't go over to his home much . . . well, it was his parents' home. They didn't take kindly to Gerald being made unwelcome at the Moores', and probably retaliated in like manner."

James's heart was pounding. "What happened in the end?"

"Hard to say. It just seemed to dwindle. Gerald came down less often. Lily seemed to shrivel up over that year. She got thinner and quieter. I don't think it was a big blowout. Gerald's parents died then—within two years of each other. Gerald sold the house and farm, at a loss. A lot of it was bought up by Violet, I might add. He and Lily saw less and less of each other. We all had our suspicions, of course. Most of us believed that Violet had succeeded in coming between them. We thought it was too bad. It's only since I've grown older that I realized it was more than too bad, it was in fact tragic for poor Lily.

"Mrs. Sweeney, now, rest her soul, she could have told you more. But what I do recall is that in the following spring Gerald came down and Lily had gone off—to France, I think it was—on holiday. She hadn't told him. We heard he was terribly put out, and shortly thereafter he stopped coming. And that was the end. He married up in Dublin. And poor Lily, well, as you see, she never did marry.

"It was sad for all of them. Jack Moore missed him. He was just a lad in those days, but he'd taken a great liking to Gerald. He was like the father or the brother Jack never had. Living up there amongst all those women! He and Gerald used to ride together, I remember. Mmm. Jack was very despondent around that time. I saw a change in him when Gerald stopped coming. Like the rest of us, he probably thought Gerald and Lily would marry and there'd be a bit of life, a bit of *family* life, around the place. Ahh me . . . Violet's a hard woman."

James hoped that Mr. Sweeney believed his story when he made his departure so abruptly. It *was* conceivable he had forgotten an important client meeting. If he were a dolt!

He wasn't sure himself why he had felt compelled to leave. But he did know that he needed time to think, to fully grasp the information that Sweeney had sprung on him.

Why indeed hadn't Gerald been personally handling this case, considering the relationship he had with the family—with Lily? Sweeney's question had been a good one.

James calmed down as he drove. It was Violet who was in trouble. Not Lily. Now, if Lily had been on trial, the question would have been truly valid.

He'd been overreacting. Gerald hadn't been holding out on him after all! Hadn't Gerald told him that he wouldn't have worked well with Violet, stating that he'd always found her difficult? Gerald had merely omitted how difficult! He'd married and made his life in Dublin. And perhaps he still did occasional legal work for the Moores over the years—not out of friendship for Violet, but out of remembered fondness for Lily.

James sighed. He had thought the answer to everything lay in Kilmartin. Everything that Jack had seemingly done had been drawn to that fine point, that single focus. And yet?

Jack hadn't gone directly to Kilmartin. He could have. His flight from London had landed at nine-thirty A.M. at Dublin Airport. Allowing for travel time, that would place him in Dublin center at around eleven A.M. Why hadn't he gone directly to Kilmartin that morning? Why hadn't he rented a car at the airport and gone straight there? If Kilmartin was his ultimate goal, and ironically, where he met his ultimate end, what had held him in Dublin? James thought rapidly. He couldn't remember the details he now needed. What time exactly had Jack Moore checked into the Shelbourne? Had he mentioned how long he'd be staying? Why did he break his journey and go to the trouble of checking in? He hadn't phoned anyone, at least from his room. That had already been checked. Perhaps he had stayed in Dublin, unsure of his welcome in Kilmartin. Maybe the transatlantic flight had tired him out? It made sense. Or maybe it was the Shelbourne Hotel and not Kilmartin that held the key?

Back in Dublin that evening, James stood up from a small writing table and walked over to the window. He pulled aside the curtain and looked out on the darkness that shrouded St. Stephen's Green. The park was locked. The black wrought-iron railings glistened, their outline picked up in the amber light of the street lamps. He glanced to the left, seeing with an inner eye his own darkened office in Fitzgerald's firm, in the building that lay diagonally across the Green. He glanced down to see the people scurrying, heads shielded by umbrellas, at this hour perhaps rushing to the Gaiety Theatre two blocks away, or to stand in the long line outside the Green Cinema. He pictured the College Club just a few doors up the street on the same side as the hotel. It would be virtually empty now. He thought fondly of Matt. Ordinary life seemed so distant. His office, the club, so near at hand, yet he seemed cut off from them by more than the thick panes of his window and the tiny white decorative balcony that clad that window on the outside.

He glanced around the hotel room. It had been an absolute fluke that the room Jack Moore had taken at the Shelbourne Hotel on the fateful day was actually vacant. The clerk hadn't even shown surprise when James had requested the room by number. Perhaps lots of visitors had favorite rooms. This room certainly was magnificent; its style was heavy, with dark mahogany furniture and Georgian prints of Dublin in gold frames against the dull green matte walls. Drapes of gold fabric dressed the two high, sash windows that offered an impressive view of the Green and of the city and the mountains beyond.

James dropped the curtain and cut himself off further from the outside world. He walked back to the desk and read what had taken him the last few hours in the quiet of this room to put down on paper. Each page bore the name of a person. He drew in his breath and read over what he'd written.

Under the name of Jack Moore he had listed:

· Knew he was dying.
· Consolidated his fortune.
· Designed a will that left the fortune to his natural daughter.

Therefore, it follows:

· He knew of the present identity and whereabouts of his daughter.

Questions:

· Had he contacted Kathleen Walsh about their daughter?
· Had he contacted investigators to locate her?
· Had he contacted Violet or Lily or Rose?

James sighed. And how could he establish if Jack had done any of this? He sat down and underscored the next few points.

· Jack had come to the Shelbourne Hotel, to this room, to meet someone?

- To contact someone?
- Who?

James wrote on the paper what he believed. The turning point in Jack's plan was connected with the hotel. He wrote the word Hotel with a question mark. Was it the location of *this* hotel? Could it have been any Dublin hotel? James set the paper aside and looked at the next name, Lily, and listing.

- Lily hated Violet enough to lie. Motive? Revenge?
- Possible other motive: Lily knew about Jack's will and wanted Violet out of the way. Violet as a convicted murderer would lose all rights of property and inheritance. So Lily would inherit Jack's fortune, with Rose.
- Lily knew about the will.
- Lily did not know about Sarah.

James canceled those lines. How could Lily know about the will or about Sarah? Unless Jack had told her? James wrote this possible idea down on the paper and moved to the next. Violet.

- Knew about Jack's visit.
- Knew about the will.
- Knew about Sarah.
- Had the physical strength to stab Jack.

James paused. Why was it he could accept Violet stabbing her brother and not Lily? Because Lily had loved Jack in a way Violet had not. He groaned inwardly. He didn't *know* that. What was missing here? He felt it nagging him, and the nagging was familiar. He pictured Violet stabbing Jack in the barn . . . That was it! The hearse.

He took a new sheet of paper and labeled it "Hearse." Of course. That was still the unanswered question. It was the question that had bothered him most at the start of this whole mess all those—what now felt like years—months ago!

He stared at the paper, and then wrote quickly.

· Where did the hearse come from?
· Sinclair was sure it was a Dublin car.

He jotted down from his own notebook the description of the car.

· Had Violet hired the hearse?
· If not Violet, who hired it?

He wrote Hearse at the bottom of Violet's page and moved on to the next. The Walshes.

· The brothers hated Jack, planned to kill him, and had hired the hearse.
· Therefore it followed they were in contact with Jack and knew his movements.
· Therefore it followed that Jack had contacted them. Had he arranged to meet them at the Shelbourne?

James smiled at his mental picture of the four Walshes in the elegant lobby of the hotel. No, they would have operated on their own turf.

· Kathleen was in constant contact with Jack over the years, and also knew of Sarah's existence. She wanted his inheritance for her child and plotted with her brothers to kill him.

James paused in wonder at what he'd written some hours before. He pictured Kathleen Walsh's face as he'd seen it in London. As a young girl she'd hated Violet Moore. And she hated her now as an adult even more. But her fear had been genuine. He saw again that look of pleading, asking James not to betray her, not to destroy her life with her doctor husband and her two sons. No. James shook his head. No way. But the combination of greed and hatred was lethal—it could make anybody do anything.

"God!" James said aloud and stood up. It seemed he was capable of suspecting everyone. He felt corrupted and tainted and in need of fresh air. He glanced at the clock. It was near midnight, and he was no closer to a solution. No, he'd work on—all night if he had to. He knew the solution was in front of him, but he couldn't see it. He rang down for a bottle of Black Bush and a basket of ham sandwiches. While he waited, he took a quick shower and changed back into the clothes he'd been wearing, feeling fresher and revived.

The whiskey was good. The sandwiches were good. He took up the next piece of paper.

It was blank. James yawned. He brought the paper and pen over to the queen-sized bed and lay down. He kicked off his shoes and leaned back, and in the best tradition of tired solicitors, slept on the problem.

The doorman was only too happy to talk to James. He would have done so, he insisted, even without the generous tip. Yes, he'd spoken to the poor dead Yank, before he was dead, you understand. He remembered him because of his American clothes, very good quality they were, and understated too. He'd seen lots of Yanks and every other type of foreigner. Mr. Moore, yes, from the newspaper reports. Mr. Moore had stopped on the step for a chat. Nothing important. The usual palaver about the weather. It had been sunny, and so, worthy of comment. About Dublin and how it had changed and how it hadn't changed. Nothing remarkable. He'd remembered it because he had relations in Wexford, but not anywhere near Kilmartin. Oh, yes, Mr. Moore had left on foot. He'd wanted to hail a cab for him, but Mr. Moore said the day was too fine to waste and he would walk. He hadn't seen him after that, as he'd knocked off work around midday.

James stepped out of the hotel lobby and into the stream of people passing up and down the pavement along Stephen's Green, people rushing to work, as he would have to later that day. Already Gerald would be wondering at his absence. He walked slowly, buffeted by the rush of pedestrians. He began to see this part of Dublin with new eyes, a part of Dublin he thought he knew extremely well.

He continued methodically, glancing at the signs over each and every establishment he passed. Using the hotel as the center of a mental circle, he divided the area into four quadrants. Moving north, away from the Green and nearest the hotel, he scoured what would have been the northwest quadrant. He carried his list of undertakers and car-rental firms culled from the telephone directory. He knew it was not complete. But it was a start. Along the canal, near Herbert Place, he located two of the garages, but neither was open to business yet. Turning back toward the city, away from the canal, he found a large establishment that rented wedding cars and hearses as well as daily car rentals. They were open and looked to be quite busy. Unsure of what to ask them, James reluctantly entered the small front office. But he quickly established that the firm did not have any business dealings in Wexford on the relevant dates. Walking on through the southwest quadrant, James found only one car-rental firm, but it no longer handled hearses.

He took a break and a cup of coffee at Bewley's Oriental Café on Grafton Street, and then could not resist two currant buns. He glanced at the small map he had sketched. This was such a long shot. Jack Moore would not have known Dublin well. Would he have had the patience to walk the streets? James had a second cup of coffee and finally moved on. In the southeast quadrant of his sketch he covered George's Street, and there saw a really fine undertaker's establishment, but it was closed. He was amazed that he'd never noticed these places before now, yet he'd passed all of them hundreds of times in his life as a student and since. Shops and cafés he'd never seen, and pubs he'd never even heard of! He made a second mental list of the ones he wished to return to and investigate —in the company of Matt.

The northeast quadrant yielded very little, so James returned to the first car-rental firm. He stood across the street at a bus stop, but he hadn't long to wait. Within minutes a hearse pulled out of the garage that fronted the street beside the business office. James's heart raced until he saw the car bore no physical resemblance to the hearse Mr. Sinclair had described. It was unlikely they used different styles, he thought, and walked on. He visited three more premises, and having inquired, was able to scratch them off his list. Eventually he was drawn back to the undertaker on George's Street which had been closed earlier. Their office fronted the street, but the garage did not. James hunted around one or two side streets and alleys until at last he located the firm's name on a double door made of wooden slats. He waited, but within seconds realized how conspicuous he was, standing in the narrow alley. He returned to the cross street near Mercer's Hospital and lounged along the railing that surrounded the huge granite-clad building. Mightn't he be waiting for a patient, or better still, for a nurse?

After an interminable wait, during which James read the morning paper and ate a Mars bar, he spotted a hearse moving out of the alley. Very modern, very discreet, sloped hatchback at the rear. He started walking, crossing the narrow street behind the hearse and coming alongside. His eyes grew wide. The silver trim, the filigree—and the opaque windows especially —matched Sinclair's description! The car accelerated as the traffic ahead moved forward. James examined the rear door; its hinges were invisible. No curtains on the windows either. He paused on the pavement as a woman with a huge pram full of damp sheets of wrapping paper bellowed at him: "Two sheets for five pence!" He shook his head, and she shrugged and moved on.

Gathering his wits and putting on what he hoped was the face of a bereaved but distant relative, he hurried back to the undertaker's office and entered the small lobby. A bell rang faintly somewhere in the building, and suddenly a slim pimply-faced young man appeared before him.

"May I help you?" he murmured unctuously, and James was startled.

"Yes," he said brusquely. In his most officious manner, James rapidly described how his uncle by marriage had died the previous night at the Meath Hospital, and that his aunt had her heart set on a very good funeral. The problem was that his uncle had particularly requested a simple coffin—plain pine— nothing fancy. His aunt, not wishing to deny his request, at the same time did not want to be "burying him poor," which would look very bad in front of the neighbors.

The young man bobbed and nodded, alternating sympathetic noises with expressions of interest—this was a delightful challenge indeed. The fact that the conversation revolved on the cost and the style they could offer didn't disturb him in the least.

"The aunt, she's very determined to have the absolute latest type of hearse, the most up-to-date. The very best! To compensate for the coffin, you understand."

The young man nodded earnestly. "I think we may have the very solution to your aunt's predicament."

"Then you know exactly what I want?"

"Indeed and I do. You see, sir, we've gone quite upscale. Now I know the older generation, our 'senior citizens'"—his unctuous voice stressed this American import—"sometimes they want the very latest, and *that* we can give them."

"Well, perhaps I could see what you have to offer," suggested James. "I know what the aunt wants and what she won't abide!"

213

The gaunt young man moved with alacrity, leading James through small rooms and corridors that connected the ancient buildings to each other. They walked along a covered passageway that led ultimately to a small parking lot whose doors opened onto the alley where James had been standing only an hour before. Two more hearses identical to the one he had just seen stood there gleaming. James was shown their features in detail. The young man looked at him expectantly.

"I, of course, see the advantages," James lied blithely. "If only there were some truly unique feature I could mention to my aunt. You see, she's terribly concerned about the neighbors."

"But of course, sir. And rightly so, this is the time in one's life when one must be most concerned with one's neighbors."

James was startled to hear his own accent mimicked so well, so subtly, and yet without the slightest hint of irony. He looked sharply at the young man, who showed no emotion.

"Our selling point with these has been that they are unique in Dublin. If you'll only mention to your aunt that our hearses have completely opaque windows, to prevent the idle onlookers from observing the class of coffin within! No other firm uses them!" he added triumphantly.

James's delight showed on his face as he took the young man's card and promised faithfully to recommend him to his aunt.

Back on the street, he stopped to phone Maggie at the office, hoping his voice, which sounded tired enough, conveyed the extent of his flu.

"Various people were wondering, James." Maggie stressed the word people. "It's been a while since we've seen you."

"Tomorrow, absolutely tomorrow. There's nothing urgent on, is there?"

"Well, I imagine that ten-year-old disputed will you've been working on will keep for yet one more day. No, apart from the Moore case, there's nothing else urgent on your agenda."

Rain was beginning to fall as he left the booth. He took a taxi back to his apartment and changed, grateful to get out of the clothes he had been living in for the past two days. Thrilled with his progress, he still realized there was a nagging problem. The young undertaker had insisted they had not handled any funerals whatsoever in the county of Wexford.

James threw on his raincoat and, taking his black umbrella, drove his very conspicuous car back into the heart of Dublin. There was no way around it. He had to park the car near enough to the alley to see the rear doors of the undertaker's establishment. The wait was a long one. James fed the meter every thirty minutes and shrugged off the looks of the passing policeman. At four-thirty he left the car and stood in the downpour near the mouth of the alley. At a quarter to six he was rewarded by the sight of two young men in their chauffeur's livery locking and padlocking the doors. As they ran down the alley with heads bent, he moved quickly to block their path. They glanced up—fearfully, James thought. He showed them the two ten-pound notes in his hand, and they moved with him across the narrow street and into the Little Brown Jug. The pub was filling with after-work revelers and residents and interns from Mercer's Hospital across the street.

"What's this about, then?" said the elder of the two gruffly.

"Are you the polis?" asked the other in a broad Galway accent.

"No, I'm a solicitor. I've nothing to do with the police. I just need some information, and I will pay well for it. If you can't give it to me, then perhaps you can tell me who could?" He smiled warmly. The two men looked at each other, and the elder one spoke.

"Whadya want to know?"

"Anything you can tell me, maybe about a rich Yank, maybe about a trip to Wexford?" James looked expectantly at each of them. He couldn't give too much away, but at the same time he had to let them think that he already knew quite a lot.

"And you'll pay?" said the older youth.

James showed him a wad of notes.

"And you're not the polis?"

James shook his head and ordered three pints of stout. When the drinks came, he put a fifty-pound note under the glasses. The elder one drank and took up the money.

"The polis were already around. They talked to old man Ellis. He told them the truth. This firm has not had any calls down to Wexford—ever. You know this outfit, they only handle the Dublin swells."

"I understand that part. But what can *you* tell me? A Yank came to see you, didn't he? Much like I did just now. Am I right?"

"Yeah, only it was in the afternoon, see. The other two cars were out. We was just hangin' about. Nothin' was on, but we stay in case there's a call to a hospital or the morgue, you know, or a house for that matter." The younger man spoke rapidly, nervously.

"Shut your mouth. I'll do the tellin'."

He shriveled into his corner and drank his pint, watching with huge eyes. He was very young indeed. The elder slid the money into his hand.

James ordered again and put a second fifty pounds under his own glass.

The older youth spoke again.

"This Yank, he comes up to us and sez, like, he wants to play a great practical joke on his family. I knew he had lots of the foldin' stuff by the way he was dressed, like. So he sez he's home on 'holiers' from the States and that his crew of spinster sisters were alus after 'im. He sez he wants to give them a right fright an' make them see sense. He's roarin' laffin', talkin' to us." The youth smiled at the memory of it. "Jaysus, we thought it was a great gag to pull off and sez we'll help 'im. He said he wanted it to be all cloak and dagger stuff and no one was to know and could we pull it off. We sez surely. You see, like, me and him, we keep the keys to the lock-up when we leave at night. We work such godawful hours that we're back here at the crack of dawn. And old Ellis, he trusts us like." He looked sharply at James.

"No doubt." James smiled and moved the fifty pounds toward the center of the now dripping table. Brown sworls of Guinness stout soaked into the thin green paper.

"We was to take one of them hearses and drive it to the Phoenix Park, near the obelisk. He said we'd see a box there. We were to take it and drive to an address down in Wexford, a place called Kilmartin, and leave it on the doorstep of this big house. He said he'd pay us two hundred quid. He was full of the joys, laffin' and jokin'. A nice man, sir, a nice man. For a Yank." His voice fell.

"We took his two hundred quid, and that night we did as we was bid. When we got to the obelisk, there was the box—"

"You mean a coffin?"

"Yes, a wooden one, one of the old-style ones. It was on the grass, and there wasn't a soul around, not even the prossies. I was glad for that. O' course it was pouring with rain. We put the box in the back. It was heavy enough, and nailed shut. We didn't look into it since it was nailed tight. Nor did we see a livin' soul around the place. We stood for a bit, but no one came out to us from the shrubs like. So . . ." He took a swig of his pint and lifted the money. The younger one's hand shot forward and folded it into his own palm. The elder shrugged. And ordered again.

"He was a man of honor, sir. A man of honor," said the younger of the two. "The next day we got the rest of the money. Two hundred more quid. A messenger came here—to the back of the premises, I mean. You know, one of them lads on the motor scooters, a courier they're called. He gave us an envelope, 'Jim and Joe' was all that was written on it—that's us, right? Two hundred quid. A man of his word he was." He sighed.

"Did you deliver the box?"

"O' course. Whadya tink we are? We did as we was bid," said the elder. "We'd had a bit o' trouble down in Kilmartin, finding the house. It was breaking daylight when we dumped the box. We fair sped out of that place. We had to get the car back, y'see. And wash it down so's Ellis wouldn't have hint nor hair of what we'd been doin' in the night." He leaned back. "And he didn't. We pulled that off and made us'selfs four hundred quid . . ."

"Less the petrol?" added the second youth.

"Right. Bizarre, that's what I call it. Bizarre." He stressed the first syllable.

"And that was it?" The mood was affable, amiable now. The pints and the pounds were having good effect.

"It was. Until we read of it on the papers. The polis were 'round like a shot. They didn't question us, just old Ellis, but natural like, he mentioned it to us. Bizarre, he sez to us, and we agreed."

"You didn't come forward with what you knew?"

"And lose our jobs!" the younger lad fairly shrieked.

James nodded with understanding.

"He was dead, wasn't he? The poor old sod. Just like a Yank. Come home, splash the money around and get hisself murthered."

James didn't attempt to follow this logic, but it seemed to console both of the hearse drivers.

"And you told no one?"

"Hey," said the bigger man, "didn't we say we gave the Yank our word? We told no one. Just like he said. And he paid us well, he did that." He eyed James over his glass.

James took out another fifty pounds and stood up.

"A man of honor, he was. He'd give the Yanks a

good name, he would, a man of honor. Just like us," he added, a bit slurred.

"Indeed," said James. "Well, have a drink to his memory, then." He nodded and moved quickly off into the crowd, but they made no move to follow him.

James walked slowly back to the car. He'd lost his umbrella, but he took no notice of the rain, delighted as he was to be vindicated at last.

"I said from the beginning it was the hearse," he told his car, whose window was now blanketed with tickets. He sped back to his flat.

A few phone calls and the stage would finally be set.

—— *Chapter Twelve* ——

James spotted Sarah Gallagher before she saw him. She was seated on one of the comfortable floral-covered sofas in the front lounge of the Berkeley Court. He wasn't the only one to have seen her. He stood leaning with his back against one of the pillars, watching as she spoke briefly but sweetly to the middle-aged couple who were obviously asking for her autograph. When two young women approached on the same errand, he intervened.

"Sarah?" he said quietly as she scribbled her name on the hotel brochures the girls had handed her. She looked up questioningly, and an expression of delight passed across her face. She stood up then and said good-bye to the girls.

"James," she whispered as she put her hand on his arm, pressing it.

"I am so sorry for being late. Something urgent had to be taken care of—at the office."

"It's all right, darling, you're not very late. I'm just so glad to see you."

"Shall we have a drink in the bar before dinner?"

"Certainly," she said simply.

James was proud to be walking by her side. She was dressed in a linen suit of pale blue, her favorite color, a shade that flattered her ivory skin. Her dark brown hair was pulled back in a simple chignon at the nape of her neck. And the style suited her oval face and striking features. She walked with an easy grace, with the gait of a natural dancer. He was conscious of people noticing them, and not only because they might have recognized her as the famous violinist. He knew they made an exceptionally handsome couple. She linked his arm with hers as they walked, and he shivered, thinking fleetingly of what it would be like to be walking down the aisle of some small church with Sarah as his bride. He glanced at her face. She didn't look at all like Kathleen Walsh. But shaken by that momentary thought, he pushed it away, back to the depths where he had buried it.

They both ordered gin and tonics with lots of ice and lemon. The day had been surprisingly hot for the end of April. Dubliners had been strewn about the grassy lawns of Stephen's Green and along the banks of the canal, lying prone and unselfconscious under the welcome heat of the sun. Like young children, they lounged at their ease, shoes kicked off, jackets thrown aside, trousers and sleeves rolled up, as if they'd just discovered sunshine. The mood of the city was a holiday mood, happy, carefree. In contrast to his own, thought James sadly.

"You're unusually quiet, James," Sarah said, her low tones like a balm to his ears.

"Am I? I apologize."

"Don't apologize. You can be yourself with me, whatever self that happens to be, on whatever day it happens to be." She smiled into his face as he blushed slightly.

They ate a very light supper of smoked salmon, a salmon mousse, some very delicate pâté of liver, and

221

thinly sliced brown bread. James had ordered a bottle of light chilled chablis. They chose a fresh fruit bowl and sorbet for dessert, and a bottle of chilled liebfrau-milch.

It was an extremely pleasant meal, and James listened intently to Sarah's description of her recording sessions in London, which had gone on for some days. But he watched her face even more intently, noting every expression, memorizing how she held her spoon, the sophisticated way in which she delicately held her fluted wineglass.

"James, although you look as though you are hanging on my every word, I don't believe you've heard a single one of them," Sarah said, laughing, but with a question in her voice.

"Oh, no, I've heard everything you've said. I just love watching you say it!" It was Sarah's turn to blush. She glanced away at the other guests in the dining room. There was a low, pleasant murmur of happy voices, with faint recorded music mingling in. James lightly touched her hand as it rested on the white tablecloth. She interlocked her fingers with his. It was then that they both sensed that somehow this night was different, the mood was different between them. There was a shared sweetness, a tenderness, a sadness almost.

They drove in comfortable silence to Dun Laoghaire. James parked the car and they walked the length of the south pier, merely chatting, holding hands just like the other hundred or so couples who passed them. The heat of the day had freshened with an offshore breeze, light and cooling. Young families were there with babies in strollers, older couples with their spinster daughters, men of all ages who walked briskly and alone. Yes, there was a Sunday feeling about the place, a holiday feeling on the long curving granite pier that thrust itself out into the Irish sea.

A few boats bobbed at their moorings. And as inevitable as the tide, the nine o'clock ferry for Wales sounded its whistle at a quarter to the hour. A signal of departure, a symbol of partings and of new beginnings. They watched in silence until the ferry was out of sight, and James felt again the primeval soothing quality of the sound and the sight of the lapping waves. They stood a long time at the very end of the south pier, until almost everyone else but the fishing enthusiasts had turned back. They were alone at last. Sarah was still silent.

"Sarah?" James said, looking at last into her lovely face. "I love you."

"I know, James. I think I love you too," she said in return.

They didn't kiss. The moment seemed too full, too tender. James had tears in his eyes and he almost sighed with relief. Sarah leaned her head on his chest and he folded her in his arms as gently as though she would break if he pressed too tightly. And so they stood until the stars began to brighten in the now darkening sky.

Eventually they returned to the car. Initially James had thought they would go to an old pub he knew in the Dublin Mountains, which on such rare, warm days as this, placed tables outside its doors. The shabby little pub commanded a magnificent view of the city of Dublin and the sea that surrounded it. On summer nights the white and amber lights of the city would flicker and shimmer through the evening mist, rendering the city a magical place always. But somehow now James didn't feel it was right. As he turned the car toward Monkstown, Sarah nodded, wordlessly answering his unspoken question.

When they parked in front of her parents' house, he knew she wouldn't ask him in. They sat holding hands like two lovestruck children. Then she kissed him lightly, lingeringly, sweetly on the lips. He stroked her hair for one brief moment and then cupped her face in his hands, memorizing its every lineament.

"Sarah," he whispered hoarsely, "whatever happens, please remember that I love you as I have never loved anyone before. And never will again."

"James, I'll see you tomorrow night . . ." she started to say with a question in her voice. "Won't I?"

He kissed her quickly on the tip of her nose. "Go now. Go quickly."

She got out of the car and ran as lightly as a child toward the house, and like a child, she didn't look back. As James put the car in gear, he whispered his final farewell and watched until the door closed.

He drove for a long time, up into the mountains till he reached Killakee, then turned swiftly into the Featherbed that ran the ridge of the Sally Gap. The road, lit by a half-moon, was deserted, and he cruised through the dark, reviewing in his mind what had just transpired and what this very long day had meant for him.

When he had got to the office early that morning, Gerald had already arrived. Within seconds he had buzzed for James. James had sensed his annoyance, but didn't acknowledge it. Briefly, he outlined what he had learned in Boston, his conversation with Jack Moore's doctor, his conversation with Solomon the lawyer, including the news of Jack's immense fortune and the Swiss bank account. He had watched to see Gerald's reaction to the size of Jack's estate, but Gerald merely grunted.

At that point Gerald had said, "And the will, James? All this is very well, but I sent you out to Boston to get a copy of the will."

James handed the papers to Gerald and watched his face surreptitiously. But nothing remarkable showed there.

"Well, it is an unusual document, to say the least," Gerald said at last.

"I haven't seen anything like it in my experience," commented James, and his experience was considerable.

"Mmm, no, I'm sure."

He had spent close to two hours with Gerald, who had been quite annoyed that he had failed to turn up at the office on Monday or Tuesday. But James had not offered any excuses.

As James stood up to leave, Gerald added, almost as an afterthought, "Violet and Lily and Rose are in for quite a surprise."

"Surprise?" James said casually.

"Well, I don't believe they have any idea of the extent of Jack's holdings. I don't think they have even considered that they would stand to inherit anything."

"Personally, I don't think it's even crossed their minds. But I'm glad you mentioned it. I phoned Violet last night from my flat . . ."

Gerald looked up in surprise.

"You see, Gerald, even though I was recovering from the flu or jet lag or whatever it was, I was still working," James said lightly, laughing in his usual way. "I told her," he went on quickly, "that I needed to speak to her, and to Lily and Rose as well. And I indicated that it has to do with Jack's will. I'll need to start probating, you know, or the firm will, since as their solicitors, it's our job. And Gerald, I'd like to start as soon as possible, because this will be new territory to me."

"How so?" Gerald was sharp.

"Well, for a start, I imagine I'll need to seek precedents, I don't know how complicated the American tax situation will be. I need to establish if he can be viewed as an Irish citizen residing abroad. He had American citizenship, you see. And I'll need to read up on the Swiss banking laws. You know, I've never handled anything quite like this. I might have to ask for an extra clerk to do some legwork for me, if that's all right with you, Gerald."

"I suppose so. Take that new girl, Miriam. She's bright and she's expressed an interest in inheritance law already. It will be good experience for her."

"There's another favor I want to ask of you. I'd like you to accompany me when I go to see the Moores tomorrow. I made the appointment for five because I thought later in the working day might suit you better. I took the liberty of checking your appointment book." James held his breath for the answer.

"You seem to be taking matters into your own hands of late. What do you need me down there for?"

"My feeling is that the will and its contents will be a shock to them. And that the amount of money involved might merit the presence of the head of the firm. And, I might add, it would give *me* a bit of confidence too. Violet tends to treat me as though I were still wet behind the ears."

There was a long pause. Finally Gerald assented. "All right. Let me know in the morning what time you intend to leave. I expect we'll make better time in your outrageous car than in mine."

"Right, I'll get back to you."

James recalled how he had literally sagged against the door to his office once he was safely inside. All the wheels were in motion now. There could be no turning back.

His head was clearer as he turned his car for home. A good night's sleep was essential. He dreaded the drive alone tomorrow with Gerald, but trusted that if they kept to the other cases the small law firm was engaged on, the time might pass quickly enough. Yes, he would be very, very glad when tomorrow was over.

They had only been waiting a few seconds on the granite front step of the Moores' fine manor house when the heavy door swung open and revealed Kevin smiling warmly.

"Mr. Fleming, it's good to see you again." Kevin shook hands with Gerald as James introduced them, Kevin's face showing the proper awe at meeting the famous Kilmartin solicitor. Gerald nodded noncommittally, and looked surprised as Kevin accompanied the two of them into Violet's sitting room.

The three sisters were having tea. Violet, cup in hand, was standing by the unlit fireplace, its empty grate supporting a huge array of lilac sprays. She nodded at Gerald and James but did not greet them. Rose, seated at the low table, also nodded, and smiled shyly.

"Tea? Mr. Fleming? And you, Gerald, it's been so long since we've seen you." Rose poured two more cups of tea, which Kevin handed to the two men.

Lily, who had been standing at the window and had obviously seen them drive up to the house, finally moved from her place and approached them.

"Do sit down, Gerald," she said softly, barely glancing at him. "And you too, Mr. Fleming." She herself sat in one of the wing chairs that faced slightly away from them and toward Violet.

There was a heavy, uncomfortable pause. James waited.

"Well, Violet, Lily, Rose," Gerald finally said, as he shifted his weight on the small straight-backed chair. He nodded at each in turn. "I think my colleague, James, would . . ." He glanced at James, who was busy reaching for another piece of tea cake. "James would like me to conduct our business here today. As you know, we had assumed that Jack, your brother, must have left a will. It only stood to reason that a man of his financial astuteness would have done so. Or have been forced to by a sensible American lawyer." Gerald attempted a laugh at his own slight witticism.

He continued, "It seems our assumptions were right. Jack did indeed leave a will. Investigation revealed that it was in the States, in Boston, and James went out to get a copy of it. We did this since we were acting on your behalf as your solicitors. Now I must inform you about the will. But I'd like to also mention that I, we, at the firm would be happy to continue in our capacity and would, as a result, like to begin the process of probating the will . . ." Violet stared at him in astonishment. "That is," Gerald coughed slightly, "just as soon as Violet is acquitted at her trial, which of course I fully believe will be the outcome of this unfortunate business.

"Now, to the matter in hand . . ." Gerald paused to reach by his side for his briefcase. While he did so, and unlocked it and took out a sheaf of papers, all but Gerald heard the front door bell ringing. Kevin left the room wordlessly, glancing only at James.

Gerald looked up. "I'm glad that young man chose to leave. I was surprised you allowed him to be present . . . this information is very much for your ears and eyes only."

"Then may I see it, Gerald? For God's sake, you're making a mountain out of a molehill . . . as usual!" Violet's voice was icy. She strode across the room with her hand extended. Gerald stood up abruptly, glaring at her.

"Violet, if you don't mind. There are three of you involved. Or have you chosen to forget about Lily and Rose—as always!"

The argument was interrupted as Kevin yet again opened the sitting-room door. Gerald swung around, on the point of speaking, when James put a hand on his arm.

"Mr. Fleming?" said Kevin, looking from one man to the other. "Inspector O'Shea has arrived . . ."

And O'Shea followed Kevin into the room, shedding his light coat as he did so. Gerald's mouth opened in astonishment. All eyes looked from O'Shea to James, who took a silent and very deep breath.

"Fleming! What is the meaning of this? Did you know O'Shea was coming? Quite obviously you did—I can tell from your expression." Gerald was livid.

Violet stepped back from her confrontation with Gerald, eyeing O'Shea and visibly trembling.

"Please. Please be seated. I know that we are here certainly to discuss Jack Moore's will. But there were one or two matters that I wished to clear up at this time. Certain knowledge . . . No, let me say I have come across certain information very relevant to Violet Moore's case. And I wanted all of you together when I brought it to your attention . . ."

228

"This is outrageous," spluttered Gerald. "Fleming, you got me down here on some bloody ruse—"

"But the will—"

"The will my foot, man! I don't like this subterfuge on your part, no matter what the outcome. Fleming, you're fired!"

James winced, but continued after a moment, "Please, Gerald, it would be better if you were here to discuss the issues. I am not leaving. Whether I'm in your employ or not, I must discharge my duty." He glanced at Violet. "Miss Moore, perhaps we could all have some brandy?"

Violet wordlessly waved to Kevin, hardly removing her eyes from James's face. Kevin quickly served large measures of brandy to all but Rose, who continued knitting as though oblivious to her surroundings. Lily stood up to take her glass and positioned herself behind Violet, who was now seated. Gerald at last sat down and drank his brandy slowly, eyeing James and O'Shea.

The mood of tension had lessened slightly, and James continued with more confidence.

"I think perhaps the best way to deal with all I have to say is to tell you a story, a narrative in which I have attempted to fit all of the events, all of the personalities, all of the information that I have.

"This story, which I believe had its roots in years and generations gone by, has its origin with three sisters and a brother. Violet, Lily, Rose. And their brother Jack.

"When they inherited this farm on the death of their mother, Violet—being the eldest, and perhaps the most strong willed, at that time at least—took over the running of the farm, and yes, the running of her siblings' lives.

"Violet had one single goal: to hold on to the property and improve it in every way. She had little time for her family, less time for a social life, and no time for men." James paused and sipped his brandy as Violet stared at him in silent fury.

"Obsessed by her goal, she failed to note that her sisters and brother did not entirely share her, let us say . . . single-minded enthusiasm.

"Lily and Jack . . . and Rose too"—James looked kindly at Rose, who had looked up gratefully when he added her name—"they wanted what the rest of the world might term a more normal life. They too wished for the farm to prosper, but not at the expense of the rest of their lives. Lily? Lily had wanted to marry and have a family. Rose, who, I think, might not have looked for marriage herself, at the same time wanted Lily to marry. And Jack too."

"In fact, Lily had a number of suitors. Violet worked hard to discourage all of them. But there was one, one young man who was more persistent, more tenacious, and, I believe, more in love with her than the others. A young man from the locality who had made up his mind to leave the difficult life of farming and who made a great success of his chosen profession, the practice of law." James glanced at Lily, who was watching Gerald. "I know now that that young man who loved Lily Moore was Gerald Fitzgerald."

"In the name of God," exploded Violet, "what has this palaver have to do with us, with anything?"

"It has a very great deal to do with your case, Violet," James said hoarsely, his tone now indicating he would not be silenced by her or anyone else.

"Lily and Gerald, both very young, in their early twenties, saw a life ahead together. A normal, happy life. And during those happy courtship days, Jack, who was rather younger—a boy, really—became very fond of Gerald. Perhaps he saw in him both a friend and a brother—brother-in-law, as he soon would be . . . or so thought Jack. As did Lily. And Gerald. And Rose. Rose too saw Lily's proposed marriage with Gerald as bringing new life into her own life.

"However, there was one family member who did not view the marriage in this way. Violet, who had broken up every other relationship Lily had attempted to have, tried to destroy this one too. There were to be no interlopers in the Moore family. No outsiders becoming involved in the farm. I'm not sure how she achieved what she clearly set out to do. Perhaps one day Lily might tell us . . ." James watched as Lily lowered her head, silent as ever. Then the sudden sound of Gerald's voice, hoarse with rage, broke that silence.

"I'll tell you, Fleming," he burst out, looking not at James, but at Violet. "She worked away at her night and day. She picked away at what little confidence and trust Lily ever had. She filled her head with stories of men, men who drank, men who played around, men who abused their wives physically and mentally. But Lily held out. She knew I was not one of those men. And then she started on Lily herself. How Lily would not make a good wife to me, that she was only a clumsy country girl who would be a misfit in Dublin. She convinced her that she would not only not help my law career, but would hinder it. Deny it as you will, Violet, but it's the truth." Violet sat stone still and Gerald turned toward the others. "That was far more successful," he said, his voice sarcastic now. "Lily had self-doubts, but we discussed them and I assured her I had no need of this fantasy Dublin society wife that Violet was creating. But Violet had succeeded in sowing seeds of doubt. Lily was weakening. She now needed time to think, whereas until then we had been rushing headlong into love. Oh, and then Violet saw her advantage . . ."

He turned to face Violet again. "How can anyone so thick have been as shrewd as you? How could you have known the right buttons to push?"

He glanced at James, half seeing him now, looking back with an inward eye. "She wore Lily down. She said I would expect many children. That as I prospered I would want a large family, sons to follow me into the law practice. She talked to Lily of the horrors of sex, the brutality of sex with a man.

"I know you well! You must have made it sound like two rutting sheep in the field. And then she spoke of pregnancy and childbirth. There too you had your bloody rural examples to throw in her sensitive face. Oh, Lily had seen ewes die after dropping twins, and Lily had seen cows dying in agony with two-headed calves protruding from their swollen bodies. I know, because I saw it too, and more, and I chose to leave this bloody awful cruel life behind me!" Gerald's voice was cracking with emotion and his finger repeatedly jabbed the air.

"Oh, yes, I would leave it and take Lily with me. But Violet painted such a picture of the marriage bed and the confinement bed that she was scaring poor, dear Lily half witless. Lily, I ask you?" He glanced wildy around the room. "Lily, so full of affection, so full of fine, delicate feeling . . . Lily, who should have been taken away from this rough life.

"Ah, but Lily had no mother to advise her, to assure her that marriage and love and trust and children on her lap and at her knee would bring her happiness, physical happiness, spiritual happiness. As if that unnatural woman who bore her would ever have advised her thusly." Gerald paused, but only for breath. "No, there was no loving mother. Only that bitch who sits there now before you!" Gerald's voice dropped. "There was no one." His voice fell to a whisper. "No one." He leaned back and looked toward Lily, who had hidden her face in her hands. Rose had stopped knitting.

"The result was . . . ." James's voice was quiet. "The result was that Lily did not marry the man she loved and who . . . loved her." Gerald bent his head. "Lily remained on the farm, looking after the accounts, tending the hens, and keeping away from the physical work for which she held a deep distaste. Jack, who had come to have hopes of a happier life, we can assume, was devastated—"

"Oh, he was," Rose broke in unexpectedly. She

looked around her. "Why, you must remember, Lily? And you, Violet? Oh, Mr. Fleming," said Rose in her rapid, breathy way, "Gerald wouldn't have known, he was gone then, but Jack, oh the poor boy was terribly sad. He loved Gerald. I knew it. We used to lie in the hay after the milking was done and chew straws, and we'd speculate on the wedding, and how we'd both be able to go up to Dublin for visits. How it would be so good to have a real brother in Gerald. And I used to say to dear Jack that perhaps he too could be a solicitor like Gerald, and that perhaps Gerald would help him. But Jack had no ideas of that. Jack loved the farm. This is where he'd stay, he'd tell me. This is where he'd make his life and fortune." She crossed the room to Gerald. "Gerald, Gerald, sure he loved you like the big brother he never had. And do you know one of the things he loved to do with you most of all? Riding. Remember, Gerald?" She waited. "Gerald, you do remember that, don't you? Jack would ride with you morning and evening. You do remember . . . ?"

"Rose, for God's sake." Gerald groaned and stood up, flexing himself, shaking her off.

"I beg your pardon," said Rose suddenly to James. And she wiped away the tears from the corners of eyes, with her fist, like a young child.

James felt completely overwhelmed with the emotion that filled the room. He wondered if he could go on. He opened his mouth, but no words came.

"Fleming! Please continue," said O'Shea in a civil voice. "Perhaps another brandy would do . . ." Kevin returned to the sideboard as James tried hard to settle his thoughts and concentrate on the order of his approach. He started again, slowly, at first, addressing O'Shea.

"Things went on rather as before. Except that now Jack was getting older. Jack as he matured began not only to take an interest in the running of the farm, he was also beginning to express his own ideas, his own goals about the improvement of the farm, the herd, and so on. And around the same time Jack too fell in love . . ."

"Love!" Violet snorted. "Is this a love story you're telling us, Fleming? Is it for this nonsense—about love—that we are forced to sit here, prisoners in our own home?"

"Yes, perhaps it is a love story after all," said James quietly, his tone full of a strange foreboding that silenced Violet once again.

"Jack fell in love with one . . . well, with a local girl, a young Catholic girl, whose family Violet despised. But Violet wasn't as quick to spot the dangers as she had been with Lily. Knowing and caring nothing about . . . love," he glanced at Violet, "she assumed Jack was 'playing around.'

"And so we come to the night that Mike Walsh died. Jack Moore killed Mike Walsh." James waited for the effect of his words.

"Come again?" O'Shea blurted out with rising interest.

"Jack Moore killed Mike Walsh. He confessed it to Violet." At this news both Lily and Rose reacted, Lily moving around the chair to confront her older sister.

"I don't believe it! You'll do anything, say anything to destroy Jack's memory." The words flew out of Lily's mouth.

"It's a lie," shrieked Rose, also addressing Violet, who merely looked past them, stony-faced and staring. "You have no right," she hissed.

"I have every right," said James.

"Go on," said O'Shea.

"Mike Walsh had left the pub after his quarrel with Jack and had laid in wait for him—to have it out, I believe, but not to kill Jack. But they were both drunk. In their brief struggle Jack pushed Mike Walsh, who went down heavily into the ditch and struck his head—"

"He was defending himself!" cried Rose. "Why

didn't you ever tell us?" she screamed at Violet. "Never, all these years, and we didn't know why he'd gone away. I thought . . . I thought he didn't love us anymore . . ."

"Be that as it may," said James, "he knew that he was responsible for Mike's death, and he was frightened. He ran to Violet, his older sister, and told her. She then—in a stroke of evil genius—saw her chance."

"Her chance?" said O'Shea.

"To get rid of Jack from the farm. She used his fear and fueled it. She told him to flee, and she helped him to do it. And after that gave him an alibi the police trusted. But all this time she led Jack to believe he was still wanted by the police."

"Oh my God," said Lily quietly.

"But there was more than just Jack that Violet wanted to get rid of."

"What do you mean?" asked Gerald.

"Only Violet of all of you knew that Jack's girlfriend, Kathleen Walsh, was carrying his child. She saw her chance to get rid of not only Jack, but also to separate him from Kathleen, and from their unborn child . . ."

"So Jack had his own child after all," said Rose, smiling through her tears.

"Yes, Rose, but he never saw her. Violet kept Jack in London by feeding him lies. She kept Kathleen in a convent, which took in unwed mothers, by feeding her more lies . . ."

"And the child?" Gerald's eyes were bulging from his head.

"Violet told Jack the child died, but in fact their child lived. Violet also convinced Kathleen that Jack had abandoned her and persuaded her to put the child up for adoption . . ."

"You know this for fact?" Gerald shouted.

"I know the young woman the child became," James whispered into the silence of the room.

O'Shea began to speak, but thought better of it.

A sigh suddenly escaped from James involuntarily. He saw O'Shea anxiously staring at him.

"And what does all this mean?" O'Shea asked.

"Violet," James began again, "believed all was well. But eventually Jack had his suspicions in London and returned secretly to confront her." Lily and Rose stared incredulously at Violet.

"He was demented. He had lost his home, his share of the farm with which he had bought Violet's unneeded silence. He had lost the girl he loved, who had left Ireland forever. And he had lost the baby Violet had told him had died at birth." Gerald groaned audibly.

"He was demented. And he was also violent. Violet, for once frightened of something or somebody, sought to save her skin by confessing to Jack that the baby girl had survived and had been adopted. She thought this would console him. But far from consoling him, this news enraged him further. And when he left, this time it was for good."

James paused, not knowing how to continue, feeling that he was himself in danger of becoming a force of destruction equal to Violet. He sat down and mopped his face.

At last Gerald spoke. "He never told me."

"No?"

"No, he never told me about the child."

"I didn't think so," James said softly, gently.

"Did he tell you?" For the first time Gerald spoke directly to Lily.

She shook her head, but held his eyes briefly with her own.

"Can you make the connections for us now, Fleming?" asked O'Shea.

"Yes, I think so," resumed James, staring without seeing the lilacs as they randomly dropped their petals on the hearth.

"As far as we can determine, Jack left London

shortly thereafter. Emigration records show he entered the United States through New York and went almost immediately to Boston. There he began working on construction sites. Through friends he made and connections he forged, he worked his way up the ladder in a manner that is very possible in the States. He began his own construction company, which went from strength to strength. To put it briefly, he made a great deal of money and he invested it wisely. He took an interest in stocks and shares, working through a very astute and successful broker. He never married —that I think you'll agree was very significant?" James looked around the room at his companions.

"Meanwhile Kathleen, who had stopped and then remained in London, eventually made a good marriage and put the past entirely behind her." James stressed this fact. "And I believe that she and Jack never had any contact over these last twenty-seven years.

"Within the last year, something happened. Jack Moore discovered that he had an incurable cancer."

Violet gasped, as did Rose. "How do you know?" Rose murmured.

"I met with his personal physician in Boston," James said simply. But he watched for O'Shea's reaction.

"But why didn't this come out at the inquest? What about the autopsy?" Gerald asked.

"Because the immediate cause of his death was so very obvious. The point is, Jack knew he had the disease and he knew how much time he had left to him.

"On the surface he immediately began to deal with his financial and business interests. We have a list of his assets and holdings from his accountant. We also have the evidence of the sale and making liquid of virtually everything he owned. This he transferred into cash . . . as far as we know to date, all of this was done quite legally. When the will is probated, we or whoever is involved will be able to learn more. I do have the will and the rough figure that the accountant had given to Jack attached to it. The money is safe and its location is known."

"Well," said O'Shea impatiently, "what is this magic number?"

"It approaches three million dollars." Violet, Lily, Rose, and O'Shea—all but Gerald, who knew the figure—gaped at James, momentarily speechless.

"Three million dollars." O'Shea whistled. He glanced speculatively at Violet. And then caught her eye.

"If you think that I knew of this, if you think this gives me a motive," snapped Violet, "then you are very much mistaken."

"I must agree there with my client, O'Shea," James said, smiling to ease his defensive tone. "You see, I believe that no one, no one but Jack's accountancy firm and perhaps the tax people, had any knowledge of Jack's real worth. Neither Violet nor Lily, neither Gerald nor Rose, knew this. Am I right?" The four nodded.

But Gerald added in a subdued voice, "I knew he was wealthy."

"And you, Lily? Did you not know, perhaps from Gerald, the sum of Jack's fortune, perhaps the terms of his will?" James's expression suddenly hardened, but Lily merely sat as erect as ever and determinedly shook her head. Neither she nor Gerald looked at each other, but O'Shea watched them like a hawk stalking new prey.

"It's not important," said James, to O'Shea's visible surprise. "You see, Jack had devised an underlying strategy. On the surface he was consolidating his fortune in view of the limited time left to him. But underneath, he had a definite purpose for massing his money. Firstly, he needed to use some of it—it turns out, not a great deal. Secondly, he wanted to make it simple for his intended heir."

"Heir . . ." echoed Gerald, sagging in his chair.

"I'm afraid I've got ahead of myself," said James, bitterness now filling his voice. "Jack had devised a very diabolical plan. It is my opinion that he had been hatching this plan—or rather, plans—for years. The single end of each, the common goal each shared with the other, was—the vengeance he planned to wreak on the woman who had destroyed his life: his sister Violet. I can only imagine how Jack Moore filled the empty nights and weekends, when he was not occupied with his work, when he chose to remain friendless, unmarried, childless. His revenge was his entire emotional life, he fed it and nurtured it instead of the children he had had a right to nurture and cherish. Perhaps he fell in love with his revenge, almost reluctant to enact it and end it. Because when that plan of vengeance was fulfilled, he no longer had any reason to live."

"Preposterous!" said Violet, but her voice was low.

"I don't think so. You, better than anyone, know that, because you saw him that night years ago, a man destroyed in front of your eyes. But when he was told that he was dying, that he was about to die, it became a matter of urgency to carry out his revenge. Now he was no longer afraid to execute the plan, he was afraid he would leave it too late. It was, you see, a very daring and cunning plan, but he needed help. Some of that help he could buy with money. But the crucial help he needed he could only demand from others who had suffered at Violet's hands, from others who had shared his hatred and his desire for revenge . . ."

Suddenly Gerald stood up. James shook his head kindly at him. "Please, Gerald," he whispered directly to him. "Even if you leave, where will you go?" O'Shea had moved unobtrusively toward the door, catching Kevin's eye, but they did not need to act. Gerald walked with dignity to the sideboard and filled his glass and James's. He nodded.

"Yes, Jack needed help. Jack—unknown to the

others in this room—had kept in contact only very occasionally with Gerald. Gerald let him know how the farm had prospered, and told him, more importantly, about Violet, her habits, her health . . . am I right?" Gerald looked away.

"When Jack learned of his illness, he chose to act. He contacted Gerald, and after obtaining his promise to help—perhaps by mentioning the amount of his fortune and the terms of his will . . . ?" He looked at Gerald, who did not respond. Lily filled her glass and went unexpectedly to sit beside Gerald, still without looking at him.

"Gerald promised to help. Only one more recruit was necessary. Someone who lived in this house, someone who could carry out the crucial spadework on which the plan hinged." Still no one spoke. James continued, his jaw tense and tired now.

"Much of the planning was done by phone. When Jack arrived in Dublin in secret, he finalized his plan with Gerald and took care of certain outside details personally—"

"Get to the point, man!" O'Shea boomed, startling James. He hardened his heart then, knowing he had been delaying the evil day.

"Right! Firstly, Lily—according to a rough time-table, I imagine—obtained from the kitchen a sharp carving knife with Violet's fingerprints on it. Some-how she conveyed this knife to Gerald, who at this time had led all of us—I mean at the firm—to believe that he was at home ill. Meanwhile, Jack himself had hired the hearse which, as we all know, was seen by a number of people in Kilmartin, and which I have located, along with the drivers. He also arranged for a simple wooden coffin to be transported to the Phoenix Park and left at a prearranged spot. On the night, or rather, the very early hours of the day on which the body was found here in Kilmartin, Gerald and Jack went to the Phoenix Park. I can only . . . no, I can't imagine that scene . . ." James stared hard at Gerald.

"All right! All right!" Gerald leaped to his feet, waving away O'Shea, who had moved toward him. He swung on Violet and glared at her. "No, none of you—least of all you, Violet—can imagine that scene, but I will describe it to you. So you, as I, will see it to your dying day. Yes, I drove Jack to the park. I felt as though I were caught in some nightmare, truly, but I made no effort to shake myself out of it. Jack was calm and level-headed, and that helped me. I had brought the knife with me, carefully wrapped. Jack had remembered the gloves."

"Oh, God," Rose moaned. "Oh God."

Gerald continued unheeding, staring only at Violet's transfixed face. "We went to the spot, and there was the coffin as arranged. I couldn't believe it when Jack actually stood in the coffin. He actually said this would help me! My God! Yes, he stood there and shook my hand, reminding me to fulfill the solemn oath he made me take earlier, to carry out the rest of the plan. He drew on his gloves and I handed him the knife. He opened his coat . . . I didn't watch the rest. I didn't turn around until I heard his body fall against the wood of the coffin. Can you believe it, he had even made sure the coffin was a light wood to make it easier for me to move. He had thought of everything.

"I was scared witless. I think now I *was* witless. I took the hammer and nails from the car, I straightened his body and clothes, took his gloves and the knife. He was dead. He *was* dead! I know because I checked," Gerald asserted, although no one had spoken.

"You were able to move the coffin yourself?" James queried.

"Yes, I nailed it shut. And I dragged it. We had placed it on a large sheet of heavy plastic. That helped a bit. It took some time, but it was an efficient method. Jack had thought of that too. I removed the plastic sheeting. That was tough. I took the hammer and the knife and the plastic . . . and I left the coffin by the side of the road, in the dark. I waited in the rain until the hearse came. Up until that point I was never sure the plan would work. But once the coffin was in the hearse, I felt it was beyond my control."

"And the knife?" snapped O'Shea.

Gerald looked at Lily, who still did not speak. "I had arranged to meet Lily the day after the body was found. In the confusion, no one noticed or cared that she had to run an errand. I met her on a local back road and returned the knife, carefully wrapped."

"And she planted it!" said O'Shea matter-of-factly. "She planted it as she planted the idea of her seeing Violet in or near the barn. Clever! Clever. She even used Kevin's actual phone call, a call she could never have predicted, to buttress her story . . ."

"Yes, I had phoned that night," Kevin reconfirmed. "And I was calling about the cow . . ." He shook his head almost in shock, staring at Lily.

"You played us for fools," said O'Shea, bitterly trying to evoke a response. "You planted the knife and we found it. You gave us the weapon and, oh, how well-timed, you gave us the damning evidence that you saw Violet at the barn . . ."

"Oh, it was easy," said Lily, her voice unlike her own normal tone. She stared at O'Shea. "Fools, you said. Yes, you and all the rest!" She spat out the words. "None of you knew how I hated Violet and my life, and none of you ever knew how I loved Gerald." She briefly touched his arm, but he didn't move.

"Can you tell us, Lily, because I think I know . . . ?" James's voice was tender. For a moment.

"When Daphne, Mrs. Fitzgerald died, Gerald and I . . . we realized that what we had felt, that what our brief meetings over the years had sustained, was still there." Lily's voice was soft now and gentle. "But still we didn't act. It was taking time, I think, to come to realize that we were finally free of all that had prevented us, from oh, so long ago. It was as though our mutual hatred of Violet held us in thrall. When Jack contacted Gerald with the terrible news that he was dying, it was as though his virulent hatred was a catalyst. I hardly questioned what he asked me, had asked Gerald to do. I was only sorry that he wouldn't let me see him when he came to Dublin. He told Gerald he thought I would . . . weaken. Maybe I would have . . ." Lily suddenly leaned back. Her face looked wizened and wrinkled, and her pallor made her appear waxen and corpselike herself.

James could hardly bear the silence in the room, punctuated by Rose's crying. He couldn't bear to see the vacant faces of Lily and Violet; the worn and beaten face of Gerald, his mentor and boss; the astonishment still registering on the faces of O'Shea and Kevin. He stood up, walked to the window, and stared blindly out at the gravel and the lilac bushes. He couldn't remember the day or the date, his mind was so fatigued.

"Suicide," said Violet with a hint of triumph. Each in turn looked at her. No one spoke. "Suicide," she repeated.

Lily stood up and walked to the window.

"Lily, I swear to God," said Gerald, "he never told me about his daughter. I thought the money would be ours . . ."

"After Violet was convicted?" James asked.

"Yes," said Lily. "Yes. It would have been myself and Rose then. And when Gerald and I married, he would have shared in it. We knew it had to be a fortune . . . somehow it seemed right . . . it was justice finally being done."

Rose seemed to have drawn herself into some protective shell, but yet she murmured to Lily: "You would have let Violet go to jail, you would have used Jack's money to look after me?" Her voice was bewildered and faint.

James began again. "Gerald, there was just one thing you had to leave to fate. You had to assume that Violet would telephone you to take care of the funeral

243

arrangements and so on. You took her call. My, but you must have been relieved! And then you turned it all over to me. You mustn't have thought much of me . . ." James's voice was bitter and sad. "And then you arranged to be in London—to make my handling of the case plausible, to remove yourself from the scene of the crime! You used me," James said flatly.

"For your information, Fleming," Gerald said, directing his voice at James's back, "it was not essential that Violet contact us first, or indeed at all, though I guessed she would. It was convenient, yes, because I could exercise control over her defense and monitor developments more closely, but it wasn't essential. Jack's plan was perfect—it had an inevitability of its own. His plan did not require any additional input from me after his body was discovered by Violet!

"And as regards using you as a pawn?" His voice rose. "What I want to know is—how long have you been working against me? You consciously misled me when you let me believe that Jack and Kathleen Walsh's baby died! You knowingly lied to me!"

James said nothing.

"Then tell me this, have you actually traced her? You know that she is alive, you know where she is?" Gerald's voice was nearly as bewildered as Rose's.

"Believe me," said James, without turning. "Yes, I've seen her. We've talked, but she . . . she knows nothing."

"Nothing?" O'Shea was skeptical, alert as always.

"Nothing." James's tone was infinitely convincing. He paused for a few minutes and then said, as he turned and looked sadly at Gerald and Lily, "Jack betrayed you both."

Gerald nodded, the full impact of that reality having already reached him. Lily began to speak, but her voice broke and she cried at last—silent, tearless, racking sobs.

"I'm lost," said O'Shea.

"O'Shea—Gerald knew the terms of Jack's will . . . from Jack, I might add. It was very simple. It said that he was leaving everything—which turned out to be three million—to his nearest relative. Since Gerald didn't know about the surviving child, Jack's natural daughter, he rightly assumed under those conditions, that Violet, Lily, and Rose would inherit. As the aim of the revenge was to convict Violet of Jack's murder, to send her to prison or worse, for something she didn't do, then only Lily and Rose would inherit his fortune. And Gerald, by marrying Lily as he always wanted—would also share in the wealth. In one fell swoop they would have wreaked both their revenge and Jack's. Violet would rot in prison, slowly going mad from the knowledge that she was convicted of a crime she didn't commit and losing the one thing for which she had lived, her property. Jack would have succeeded in doing to *her* what she had done all those years before to him. He would have taken everything that made life worth living away from her. And Lily and Gerald would in that single stroke have also acquired immense wealth. Wealth that would have freed them. Or so they thought. It was to be the most poetic of poetic justice."

"And now?" O'Shea looked at James.

"And now, Jack's daughter will stand to inherit—if, as I think, Jack did everything legally in the States regarding the disposal of his fortune." James sighed. "Yes, Jack's daughter will inherit his millions . . . and inevitably, with his money, the knowledge of who her parents were . . ."

O'Shea watched James closely. "You obviously know her. Does she—"

"Absolutely not. I already told you. She knows nothing. Jack never contacted her. I suspect he had her traced by professionals, private investigators. It would have been simple, with his money. If *I* did, then they could have done it."

Studying James for a long minute, O'Shea said

finally, "There's more to you than meets the eye, Fleming."

But James merely shrugged, turning back to his window, his only image of escape from the horrors of this stifling room. He continued to stare unswervingly at the sodden lilac bushes now bent to earth with the weight of the rain and with the heavy wind that had risen and was now rattling the bones of this very old house.

He continued to stare as O'Shea led Lily and Gerald to the waiting car. He stared, and behind him Kevin cleared away the glasses and silently left the room to see to the cows. Natural life went on, thought James wildly. Life outside this room went on. And so he chose to stare out, ignoring Violet and Rose as they finally looked at each other, looked into each other's eyes, and saw nothing there that would enable them to go on together. And yet they would. He stared until they in turn left the room. Only then did he let the tears roll down his face as the raindrops rolled down the glass in front of him.

"So the charges were dropped against Violet Moore?" Matt asked as he poured another cup of tea for James. They were alone in his office, surrounded by towering stacks of homework books and endless team photos on the walls. The school was eerily quiet, the pupils having left for the day. James shut the door.

"Yes, as soon as Gerald and Lily made their statements, their confessions, really. I'm representing them both, but that is merely routine." James sighed. "Gerald's been a real soldier about it all. It bothers me . . ."

"What?"

"To see him so . . . so beaten."

"For God's sake, James—"

"I know, I know but . . . he's asked me to take over the firm. To buy it out. He'll never be able to practice again, being disbarred. I said yes. The name will be changed too . . ." He smiled at that, and looked up at Matt. Matt nodded, reassuring as ever.

"My mother's helping out. He's giving me a good price, but I don't have the capital. She says I might as well have what I'd be getting when she died. You know how funny she can be. We discussed it with my brother, and he doesn't mind. He'll be setting up his own practice shortly. I believe he might open his surgery in her house. Now there's an image to conjure with!" James laughed, but half-heartedly. He was tired.

"But tell me this, what do you think will happen to Gerald and Lily?" Matt was anxious for all the details, he wanted every loose end tied up. James sat back and crossed his legs, inadvertently clipping the edge of a towering stack of books. As he went to grab for it, it came to meet him, and in an instant the entire history assignments of Class 2B were in his lap. All twenty-six of them. Five minutes later James answered the question.

"I do believe they'll get suspended sentences . . . at their ages. They didn't kill Jack, although it's hard to separate that out from the whole tangled mess. They concealed knowledge, they obstructed justice, they attempted to divert justice—you know—by planting the knife, by incriminating Violet. God! It might have succeeded . . ."

"Mad, absolutely mad!" Matt whistled.

"You mean Jack? Yes, I'm afraid so. I think the cancer tipped the balance. Perhaps if he had lived, he just would have continued to fantasize, to plot and plan. I believe the cancer unhinged him . . ."

"And hatred and bitterness and greed 'unhinged' Lily and Gerald too?" Matt sounded skeptical.

"Oh, Matt, how else can I look at it and carry on? It's hard, really hard, to see these people in the clear light of day. I had come to know them . . . they're names, just names to you."

"So Gerald will retire. And Lily? Don't you think

it's unfair that they will be able to live out their lives together in peace . . . as though none of this had happened?"

"That, at least, won't be happening . . . Lily stayed with Gerald one night in his Dublin house, the night of the day they were formally charged and released on bail. Can you imagine? Gerald a felon, standing before a judge. Gerald, whose whole life was the law!" James shook his head, and Matt saw in that single gesture the disillusionment James was feeling.

"And Lily, you started to say . . ."

"Lily went back to Kilmartin, to the house. The three of them are there together, and I think that's how it will stay. Habit is a powerful thing, Matt. The habit of hatred binds them together in that house." He stared in front of him, picturing Violet, Lily, Rose. Picturing them in that house, in the barns, carrying on, unable to speak of what had happened, hate binding them as love might bind another family. Perhaps blood is thicker . . . His thoughts strayed to the brief note he had mailed the day before to Kathleen Banks in London, suggesting she might enjoy following the career of the prominent young violinist, Sarah Gallagher. But Matt was asking him a question.

"O'Shea? He thinks I'm the greatest thing since sliced bread!" James laughed out loud. "But that won't last," he added.

"Well, the reports in the papers have given him much more of the credit than he deserved. They barely mentioned you!" Matt laid a plate of stale biscuits on the desk. "The whole thing is virtually a dead issue. It was really hot in the staff room when the papers thought it was a murder, a juicy scandal. Everyone was talking about it, and I didn't even know you were involved." Matt scowled at James, teasing him. "But now, well, once the news was out that it was a suicide, it died a death . . ."

"Oh, very bad pun intended," James replied. "Anyway, you know I couldn't tell you what was going on, don't you?" He was apologetic with his old friend.

"Of course, of course. I know, always knew how discreet you were. How discreet you are. In fact, if you're not too tired from all your high drama, there's a small matter I'd like your particular perspective on."

James's ears pricked up with interest. "Yes?"

Matt paused and then leaned across his desk. He lowered his voice. "It's the head of my English department. He's Irish, you see, but he's been teaching in England—in Oxford, as he led me to believe. He only came this year. I was desperate when old Maughan died, God rest his soul, and I hired this man damn quick, too damn quick. I only got around to checking his references recently. They're phony. He's from Oxford all right, but I've been getting some very funny rumors back from my inquiries. It seems there was this young graduate student . . ." Matt's voice dropped as his friend moved closer. James smiled to himself. His Peru journey was postponed for the foreseeable future, but this most interesting development could well make up for that!

James let himself into his flat. He was tired, but pleased with his day. The visit with Matt had been good in more ways than one. And the bank manager had been more than cordial when he saw Mrs. Fleming's substantial savings account. The small Dublin law firm of Fitzgerald's would be his in a matter of weeks. He sighed. He hadn't been able to force himself to go into the office. "Avoiding the issue, Fleming," he said out loud, his voice booming in the silence of the flat. "Not a great way to start off as head of the firm. A raise for Maggie, that's the first thing!" He smiled to himself. He couldn't afford to lose her; she ran the bloody place!

James loosened his tie and threw himself into the chair beside his phone. The blinking red light of the answering machine distracted him. "Maggie, no doubt," he mused aloud, "with an agenda a mile long." He laughed as he punched the button on the machine, but his laughter froze when he heard the voice.

"James, darling, where on earth have you been? I haven't been able to reach you at the office." She paused. "I've just received a very strange letter, telling me I've inherited a fortune. It's postmarked Boston and it's signed by someone named Jack Moore. I was wondering if you knew anything about it . . ."